The Power of the Relic

A Novel

José V. Bonilla

An epic adventure of faith, courage and purpose unfolding in the wilderness of South America.

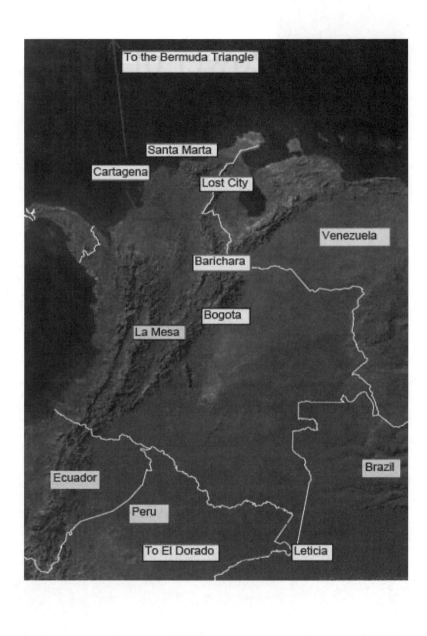

José V. Bonilla

THE POWER OF THE RELIC

© 2005 By Jose V. Bonilla.
All rights reserved. No part of this book may be reproduced, stored in a retrieval system or transmitted in any form or by any means without the prior written permission of the Publishers, except by a reviewer who may quote brief passages in a review to be printed in a magazine or newspaper.

Cover design
Jose V. Bonilla

Photographs on the book cover:
Cathedral of La Mesa
Town of Barichara
Grand Canyon of the Chicamocha River
Tequendama Waterfalls
Pedro Palo lagoon
Balsilla Muisca

FIRST PRINTING
ISBN: 0-9765151-0-5
PUBLISHED BY MILAT-BOOKS, INC.
WWW.MILAT-BOOKS.4T.COM
GILBERTSVILLE, KY

PRINTED IN COLOMBIA

DEDICATION

This book is a tribute to the educators that day to day discover in our youth, not only what is, but what can become. With great determination and much dedication, they teach our young children the power to dream, to create, to discover, to find and to reach out for a higher purpose in life.

With a deep sense of respect, admiration and gratitude.

INTRODUCTION

At the end of the 15th century and beginning of the 16th century, the European conquistadores came to the New World in search of the legendary *"El Dorado"* and *"The fountain of Youth"*. Gonzalo Jimenez de Quesada and Francisco Pizarro marched towards South America in search of the *"El Dorado"* but they did not find it. On the other hand Don Juan Ponce de Leon, traveled to Florida in North America, searching for *"The fountain of youth"* but also failed in his attempt.

Although these two coveted treasures eluded the avaricious conquerors, both of them are in the high Andean Mountains in South America. The extraordinary task to find them has been assigned to two young people who are culminating their last year of high school in La Mesa, a small town located on the slopes of the Eastern mountain range of Colombia.

This epic adventure of action and suspense begins during the Easter week of 1974 when these two young fellows, providentially chosen to carry out this task, meet Bachu, a native Indian who has lived for almost two thousand years in a wonderful underground temple near Bogotá, awaiting their arrival. Without them he will not be able to carry out the mission of freeing his people and recovering the sacred treasures, until now lost in the majestic Andean mountains.

During this adventure these young men discover two great civilizations of remarkable technological advances: one was established in the Caribbean Sea and the other on the summits of the Andes. They have been there for thousands of years, but have remained until now in the shadows of mystery. Those people came to the New World from the Middle East and brought with them a civilization of advanced science and knowledge.

The first group settled in the Caribbean and founded a marvelous city under the sea. The second preferred the mountains where they built a great metropolis. Examples of the influence of these great cultures are the magnificent monuments of Central and South America.

There the famous city of "*El Dorado*" is protected. Many European conquistadores heard of it, but none of them was able to find it. The success of this adventure was reserved for these two young fellows from La Mesa.

CHAPTER 1

Easter week, 1974. The students of the "Francisco Julian Olaya" school in the small rural town of La Mesa are on vacation all week. The two Cousins Juan and Chepe were enjoying their time off from school. Normally Juan would be working in his Father's farm picking coffee, but on this occasion there were sufficient workers in the farm for that arduous work.

"This year I want to spend the week of vacation resting from school work. After all, this is my last year in high school" said Juan to his cousin Chepe.

"What would you say if we go tomorrow to the lagoon of Pedro Palo? We can have a picnic and swim for a while."

"That is a great idea," added Chepe as an answer. "On our way back we can stop by the San Carlos farm to visit Father Alberto. I don't know him yet but Father Carvajal, our philosophy teacher, speaks highly of him. He tells me that they are good friends and that Father Alberto is very friendly and hospitable.

"Very well then, you bring the meat for the cookout and I'll bring the rest we need for the picnic." Chepe answered as a final comment. "I will see you tomorrow!"

Juan, like Chepe his cousin, was raised on a farm. From his early childhood he helped in all activities of his Father's coffee plantation located not far from the town of La Mesa. His cousin Chepe also grew up on a coffee farm, a fair distance from Juan's family. At the proper time they started their studies in the same high school, "Francisco Julian Olaya" in La Mesa, where they cultivated a closed friendship. Juan had an adventurous and festive spirit, he composed his own folksongs and loved good music; he was always cheerful and amusing. He was tall, and of white complexion; his green eyes which he inherited from his mother made a nice contrast with his black and wavy hair. Chepe, unlike his cousin, was of medium stature, brown complexion, brown eyes and black and straight hair. Of timid and reserved character, he was extremely intelligent.

On Monday morning, the cousins met at the bus depot to take the bus that would take them most of the way to their destination, the lagoon of Pedro Palo. Each one had a small bag with the contents for the picnic. The trip from La Mesa to San Carlos was rather uneventful. Nevertheless both of them appeared to be a bit anxious; something within each of them told them that this would be the beginning of an adventure for which they were not prepared. But they remained in silence when they got off the bus, having a feeling that their lives were on the verge of something new, something they have never imagined before.

The narrow path towards the lagoon could only be traveled on foot through a steep trail towards the mountain, but the fresh air in the atmosphere did make it an easy journey. From time to time both young men took a short rest, turning around to see at the distance the small town of La Mesa that watched in silence over the travelers who ascended the mountain.

After few minutes of rest they continued the course towards the lagoon. The morning was still quite cool; the temperature probably did not reach yet ten degrees. The grass looked shiny with the morning dew. The weather was actually quite nice with the warming rays of the sun. Some trees were starting to bloom and the intense green color of the grass was witness of the strong rains that had fallen in this area during the last few days. The scenery was simply peaceful and enchanting. After a few minutes of ascending, they stopped again to observe the mountains at a distance, which appeared in an artistic and majestic arrangement behind La Mesa.

The shrubs at both sides of the path appeared as if they were painted with a greenish - blue color tracing the route towards the top of the mountain. It was not possible to get lost; the trail was narrow but well defined. It was not highly traveled. In two locations the path was blocked with a wire fence to prevent passage but the two cousins went forth between the wires taking care to avoid hurting themselves or tearing their pants or shirts. The pleasant climate, the scent of the wild flowers, the fruits, the wild mushrooms, the humid aroma typical of the forest, allowed them to appreciate nature in its entire splendor.

"The cool temperature offers a relaxed atmosphere that invites us to rest and meditate," said Chepe, as he looked for a clear place on the ground to sit and rest for a few minutes.

His cousin Juan followed his example without saying word. A shrub of wild red berries appeared to offer its fruit to the travelers; some already had fallen to the ground for the benefit of the birds and the insects. They had not seen these delicious berries for a long time, so they tried to taste them but it was a little difficult to gather them from the branches covered with thorns. Now they could hear the cheerful singing of the wild birds that normally live in the hills alongside the water, indicating its proximity. After passing another metallic fence used to maintain the cows in the meadow, they took a final ascent that took them to the peak of the mountain, about a thousand five hundred meters above sea level, from where they could finally observe the calm waters of the lagoon.

They continued towards the lagoon through a narrow path. It was about ten in the morning, and the rays of the sun warmed up the atmosphere a little more. After a short break to take refreshment and a brief rest, they continued towards the borders of the waters that hid timidly behind the ferns that surrounded it. The green prairies invited them to a good rest under the lukewarm rays of the sun. There were bonfire leftovers on the ground, a sign of previous visitors. They chose that place to leave their bags with the food and refreshments to make a bonfire later to prepare the lunch. The lagoon of Pedro Palo had one of the most beautiful landscapes of this region. Its large surface and great depth were still unknown. Its clean and crystalline water with tonalities of many colors according to the time of the day was surrounded by colorful forests and prairies. It was an ideal place for a morning stroll. The place of greatest attraction was a small cove in the east side with green and smooth meadows of an incomparable beauty.

"Let's go to the other side" suggested Juan. "There is a magnificent view from there. We will be able to observe the beautiful prairies around the waters with their incredible tranquility."

Once they arrived at the selected site, they sat on the grass for a long while without pronouncing a word. From the west, where the hills are higher, they could observe the lagoon in all its extension. To the south a high and imposing mount rises. The wild ducks and other birds offered a mysterious choir that lost itself in the distance of the forest. The calm and pure waters, emerald green, reflected the image of the trees that surrounded it from the south.

Chepe rose up and looked around trying to absorb all the beauty and mystery of the landscape. At that moment a fog originating from the forest began to move over the waters, until finally covering the lagoon completely.

"Juan!" murmured Chepe; in low voice as if he had discovered a secret. "The waters have disappeared! They can no longer be seen!" The song of the wild ducks could be heard at the distance, adding an additional mystery, but the lagoon remained under those white curtains, that were slowly retiring magically towards the forest, in the same manner as they had appeared.

"It seems as if this lagoon is enchanted" Juan finally said, trying to break a type of hypnotism that this had brought to Chepe. "The legend says that the enchantment of this lagoon is due to the powers of the legendary Juan Diaz, a man of great power in the days of the Spanish Colony, also known as *El Sevilliano*." "All you can see from the top of La Mesa was his property. It was populated with cattle. Of special notice was the "Casa Grande" or "Great House" of Juan Diaz. It was built in the neighborhoods of Tocaima, with all lavishness available at that time: extensive, solid and strong like a castle. The materials to build it were brought from Santa Fe; and the blue tile, glass for the windows and the beautiful ornaments were brought from Spain. Wishing to immortalize himself, he built this ostentatious house that could serve as a residence for the king of Spain. In its warehouse he always had a reserve of the best Spanish wines."

"Juan Diaz, *El Sevillano*" continued Juan, "had arrived from the Spanish peninsula with a very bad reputation and like many other Spaniards, in search of fortune but without a well-known profession. Since he was not of noble blood and he did not work for the king, his task seemed to be more difficult. He could have dedicated himself to discover and conquer new territories through plain courage and audacity, but he was cowardly and incapable of surviving the difficulties at the time. He was deeply troubled with the rigors of the climate and other deprivations that all the Spaniards had to endure. Nevertheless, luck soon changed for *El Sevillano*. He had a black slave called Domingo who served him and accompanied him in all his expeditions. In one of these, the black slave was sitting, without realizing it, near an anthill. He noticed that the sand removed by the ants was shining. When coming near to take a closer look, he discovered that it was gold dust. He went out to investigate further and found that it was a large gold mine. Full of joy he went to take the great news to his master, requesting from him in exchange for so much wealth, only his freedom. Juan Diaz called him his friend and his companion and he offered to release him and promised to divide with him this fortune. But once he saw the rich mine, from where the gold could be extracted without much effort, he was moved with greed and became afraid that Domingo would share the discovery with anyone else. He killed him with and extraordinary blow to his back.

This way his fortune changed forever. His property began to be well-known as "La Mesa de Juan Diaz". He reached such a high position, that the nobles gathered at his house to play dice every night and to savor his exquisite wines. Many Spaniards called him compadre. He had the votes of the town hall and nothing was done in these fields without his approval; nevertheless, nobody liked him and all murmured in low voices. Nobles, rich people and all the town folks would have celebrated his death with great joy. Everyone asked themselves how *El Sevillano* had amassed such great wealth. Nobody knew where his gold mine was located, because he kept this secret very jealously; nobody had accompanied him, nobody had worked with him, and even today people speak of the famous gold mine of Juan Diaz but the search for it has been in vain. It is said that it is near the town of Tena, somewhere not far from this lagoon. There were rumors against *El Sevillano,* accusing him of the death of many of his dependents; and there were rumors that he had made a pact with the devil in exchange for gold, not only selling his soul to him, but also being in charge of buying those of the good Christians. So, from a friendly, giving and helpful person that he was, he became arrogant, insolent and despotic. He mistreated his servants in public, he offended the nobles as if taking revenge for his old humiliations, until he become an intolerable and cruel human being. All suffered because they were indebted to him, some living in houses located in his property. They feared his secret machinations, and some feared his diabolic arts; but no one dared to face his anger. His arrogance and irreverence took him to an unfortunate end: On Thursday of Easter week, the standard of the Christ was been carried in a sumptuous procession prepared as never before, worthy of the wealth of *El Sevillano.*

At three in afternoon a great number of faithful believers had been crowded at the doors of the church and the passage of the procession had advanced through the middle of crowd, when Juan Diaz appeared to receive the standard of the Holy Cross. A thunderous ray of light crossed the skies, and a formidable thunderclap resounded in the air. The multitude stopped terrified, and at the same time a furious storm was unleashed preventing the procession from moving forward. Juan Diaz, full of rage, started to curse to the surprise of the horrified multitude.

Good Friday is a day kept with religious solemnity by all believers, and in those times it was kept with great severity and rigidity. All fasted; not even the children could eat meat, and the most religious had only bread and water. Neither a shout, nor a voice, nor a bell was heard throughout the city. The day and the night celebrated the sacred ceremonies or the meditation of the passion and death of the Christ. The perverse Juan Diaz, in an act of incomprehensible extravagance, decided to celebrate the night with a splendid dinner in his house on Good Friday, after the procession. He was able to get some of the less faithful young people and some of the nobles indebted to him to commit to attend. His house was all lighted in dissolute celebration. The people from the town, that had attended the procession, went to *la casa grande*; and when seeing the great celebration that was taking placed there, they began to protest at the profanation of the greatest of the holy days. As a sign of additional defiance, *El Sevillano* ordered some of his most trusted man to distribute brandy to everyone; and after two hours the town had forgotten that it was Good Friday. Later on, realizing what they had done, the sorry and angered guests shouted: "Damn you, Juan Diaz, and cursed be all your wealth!" "Not even God can take it from me!" was his arrogant and quick answer. At that very moment a vague sound began to be heard in town; the horrified multitude started shouting in fear in the streets. The noise increased until becoming a thundering, terrible and colossal wind extinguishing all the lights. At the same time a great water wave swept through the party hall. It was an impressive flood of the Bogota River, which took everything it found on its way including the blasphemous Juan Diaz, his huge house and everyone who was with him.

The legend also says that even now, after his death, Juan Diaz occasionally visits his former lands. From time to time he does it through a mysterious control he has over this lagoon. With the dense fog from it, he takes short visits to La Mesa. In the beautiful mornings, suddenly the town covers itself with that dense fog that makes it impossible to see even just a few meters of distance."

Chepe remained in silence for a few minutes observing the beautiful landscape.
"Very interesting" he said finally looking directly at Juan. Now it is time to have lunch. I am so hungry that I could eat a whole horse by myself. Saying this, the two of them returned to the place where they had left their bags. They made a small bonfire to prepare a simple but delicious lunch with country flavor: meat, homemade bread, cheese, and fruit juice.

They ate their lunch near the lagoon but this time they did not dare to swim in it as they had done in previous occasions. They stayed a few more hours enjoying the beauty, the peace and the tranquility that this place had to offer. Towards the evening they started the way back down to the road that goes to La

Mesa. After talking with some people at the convenience store in San Carlos, they went towards the monastery to visit Father Alberto before returning home. The trail crossed the highway, next to small and colorful farm houses. Before getting to the path that would take them to the monastery, they had to jump over a stone wall, since the main door remained locked for security reasons. They walked for about ten minutes towards the place where Padre Alberto lived.

"A new adventure is waiting for us ..." thought Chepe as he walked down the short trail.

The path was surrounded by trees and flowers of lively colors. This was a stone road characteristic of the highway constructions of the period of the Spanish Colony. The architectural splendor of this place was a silent witness of admirable histories of conquistadores and horsemen of past centuries who took valuable treasures from this land over to Europe.

Here the landscape was totally different from the place they visited by the lagoon: the gardens were well cared for, and the cultivation of fruits and coffee along with various domestic animals around the farm offered a comfortable and stress-free atmosphere. Here you could enjoy the solitude, the romantic and spiritual atmosphere typical of the Andean region. At first this monastery was occupied by the clergymen of mother Spain and now it was used by priests dedicated to the study of sacred writings. Father Alberto was at home this evening. He was very friendly and hospitable, just as Father Carvajal had described him. As soon as he knew that Juan and Chepe were Father Carvajal's students, he was more excited and invited them to come in into the reception hall, which was modest but well furnished.

Father Alberto showed an excellent monastic spirit as he requested refreshments, cakes and some treats to share with his new visitors. The three spoke with great enthusiasm of philosophy and history for a long time. At the end of the conversation they talked about the period of the Spanish Conquest and the Colonial period. His appearance and his high spirit seemed to change a little, as if these subjects brought bad memories to him, but he tried in vain to disguise it. "Young men, do you know, that much of the gold and emeralds that the Spanish conquerors took with them on the way to Spain, is really under the sea?" said Father Alberto, in a somber tone. Then he continued, "Not many people know the exact location where these treasures are, but there are certain clues in some maps that may indicate their precise location. Some people think that some of those maps are in our region and that they contain precise indications as to the places where the ships containing such treasures sank. He who can find these maps will also be able to find the treasures that lie there," said Father Alberto in a lively tone. This last piece of information got Juan's attention who then dared to ask:

"Father, you know where those maps are?" "Not exactly, but I have a very good idea of the place where they possibly are hiding; the problem is how to get to them" replied Father Alberto "During the period of the conquest some tunnels and caverns were constructed in this area; not very far from here, on the way up from the town of Tena. But with time these tunnels have collapsed or disappeared. There are credible indications that some maps that contain the data of the traffic of gold towards Spain were hidden in those tunnels."

"Father, you know how those tunnels can be found?" inquired Juan. "I could not say that with certainty, but it seems that some of them are in one of the properties on the way that leads to Tena, but it seems that it would be very difficult to locate them" answered the Father, then adding kindly, "my children, you are already late and must return home before it gets dark. You are welcome to come back anytime you like. It is great to have visitors like you; very special greetings to Father Carvajal and God bless you, my children" said the Father as a final goodbye.

At this time it was already a little dark, so they ran towards the road to try to take the bus at the bus stop of San Carlos. "The last bus goes by at six thirty and if we miss it, it would be a very long walk to La Mesa," warned Juan as he immediately began running as fast as his legs could carry him when he saw the lights of the last bus coming down from Bogota. The bus was now about two or three minutes away from the spot where they could board it. With an extraordinary effort, he climbed the wall to run to the bus stop. When he was at the other side of the wall, he gave a strong whistle hoping that the bus driver could hear it. And he did. It was his lucky day. He did stop for him. Juan raced to the bus and asked the bus driver to wait for Chepe who came behind almost out of breath due to his great effort not to be left behind. Once in the bus he threw himself on a seat trying to catch his breath.

"We were lucky!" said Juan smiling. After thanking the bus driver for waiting for them, he sat next to Chepe to make sure that he was in good shape. "This was a day of great adventures, wasn't it?" asked Juan very excited. Chepe moved his head affirmatively but did not say word, still exhausted from the race to the bus. "We have to find them!" continued Juan. "Find what?" asked Chepe a bit confused. "The maps, man, the treasure maps" responded Juan, then adding: "Didn't you hear what the Father said?" "Nobody knows where those tunnels are and I doubt that they exist" responded Chepe, adding further: "And still if they exist, how are we going to find them? They are lost. And what would we do with those maps in the remote possibility that we could find them?" "Ah! One step at a time," responded Juan. "First we must locate them."

CHAPTER 2

Tuesday of Easter week. It was a beautiful spring morning with dew covering grass and trees and shining like precious diamonds, with the rays of the morning sun. The temperature barely reached forty degrees. In the background, the white snow covered Tolima, and Huila peaks stood out from the formidable and majestic Andean mountains in the horizon. Before Chepe had breakfast he went out to enjoy the fresh morning and to get ready to help with the work at his Father's coffee farm. The light of the morning sun penetrated through the trees to evaporate the moisture of the wet grass. The tranquility was absolute; you could only hear the early singing of the birds and the noise of the wood peckers who got up early in the morning to caringly tend their morning tasks.

Peculiarly, Chepe's father had not risen to begin his work yet. Noticing his absence Chepe took advantage of the opportunity to do his exercises. He always tried to take care of his body and to stay in good physical shape. With this in mind, he decided to run about ten kilometers cross country, up and down the scenic hills of the farm country of La Mesa. He ran downhill to *Puente Roto*, where a small stream of water flowed by the highway towards the small town of *San Joaquin*.

From there, he started a hard ascent towards the town. Halfway up, he stopped to contemplate in the far distance the summits of the mountains behind the town of Quipile. The clarity of the atmosphere allowed him to see clearly at the far distance. The valley of the San Javier River looked splendid as did the small villages of San Javier, La Capilla and other small groups of houses seated in the valley, in front of green hills. The sun began to evaporate the dew that rested on the leafy trees and the green meadow.

On the way back to his home there was a beautiful gorge, whose waters made of this region a quite fertile zone since it provides irrigation during the time of drought. The temperature was wonderful, the sun warmed up a little and the sky appeared completely blue and clear. It was truly a beautiful day to be in the farm country. Chepe crossed the small water stream on a make-shift bridge using a fallen tree and soon he arrived home, looking forward to a good breakfast. Juan was already there waiting for him, ready for the adventures of the new day.

With a radiant smile on his face, he asked Chepe:
"Are you ready to go in search of our treasure?"
"Well, I am not as optimistic as you are; we don't even know if it actually exists," answered Chepe.
"How can't it be true, if Father Alberto said it!" answered Juan in a forceful way.
"The Father said specifically that these were only indications" replied Chepe. "Come-on, you cannot let me go by myself in this adventure! It's the most

important adventure of our life!" said Juan in an almost prophetic way.

"OK, I can go with you today only, but tomorrow I will have to help my Father in the farm. You already know that the coffee harvest is ready to gather."

"Very well; if we go today, I help you tomorrow," he added decisively with an expression of joy.

After a good breakfast diligently prepared by his mother, they started off for La Mesa, where they were planning to take a bus for Tena. The trail that would take these adventurous young men from Chepe's home to the village of La Mesa was short but steep and required them to be in good physical shape and energetic to travel it. Their minds were focused in their new adventure, so they did not talk much during this stage of the trip which they made relatively fast.

When arriving in town they went straight to the convenience store to buy some food for their journey: a few sardine cans, bread, juice and some candy. They already had the equipment required for the exploration: a small lantern with new batteries, pocket radio, nylon cord, and a Swiss army knife with all the necessary services for a field adventure. Each one had a light bag with their respective utensils and food for the day. "Ready?" asked Juan after paying the cashier and packing his food. "Yes ready. The bus is coming and we must hurry if we do not want to be left behind," said Chepe with a look of distress as they ran to the bus stop.

There they asked the bus driver if the bus happened to go through Tena; with an affirmative answer, they boarded the bus and found a seat. This road is the same one that goes from La Mesa to Bogota but a few kilometers ahead in a small village called *El Ramal* it divides into three roads, one of them going to Cachipay, another important town of the region. The main highway, is asphalted and maintained generally very well unlike the one going to Tena which was covered only with gravel, but the landscaping about that road was extraordinary and colorful with small coffee farms and a large variety of fruit trees characteristic of the tropical climate.

The trip by bus was short; it lasted only about thirty minutes. A few kilometers past the town of Tena, the adventurous young cousins got off the bus and took a narrow trail in the direction of the monastery of San Carlos. It was probably ten in the morning when they started this walk up the mountain. After a few minutes on the trail Chepe asked: "And what is the plan to find these tunnels? Don't you think that we needed directions to find the maps?" "I do not know yet, but I have a feeling that when we arrive to the right spot, when we get there we will know one way or another; there will be some kind of clue" answered Juan. "Let's move forward and I will let you know where we can begin the search.

They started walking the trail which initially was relatively flat; an easy walk among coffee plantations shaded by banana trees. The scenery could not be more pleasant and welcoming, with the delightful singing of the birds that greeted the new comers. After a few minutes the trail became steeper. Before their eyes appeared the majestic mountains of the Eastern cordillera with a lovely range of green colors. In the top a dense cloud rested behind which they could see the blue sky. It was a magnificent panorama! They continued ascending and about half way to the Monastery of San Carlos, Juan stopped to search the surroundings. On both sides of the path there were coffee plantations with orange, mandarin, banana trees and other varieties of fruits. It would be very difficult to find something in these lands covered with so much vegetation. The coffee plants were ready for harvesting. Luckily they were planted in perfectly aligned rows, almost with a geometric perfection. The coffee trees were dressed in deep red color with their fruits over the green background of the leaves, splashed with white flowers here and there. The aroma of the mature coffee and the flowers of the other trees captivated the spirit of Juan and Chepe.

After a few minutes of searching the surroundings, Juan pointed to the left side of the path and said decisively:

"I think this is this way."

Immediately he walked through some tall grass that grew next to the trail that some farmers used to feed their cows. After climbing over the wires that surrounded the farm he ordered Chepe to follow him.

"To make it simple, this is what we will do," said Juan. "First, we leave the bags hidden under this tree, this way we will be lighter to explore throughout the land. Second, we divide the farm: you cover half and I cover the other half following the coffee rows one by one."

"It is very important that we save our provisions" he added. "When we find the tunnel we will need them. So if we get hungry or thirsty we will eat of the fruits we find here in the farm," said Juan. Chepe stood for a few moments without saying a word as if slowly processing each one of the decisions taken by Juan; then he moved his head in sign of agreement.

"I agree" said Chepe to Juan placing his bag under the tree and covering it with some branches "we are looking for any clue that may indicate the existence of a tunnel; a hollow or a cave in the land can be an indication of an entrance" remarked Juan.

"We will meet here again at four in the afternoon. After this agreement both young men started off in search of the missing tunnels. They spent the afternoon walking through the coffee plantation from one end to the other, examining meter by meter all the land, looking for any clues or any details that could indicate the presence of a cave or a tunnel. The time went by quickly but the intense search was unfruitful. At the decided hour, they met by the tree where they had left their bags. Juan sat down on a rock and Chepe reclined against a tree to rest and to try to process the last events. Both were discouraged and tired but they exchanged ideas and thoughts about the events of the day.

"Well, it was an adventure without results; nobody really knows if these tunnels really exist" said Chepe, who already showed his desire to return home. Juan kept silent but he understood the situation and the reasons given by his cousin. After a while Juan began to stand up from the rock that he was using as a seat when suddenly he observed a small lizard going towards him. Being very careful on not to get its attention, he raised his feet on the rock while remaining seated, with his eyes fixed in the movements of the agile creature. Soon it disappeared under the rock. With great curiosity, Juan searched under the rock looking for the place where it had disappeared, but the small lizard had vanished between two stones located under the rock where minutes before Juan were seated.

"Look Chepe! Look, we found it!" exclaimed Juan. In an instant Chepe was next to Juan to share the great surprise. It really did not seem be anything out of the ordinary. The two small rocks only gave the impression of supporting the larger rock on top in a normal way. With the help of a large branch Juan tried to remove one of the rocks. He inserted it in the crack where the small lizard had disappeared and after some effort, they managed to remove it uncovering a big hole.

"Finally, we found it!" Exclaimed Juan with great joy who did not yet believe what he was seeing.

Chepe on the other hand, studied the situation for a few moments and then he said:

"I think it is possible to get in there, but it is necessary to open the entrance a little more.

Then Juan, impatiently said:

"Get the flashlight, quick!"

Chepe brought his small bag and getting the flashlight quickly he gave it to Juan. He turned it on and focused it in direction of the hole to see its depth. It seemed to go down for two or three meters and it leveled off into a horizontal direction at the bottom. With much effort, they removed the second rock but still there was not sufficient space for one of them to go in. Fortunately Juan had brought a small shovel that some times he used in field trips to dig out plants of interest or to prepare small lots of soil in his farm. Using this simple tool, after more than one hour of work, they were able to enlarge the entrance. "Well, now we can return tomorrow to explore this place; now we can go home" suggested Chepe rising from the ground where they had been working.

"Tomorrow? No, no! We have to do it right now!" replied Juan.

"Now? Are you crazy? It is already dark" protested Chepe, adding then, "this takes time and we do not know what we are going to find."

"Very well, we'll go in the tunnel to find out what is there and to see what we may need, OK?" Juan asked anxiously.

"Well, you go in and find out, then we will come back tomorrow with more time and energy" responded Chepe.

"Although you should go first since you are smaller and it would be easier for you…" suggested Juan.

"No, no…!" Was the quick answer from Chepe.

"OK, I go first" answered Juan with a tone of resignation. With some difficulty Juan slid on his back through the hole descending about two meters vertically. Once there, he requested the flashlight and a wood stick to examine the place for a few feet. When illuminating towards the interior, he discovered clearly the designs of a rudimentary tunnel, perhaps of a meter and a half in height by one meter wide, maintained by boards in the ceiling and tree trunks in the side walls.

"Chepe, it's the tunnel that we are looking for!" exclaimed Juan, with great joy. "It seems that is very long. I cannot see its end! Let's go and see it, Chepe!" Juan exclaimed again from the bottom.

"Bring everything and let's go and see it!"

Although the darkness of the tunnel caused some distrust and fear in Chepe, he was also curious, so he accepted the invitation. He threw the bags with the equipment and food and lowered himself through the entrance easily due to his smaller size. Juan, meanwhile, discovered in the tunnel some black creatures suspended from the ceiling.

"It is a large number of bats and we should not bother them," said Juan in a low voice.

"They have chosen this place to avoid the light and the noise of the outside, so try not to bother them with the flash light" concluded, Juan, signaling Chepe not to make any noise or sudden moves that could wake them up.

CHAPTER 3

Although the atmosphere was humid in that place, it had sufficient air to breathe normally. Both of them turned off the flash lights and continued trying to explore in the dark. Once they felt more comfortable with the new environment they placed their bags on their back and began to move forward being careful not to disturb the bats that slept hanging from the ceiling. From time to time one of them would move slowly in the dark shadows trying to ignore the new intruders.

After a few moments of traveling through the narrow tunnel, it opened into what seemed to be a large room about three meters high and about six meters in diameter. Some stalactites hung from its ceiling. Since this place was rather calm and comfortable, the two cousins decided to rest there for a while, taking advantage of the time to have a simple but nutritious dinner to recharge their bodies with new energy: a can of sardines, bread and fresh fruit juice. Once finished they decided to continue their adventure. After a while the search became more complicated because the tunnel was reduced to a small hole difficult for Juan to cross due to his larger size. After this narrow crossing the tunnel opened up again into a large room. Very slowly and carefully both of them went through the narrow passage trying to avoid any damage to their clothes or to their bags. The two young explorers took advantage of the place to prepare the space to spend the night, and then they sat on the cold floor turning off their flash lights to experience total darkness and to reflect again on the activities of the day. For a few moments they did not say a word. Finally Juan broke the silence.

"This is a good place to rest for tonight. I have a feeling that a greater adventure awaits us tomorrow."

The temperature of about sixty degrees was pleasant, so the only thing they needed was pillows for a good night of rest. They improvised pillows by using their bags, being careful not to squash the bread they still had for the rest of the trip. Eight hours later both young men were once more moving forward through small passages, through small water puddles and slippery places covered with mud. But these passages were not very difficult or scary. Everything was rather somber, with the atmosphere resulting from the absence of the sun of the new day.

"At this moment we must be almost directly under the lagoon of Pedro Palo" said Chepe.

"The end of the tunnel cannot be very far." In the morning they found time to speak of the wonders of the nature they had observed the previous day on top of the mountain that serves as a cradle to the beautiful lagoon with its charming landscapes.

The tunnel now ended in a free passage into a room three or four meters high. It seemed to be the end of the tunnel. Up to this moment neither one had been successful in the search for the maps. They examined the walls and the ceiling of the room without finding anything that could indicate their possible location. To complicate matters, they noticed that the batteries of the flashlights were starting to discharge and they had enough food just for one more meal.

"Perhaps it is time to return" suggested Chepe. "We do not have to run unnecessary risks staying here, in this dark and terrible cave, without batteries" he added. "I think you are right, but we cannot return with empty hands" responded Juan. "We have to accomplish the mission of our trip!"

Having said this, they decided to use a single lantern to save the batteries of the second one for when it was absolutely necessary. After several hours of intense search, they found a small entrance along the north side of the room which was disguised by wood posts that maintained the wall covered with a pair of boards. The narrow entrance led to another tunnel only a meter high. It was very difficult to continue, but now both of them had the determination to get to the end.

In this instance Chepe led the way with his flashlight in one hand and his bag on the other. For Juan, it was a little more difficult to crawl through this tunnel. From time to time Chepe had to stop and wait for Juan. Trying to save the flashlight batteries, now they used the lantern only sparingly to explore the way, trying to memorize each detail, moving cautiously in the dark. They continued this way for a long while in which both of them lost the notion of time.

Suddenly, in the darkness, and without realizing it when crawling on the floor Juan, moved with his foot one of the columns that maintained the precarious ceiling of the tunnel, causing a small landslide that fell on one of his legs. With a muffled scream of anguish and fear as he found himself immobilized he requested help from Chepe, who was a few meters ahead of him.

"I am wounded! Let me have your flashlight please!" cried out Juan. Chepe returned carefully, to find out the condition of his cousin. Once at his side, he examined the situation and verified that the landslide was not very large but a rock rested on top of Juan's leg, who could not feel it or move it. Both of them waited a while trying to regain their calm. "First we must remove the rock to release the leg" suggested Chepe. "Perhaps I can do it by myself if you remain still where you are."

With great agility, Chepe sled on his stomach until he could touch the rock. Looking in all directions he considered the possibility of clearing the dirt around the rock to make it roll away. With great difficulty, first by hand and then with the help of the small shovel he managed to do it. When finished, he moved backwards and asked Juan to try to move slowly. In spite of several attempts, horrified they noticed that their efforts had been in vain. Chepe slid then over Juan's body to study the situation with the flashlight. He moved his hand through the mud covering his leg to examine his condition. He brought his hand close to his eyes and then to his nose, then he cried out, "Smells like blood, it appears that is a lot but it is difficult to know how serious it is since it is so muddy."

Chepe made a second attempt to raise the leg. To

his consternation, this bended in the middle of the bone indicating that it was broken, while Juan gave a painful scream. The blood mixed with mud covered the leg of his pants. He remained immovable, moaning. But there was no time to lose, the situation was critical for both. Chepe tried to calm him and to reason with him, to plan for the next move. "We have to get out of here as soon as possible, but we cannot return the same way we came because the landslide is closing the exit. The only thing we can do is to move forward," said Juan with determination and then continued: "between both of us, we can do it. You pull me by the hand and I push with the good leg. We must find a clear spot where we can fix my leg temporarily. They struggled through the narrow tunnel for more than an hour. They were tired. Suddenly they found a space of two or three meters wide by two meter high, where they could finally rest for a while leaning against the wall to recover their energies.

Juan had lost a lot of blood and he was very weak but he tried not to show it in order not to worry his cousin Chepe who appeared already demoralized. Chepe took the bags and emptied them on the floor looking for something he could use to improve the state of his companion. He found nothing useful. Seeing his cousin in such condition, he grabbed his head with both hands and shouted with anguish:

"Help! Please, help me!" knowing full well that nobody could hear his request or come in his aid.

In the middle of his anguish, without thinking, he took off his shirt, tore it off in long pieces which he used to cover his cousin's wounds to control the bleeding and to provide some comfort. To make matters worse, their provisions had been exhausted as well. They had finished the last ration they had taken before entering the last stretch of the tunnel. The situation was precarious and both knew it but they refused to acknowledge it.

"How are we going to get out of here?" asked Chepe, already knowing the answer. He knew the condition they were in. Juan, who was completely exhausted, did not respond. Minutes latter he slept for a couple of hours to try to recover, at least a little. When he woke up, everything was dark and in deep silence. Nevertheless, he though he had heard music in the distance. "Chepe! Did you hear that, Chepe?" he asked anxiously. Chepe turned on the flashlight briefly to search around him and then turn it off. "I do not hear anything. What are you talking about?" he asked intrigued. "I heard music, I am sure that I heard music, like a symphony orchestra in the distance. They kept silence for a few minutes and in this occasion both of them seemed to hear the tones of music, something like classical music. Chepe turned on the flashlight again to search the place where the music seemed to come from. He could suddenly hear it more clearly: it came from one of the corners of the room; it was very soft but well defined. "It's music!" exclaimed joyfully Chepe. "It's music!"

With a little effort he helped Juan to move towards that corner and both of them placed their ears against the wall trying to capture each of the notes. "It's the most beautiful music, the most magnificent and perfect music that I have ever heard in all my life!" commented Chepe, adding then: "it seems like a symphonic orchestra with all kinds of instruments; but it also has words... I do not understand what they are singing..."

They spent a long while with their ears stuck to the wall, hypnotized by the captivating beauty of the music. They could hear a choir but could not yet understand the words. Chepe turned on the flashlight again to investigate anything that could indicate an exit from this room. Unintentionally he passed his hand through a small crack in the wall where the music seemed to come from. With this movement a door was opened in front of them flooding the room with light so strong, that it made them close their eyes since by this time they were accustomed to the darkness of the tunnel.

After a few minutes they tried to open their eyes, very slowly at first and then in a normal way. A soft light now illuminated a great place, totally unknown to the young explorers. Juan continued lying on the floor, immovable, due to his physical state, but astonished by what he could observe now. Although the light illuminated the center of this place, the details inside could not be seen well. The music had stopped. Everything appeared to be a great mystery.

CHAPTER 4

Chepe took a few steps to explore this wonderful and impeccable place. Suddenly he heard an enigmatic voice that greeted him from the other side of the large patio. "Welcome, we were waiting for you..." Chepe moved cautiously in the direction where the voice came from. From a closer distance he could distinguish an image, blurred at first, but little by little it turned clearer. It was the figure of a young person with indigenous characteristics. Then he stopped to observe him in more detail. The person who had just welcomed them was of low stature, perhaps measuring only a meter and a half in height. The only clothing he was wearing was a skin that covered him from the waist to half the legs. A white headband held his black and well cared short hair. In his belt of skin hung something that seemed like a sword; it was hard to tell for certain due to the strong light that surrounded him. On his left side hung an instrument of yellow color that seemed like a blowpipe or a short telescope. His face, with a wide smile, radiated tranquility, while his brown eyes, were fixed on the new visitor. "Welcome, we were waiting for you..." repeated again. As if waking up from a dream, Chepe finally answered:

"Please, help us! My companion is severely wounded; he needs medical attention and water."

"Please be still!" answered the young native, taking his right hand to his chest, then to his lips and extending it in Chepe's direction, followed by a bow.

Chepe thought that this was a form of a greeting and replied in kind with a bow of respect.

"My name is Bachu. I have been waiting for you and your cousin Juan." Chepe had many questions but did not think this was the time to ask questions with other more pressing matters at hand. He observed that behind the young Indian there was a beautiful and crystalline fountain of water. It had a beauty and clarity never seen before. The fountain seemed to spring out of a small well.

"Please I need a little water for my cousin!" implored Chepe.

"No, mortals can not drink from this water," was the surprising answer from Bachu.

"But without water my cousin will die! Even more, he is wounded and he has lost a lot of blood. Please, we need help!" He cried out again.

"Peace my friend!" said Bachu "wait just a minute here."

And going to the water fountain, he took a small crystal container, something like a miniature jar and filled it with water.

"Mortals are not allowed to drink from this fountain, but your cousin will be well soon" answered Bachu with a soft voice.

Approaching Juan with a welcoming smile he greeted him with the same greeting as he greeted Chepe minutes before. Juan fixed his eyes on his host and tried to greet him with a bow as well but found it impossible due to his pain and physical weakness. Bachu bent down to examine Juan's condition without saying a word. He untied the bandages that Chepe had used to contain the blood, then he cut the pants to uncover the wound. Juan twisted giving a loud shout due to his pain. The bone was broken in half and all the leg looked purple and inflamed. Bachu took it on his hands and extended it at the same time that he poured a few drops of water on the wound. Like a miracle, the wound disappeared, as if it had never existed. The bone healed and the leg was even in better conditions than before the accident. Chepe blinked several times to be sure that his eyes did not deceive him. For his part, Juan got up without a problem. Not only his wounds had disappeared, but his body felt renewed. He was neither thirsty nor hungry. It was a true miracle!

After this, Bachu led them through the patio to a dinning room where supper was waiting for them. It was served for three people. Bachu sat at the front of the table which was covered with a white table cloth that descended almost to the floor. The plates and glasses were of pure crystal and the place setting was of silver. He then invited Juan and Chepe to sit to his right and to his left respectively. They had a simple but delicious supper through a time of great silence which nobody dared to interrupt. The new visitors could not find the appropriate words to express their surprise, admiration and gratefulness.

"Perhaps you have many questions about this place and those who live here" Bachu said while finishing supper. "Later I will introduce you to my friends and companions. For now I will explain briefly the history and the purpose of this place."

"My ancestors lived in this region many years ago. Just about two thousand years to be precise. Although it was long time ago, I can still remember it as if it was yesterday" continued Bachu. "Yes, I remember very well…"

"It happened on Friday, almost two thousand years ago… My sister and I were in the field that morning, gathering some fruits for our family. The fields, at this time of the year were covered with beautiful flowers and fruits. It was harvest time with plenty of mangos, oranges, mandarins and wild berries, all delicious and ready to gather." Bachu said.

"But that day everything felt sad, gloomy and incomprehensible. A dense fog covered most of the fields. From eight in the morning and into the evening everything was in complete darkness. Hours later the Earth shook with great violence followed by a strong roar, as we had never witnessed before. The skies were illuminated with terrible rays of stormy lightning and thunders. The rocks split and the mountains shook with a brutal force."

"In the middle of such a frightful and apocalyptic roar, we heard a strong voice as if carried by the wind that said: "It is finished …" The voice resonated again in the air after more thunders, and lightning illuminated the sky with the brilliance and strength of the sun. "It is finished…"

"My sister and I thought that this would be the end of the world or at least the end of the world for us. The rocks rolled down the mountains and hills with great roar and violence. In the middle of this catastrophe we hid behind some shrubs of wild fruits, we hugged each other to protect each other."

"At the end of the cataclysm everything returned to silence. The mountains and the nature kept silent as if they did not understand what had just happened. When looking up towards the Pedro Palo lagoon, our greater fear was that it could break open and flow down the mountain destroying the land and the crops on the way. But the mountains were again in peace and harmony. When we looked again at the lagoon there was a dense cloud covering it as if trying to protect it."

"After a time of fear and anguish, we came out of our hiding place and began our way back with certain apprehension, trying to reunite with our family. On the way back we saw a cavern in the slope of the mountain that we had never noticed before. It was very special because it seemed to contain a light inside. I thought that maybe somebody from our people had taken refuge over there. We approached the place and did not see anybody, but the light captivated our interest. When entering we realized that it was quite clean and empty. Our curiosity took us to the end of a tunnel which at that time was in better condition than that which you see today."

"We were tired and fatigued; when arriving at the end of the long tunnel, we noticed the presence of a small water fountain. When we got a little closer, we noticed that it was different and special. Its pure and crystalline waters never seemed to exhaust. I took a little from this water with my hands and then I gave some to my sister. Right away we noticed the supernatural power that this water contained. The thirst, the hunger and the fatigue we had, disappeared at once after we drank the water."

"Later we discovered that although the time passed our bodies did not age, we were the same as in the day we drank the water for the first time. Our bodies have remained young for almost two thousand years. For that reason we call it "The Fountain of Youth." The Father prefers to call it "The Fountain of the Holy Water."
"The Father?" exclaimed Chepe almost interrupting his story and jumping off his chair.
"Yes, Father Carlos. He has also been with us for many years... of his arrival to this place I will explain to you later."
"We discovered the Fountain of Youth at the same time with this wonderful and heavenly place. It is like a window to a place that is magnificent, sacred and full of glory that we still do not know but whose shadows, as you can see is reflected in this place. Here we realize the existence of a supreme being, a being who transcends space and time, full of glory, majesty, splendor and power. We call Him with great reverence and devotion: 'The King and Lord', or 'the King of kings and Lord of lords'."

Bachu reclined backwards in his chair and continued relating his history:

"Over five hundred years ago this zone was populated with hard working natives, who had much gold and emeralds which attracted the European conquerors who came to this land in search of wealth. The first of these visitors was the Spanish Gonzalo Jiménez de Quesada, founder of Santa Fe de Bogota. The mistreatment and the extermination of the natives by these foreigners started back in those years."

"According to the instructions from Spain, the expedition undertaken by Jiménez de Quesada in his route towards the New World, had to establish peace with the natives they found in the way and collect gold from all of them to consolidate the conquest process. If the natives refused to agree to a peaceful settlement and to collaborate with the Spanish cause, the commander in chief could undertake, at their discretion, a war of blood and fire, the so called "Just war," that would allow him to take control of their goods and even to enslave them."

"As they came into the new territory of the savannahs, the expeditionary army of the conqueror, they heard the news that an active commerce of salt between the inhabitants of the productive Andean land existed. In route to these mountains they gathered enormous amounts of gold and emeralds, without much resistance on the part of the natives.

In March of 1538 they entered "El valle de los

Alcaceres", as Jiménez de Quesada called the savannah ruled by Chief Bogota, also called Zipa by his people. On the way they discovered in addition, the lagoon of Tota, where they obtained fabulous treasures. In the town of Tunja the conquistador captured Chief Bogotá and with him a rich booty of gold and emeralds."

"On August 6, he declared the conquest of this territory in favor of the kings of Spain. Such activity coincided with the arrival of the armies of Sebastián de Belalcázar and the German Nicholas de Federmán, who came from Venezuela."

"The conquest of the Andean plateau was bloody: ill treatment and abuses against the natives and the brutal murder of chief Bogotá. In spite of this, Jiménez de Quesada obtained from the "Council of Indias" the right for the civilian and religious administration of the territories taken by him."

Bachu made a pause with certain air of sadness in his face and then he continued:

"But there is always justice under heaven; as it says in the sacred book: "He who oppresses the poor in order to get rich will end up in poverty... You do not rob the poor because he is poor, nor break the afflicted one because the Lord defends the cause of them" Then Bachu continued " It is in this way that in his last years, Gonzalo Jimenez de Quezada received his own reward. For a time he dedicated his life to the profession of attorney since he returned to the savannah. He lived a rather disordered life in which he got into deep debts that took him into a permanent state of economic shortages. At sixty years of age he tried in vain to solve his problems by undertaking the search for the mythical

EL Dorado in the east of the Andean mountains. In this last venture he went into definite ruin."

"Along with Hernán Cortes in Mexico, and Francisco Pizarro in Peru, Jiménez de Quesada was recognized as one of the great conquistadores of the New World. Like many of his adventurous colleagues, he committed great excesses against the natives of the new world. The search for *El Dorado* and the conquest of the Eastern plateaus were his obsession and his perdition. Once the failure of his expedition was known, the merchants who had financed his venture began to press the old and already defeated conquistador. His goods and properties were confiscated. After having lost this litigation, the conquistador managed to obtain from Spain the mission to make peace with the Gualí Indians, who lived in the region of Mariquita. He initiated this undertaking at the end of 1573 and achieved some successes at the cost of the lives of a large number of natives as well as Spaniards."

"The sad thing about all of this is that Jiménez de Quesada held in his hand, for a short time, the map that would take him to *El Dorado* but he never realized it, due to his own greed."

"Did you say that Jiménez de Quesada had the map to *El Dorado* in his hands?" interrupted Chepe with great interest.

"That's right" responded Bachu. "*El Dorado* is still in the high mountains, by the way, directly south of here. "One of the relics that he obtained from the natives was a valuable golden *balsilla*, which remains lost in the Caribbean. It is a copy of a powerful old relic brought to the New World by people of a highly advanced culture. It contains the key to find the famous *El Dorado* which attracted the European conquistadores and became a terrible tragedy for the natives of South America."

"However, not everyone that came from Spain came looking for gold or with the idea of dominating, humiliating or mistreating the natives. Padre Carlos was one of them."

"He was a man of God, with great compassion to the natives. In the middle of the adversity of the colonization period, the voice of Father Carlos continuously resonated in favor of the natives, pleading with the conquistadores to treat them like human beings. His voice went across the sea arriving at the ears of mother Spain, which resulted in endless difficulties for Father Carlos. As a result, he himself was persecuted and mistreated by the conquistadores."

"From his childhood Father Carlos' mind was set on being a missionary; he studied to be a teacher. Suddenly he found himself among the natives in the Savannah of Bogota; in the new world, a different world, learning a new culture and teaching the Hispanics and the natives. As a missionary his greatest desire was to help the poor and the needy. In this task he worked incessantly, day and night. He lived with the Indians, he learned their customs, and he ate with them according to their simple country style they had to offer. He prayed and meditated with the poor families, kneeling down on esterillas of straw that they wove artistically by hand in their homes."

"The crucial moment in the life of Father Carlos took place when he came against the bloody execution of the Indian Chief Bogota. As a result of this defying act he underwent terrible persecutions at the avenging hands of the conquistadores. It was at this moment that the mission to rescue him became necessary."

"For more than five hundred years we were waiting in this underground palace for a special person. Someone who had been promised to us, who would come from Europe to give us new revelations and to teach us a new way of life" continued Bachu. "While we were meditating in silence by the fountain, which we did daily in the morning, giving thanks to the great King and Lord, suddenly I felt a call in my spirit. The message was very clear: I had to go in search of that special person who had arrived from the Old World and he had been given to the service of the natives and the poor, living among them, helping them and teaching them."

"That call came as a revelation but immediately I met a great obstacle: I was not allowed to leave this sacred place; the question now was how I could carry out that order. I received then a special permission from the King to fulfill this mission, but only during the night, because my contact with the mortals had ended the day we discovered this fountain, the day we drank from it."

"From that moment our life has been dedicated to the service of the King. It happened in this way: On a Friday night I went searching for Father Carlos whom I found in a straw hut in the mountains teaching some families. It was not difficult to persuade him to come with me to this sacred place to fulfill his purpose in life."

"Once in the palace, he also drank the water from the fountain. His physical state and physical appearance are the same now as it was the day he arrived here more than five hundred years ago. His youth and vigor have remained intact for ever..."

"From that moment and through the years Father Carlos has been our guide and master, studying the content of the great book he brought with him to our secret refuge. He has taught us with great humility about this extraordinary fountain of wisdom and power. When you meet him you will realize that he is truly a man of God, a servant of the King."

"This has been a very long day for you, now you must rest" said Bachu as he led Juan and Chepe to the guest room. Before they retired for the evening they were given clean clothes and a bathtub to prepare themselves for a good nights rest. Their two beds were covered with white sheets. As if a revelation had finally come to his mind, Chepe commented to Juan:

"This is incredible! It is as if everything was ready for our arrival!" "You are right" answered Juan as the only comment, as he stretched out in his bed; having said that, both of them fell into a deep sleep until the following morning.

CHAPTER 5

Before beginning the new day, they got dressed in the new clothes that awaited them next to their beds: white pants and shirt and leather sandals. After leaving their room, they took a walk through the large palace which seemed at first as a large house of medieval style. The crystalline fountain at the center of the patio was surrounded by beautiful flowers of many colors which also bordered small paths going in different directions around the patio. This water seemed to give life to everything around in a magical way. The soft sound from it was clear, fascinating and charming.

Next to the fountain was a wood bench and seated on it was Bachu in an attitude of meditation. Opposite to him, on another bench was an Indian woman of medium stature in the same attitude. Her age was approximately twenty-five years. "I imagine she is Bachu's sister" thought Chepe.

She was dressed with a long brown dress that matched perfectly with the brown tone of her skin and with her long black hair. Her eyes framed with eyebrows and black eyelashes accentuated the beauty and smoothness of her face. Her looks were those of a beautiful princess. They stood there observing these two people for a long while with respect and reverence but with great curiosity, trying to understand the meaning of this ritual.

After a while, and as if synchronized, both of them arose directing a glance towards the new visitors. Bachu greeted them with his usual greeting, taking its right hand to his chest, then to his lips and finally extending it in their direction, without pronouncing word with a final bow. Juan and Chepe on the other hand responded to the greeting in the same manner. The young woman went in the opposite direction as if trying to avoid them.

Bachu took them to the dining hall where a delicious breakfast awaited them as if prepared by invisible hands. The three sat at the table like the previous night. On this occasion, Bachu, after giving thanks for the food, invited them to enjoy the breakfast. These were served in a crystal set of dishes: bread, eggs prepared with vegetables and several fruit juices. "It's absolutely delicious!" said Juan in a low voice expressing his gratefulness. "Today will be a special day for you" said Bachu as he finished his breakfast. "You will have the privilege to walk around this place and to find out some of its great mysteries and powers. Additionally, you will have the opportunity to meet other guests, as well as Father Carlos. And most importantly, you will also find out the purpose of your visit. More specifically, what is our mission, since you will have the privilege of being part of it. But before that, you will have to take part in an intense and rigorous training to receive the power and the equipment that you are going to need in order to fulfill this mission; you have been chosen, but you will have to work with great discipline, absolutely essential to ensure your success."

Juan and Chepe did not know what to say and they were very afraid of what they had just heard. "Do not worry, my friends" continued Bachu. "Before you are ready to leave, you will receive what you need for a successful mission." After saying this, he proceeded to show them each special place of the palace.

They started towards the fountain. From here they saw a wall which seemed to be the external wall of a temple. Bachu went to the door that faced the center of the garden, walked up a few steps and looking at Juan and Chepe he said:

"This door remains sealed, it is like a window to the throne of the King. It will be only opened at the end of the times, when the final mission has been totally fulfilled.

The walls looked like pure gold and the doors were made of a magnificent white and shining material, never before seen by the two cousins. The doors were held in place by great pillars of the same material as the walls. On the walls there were also windows that remained sealed. On the pillars there were engravings of palm trees giving the appearance of a royal palace.

This place had the aspect of a gigantic cathedral not constructed by human hands nor designed by men's creativity. The ceiling was as if it did not exist, because the light that illuminated it around did not allow one to see the central cupola directly.

A chapel was fashioned in the walls of this great underground palace, with simple outlines. It was bathed by a soft light that accentuated an atmosphere inviting to meditation. Attached to the wall there were a large number of planters with flowers that complemented the garden of the central patio that surrounded the fountain. Each station was maintained by inlaid marble columns in the wall. It was a beautiful sight.

One of the most welcoming places was the big chapel; with a small celestial cupola, where an intense light emanated from the top like a supernatural lamp flooding the place where Father Carlos had his daily meditations.

"This must be the place where Father Carlos meets with the King" whispered Chepe, not to be heard. "The celestial cupola is one of the most imposing places of this palace" affirmed Bachu with solemn tone, having heard the comment from Chepe.

There were also small benches carved on the rock of the wall which could be used to rest and to enjoy the beauty of the fountain and the central patio. When arriving at the front of the fountain a majestic hanging cross could be observed at the other side. It was about twenty meters high by about ten meters wide. It radiated a light that illuminated all the surroundings. When noticing this Juan exclaimed:

"Look! Directly on top of the cross there is a sign that says: "King of kings and Lord of lords". The beauty of this place was impressive.

Along the left of the central hall, was an immense carving on the rock, where an altar was located looking in the direction of the fountain. It was softly illuminated and surrounded by a solemn silence appropriate for contemplation and prayer.

From here they took another hallway which took

them to a great room with small divisions that led to another hall located on the other side. "This is the training room" said Bachu.

From here he led them towards the south, until arriving at other rooms whose size was as the previous ones. You could say that it was a replicate. All had large windows that looked over the central garden where the fountain was located and were designated for special guests like Juan and Chepe.

In the inner vestibule, there were two rooms. Next to the door of one of them Bachu stopped for a few minutes and then he said:

"This room is for Father Carlos who is in charge of the training for our mission and the one of alongside is the one for his assistant."

The inner hall of the palace, the thresholds, the windows with their grates and the galleries around the building were covered entirely with fine wood. From the entrance to this room, around the wall, there were alternating engravings of creatures with wings and palm trees. On the inside, everything was covered with pure gold, except the central hall which had wood panels adorned with palm trees and brilliant gold chains.

Alongside the wall was another chapel adorned with precious stones and white gold. In its interior, the beams, the thresholds, the doors, and the walls were covered with gold emphasizing the carved cherubim's figures. To the left of the pulpit was an altar of bronze and to the right a circular metal fountain. The set of dishes, the censers and the ten candelabra with their respective lamps, also were of gold. These last ones were placed five to each side of the entrance, whose doors were of fine wood covered with the same metal. Alongside, opposite to the main entrance was the chapel where the special liturgies, meditations and tributes were celebrated.

"This is a special place of great respect and requires certain clothes and implements to be able to enter" said Bachu in a solemn tone. "It is a sacred room. Here is where Father Carlos renders tribute to the King and Lord and places his daily offerings. When Father Carlos comes into this place he does not leave without changing first the sacred clothing with which he celebrates the ceremony."

Next Bachu took them to a door that faces east on the outer wall. There they heard again that magnificent, heavenly and glorious music. In the midst of it the voices of thousands of people could be heard giving glory and honor to the King. They sang in a wonderful choir like the waters of the seas that lull to sleep with their power and majesty.

The place was overwhelmed with an incomprehensible, majestic, and transcendent beauty. Juan and Chepe bowed with their faces to the ground, feeling unworthy before so much perfection. Bachu observed them in silence for a while.

The glory of the King seemed to permeate through the wall that separated this place. Taking off his sandals, Bachu bowed in reverence. The two cousins remained there for a long time captivated, enjoying the impressive and celestial music; a mixture of trumpets, piano and stringed instruments, fabulously transported through the air in all the directions to satisfy those who had the privilege to hear it. Soon thousands of voices were united in perfect harmony with the instruments singing:

"Holy, Holy, Holy is the Lord, The mighty King, who was, who is and who will be eternally and for ever".

Whenever those invisible instruments sounded in thanksgiving, the choir of voices paid its tribute exclaiming:

"You are worthy, our King and our Lord, to receive glory, and honor and power, for you created all things; and by you they exist and for you they were created."

The music and the singing continued for a long time. When it was all finished, the three of them got up and walked in silence.

"This is a privilege given to us for now as passers-by that we are. When our final mission is accomplished we will be able to enter in and enjoy the fullness of the presence of the Lord and King and behold his glory that now can only be observed from a distance... as a shadow" said Bachu in a low and solemn voice.

Later on he led them to the western flank to show them the place where water flowed forth from below the wall, in the eastern direction. It ran on the right side of the garden.

"This water is used for all the daily necessities of the palace, but it never mixes with the water from the fountain" said Bachu, and then he led them to the end of the wall, to the palace's exit.

This water flows towards the garden of life. Where this water flows there is abundant life for the benefit of the palace and those who live in it. The fish in the lakes of the garden are varied and numerous. In the borders of this stream grow all kinds of fruit trees; their leaves never wither and they always bear fruit, because the water that gives them life comes from this sacred place.

The garden was an idyllic place, well irrigated, with abundance of food and always well taken care by the men who helped keep the palace. The surroundings were pleasant and calm; this was a place of harmony.

Part of the garden was surrounded by a wall. It was located on a plateau by a steep mountain; some brooks formed beautiful cascades. The air was impregnated with aroma from roses, jasmines, violets and jacinth. The singing of beautiful birds of bright colors was quite enchanting. The palm trees, the cedars and the pines offered shade to the green meadows. Next to the cascades, in the middle of all these trees, one stood out due to its leafy branches and great beauty, overflowing with fruits.

"This is the tree the life of which no mortal can eat" noticed Bachu.

Juan and Chepe fixed their eyes to that tree with astonishment for a long while. Before they started back to the palace they tried hard to remember where they had read about the legend of this tree but they could not remember exactly. The garden offered a large number of trails where it was possible to enjoy its beauty and at the same time observe a large variety of exotic plants. Each of these trails had a special detail that turned it into a magical place of dreams.

At the end of the day, after getting well acquainted with the palace and its surroundings, Juan and Chepe would have the opportunity to finally meet Father Carlos. The moment was formally set up to take place in the main dining room. The table, ready to seat six people, was covered with a white table cloth. In the center was set an arrangement of beautiful wild flowers most probably gathered from the garden of the fountain.

At the proper hour Bachu entered the room and invited Juan and Chepe to follow him. He was dressed for the occasion in a white tunic. He indicated to Juan and Chepe to sit to the left, while he proceeded to sit at the right of the table. Minutes later Father Carlos arrived, also covered with a white tunic and a robe of the same color on his head. He remained standing at the head of the table. Then a person of about twenty years of age dressed in the same manner entered the room and stood next to Father Carlos.

The last one to come in was Bachu's sister whose dress was also similar to that of the rest of the guests around the table. Before she took a seat, Bachu stood up indicating to Juan and Chepe to do likewise in order to greet Father Carlos. In silence, the four of them greeted Father Carlos and his assistant with a ceremonial bow. From the corners of the room a smooth and solemn music gave the occasion a more formal atmosphere.

Father Carlos raised his hands giving thanks for the food, and then invited everyone to participate in the delicious and abundant supper prepared with perfection. During dessert the string music filling the room turned into a happier tone making the atmosphere somewhat less ceremonial. An informal introduction of all of the people present was carried out at this time. The conversation, mixed with humor and interesting stories, was drowned occasionally with great outbursts of laughter. Bachu's, sister seating opposite to Chepe, had captivated him with her eyes. Her beauty was heightened by her immaculate white tunic, which made her look even more attractive.

For the first time Chepe could admire her black eyes, which made perfect combination with her long black hair that covered her back. They look at each other briefly in silence, and then she fixed her glance on Father Carlos to avoid looking at Chepe again. After several unforgettable hours for Juan and Chepe, supper concluded when Bachu stood up to announce the next event of the night:

"Friends and guests" he announced formally looking to Juan and Chepe. "This is a special occasion. Again I like to offer a friendly and warm welcome to you. I like to introduce to you a special person and to offer additional details about the purpose of your visit to this place. But before I do that, let me say a few words about my purpose here." Bachu retold the story again, of how they had discovered this place two thousand years ago, along with his sister and how after drinking the water from the fountain of youth their lives had changed forever. The first person to be introduced this evening was of course his sister Tachia. The eyes of everyone present in the room were fixed on her, who remained sitting while her brother related her history that in fact was the history of both.

She was a beautiful princess born in the Andes enjoying peace in her lands. With her brother she lived this historical feat that would unite them for eternity. She had the physical characteristics proper of her ancestors. Her youth had been frozen in the peak of her beauty which all considered a great blessing. She was the youngest and the last daughter of her family.

CHAPTER 6

Tachia was born at the height of the splendor of the Chibcha Indians in the savannahs of the Andean mountain range in Colombia. Like Bachu her closest brother, her heart always dreamed about the coming of the day when all humanity could live in complete peace and harmony. Her shyness, beauty and kindness hid the great power she had, which had been conferred her, as well as her brother to carry out the mission of her life. When she smiled, her face seemed to fill with light and happiness that was contagious. Although generally quiet, her voice was musical and soft; it reminded you of the enchanting singing of wild birds that cheered the heart and the spirit of the inhabitants of this mountain range.

In spite of her sweet appearance, her eyes radiated the power and the wisdom acquired in her long life in this exquisite place. A beautiful necklace of gold and emeralds adorned her neck, being symbols of the wealth and riches of her ancestors. One of her dreams was the destruction of *La Reliquia Del Poder (The Relic of the Power)*, that could put in danger the existence of the human race in this planet. She felt great nostalgia for her land and for her people, but she knew that she could never again see the land that saw her grow up and become a woman. Her presence for a couple of millennia was a special complement to the life in this beautiful place. Thanks to the powers given to her, the people of this region remained protected from outsiders and in a permanent spring.

When finally meeting Juan and Chepe, Tachia could celebrate the purpose of her life and the purpose of her people. She finally realized that they were truly the guardians and keepers of this majestic place. Along with her brother, she had been many years in the palace, observing how a threat, like a black shadow, grew in strength at the other side of mountains, in the lands of the condor. At the providential arrival of the two cousins, she was the first to know where they were coming from and what their final mission was. As the years went by, the imminent danger of *La Reliquia del Poder* was revealed. She could see things that were about to happen, but she would not reveal them until the proper time. She would maintain them in privacy, hoping that they would develop accordingly with the passing of time.

Once he introduced his sister, Bachu continued: "Our work for over two thousand years has been to take care of and to keep this sacred place. The existence of the fountain was a true mystery until the arrival of Father Carlos, who in great detail related to us about its origin and its meaning. He brought with him a great sacred book that he used to explain the power and the mystery that was in the fountain. He also spoke to us about that terrible event which we witnessed about two thousand years ago in these mountains. He explained to us that this was related to the death of an innocent man called The Christ. That he had come like a servant and a redeemer, doing great wonders, miracles and signs among men. But although innocent, this Christ was

The Power Of The Relic

condemned to death in a cross in the middle of two evil men. He was despised, stricken and humiliated; he bore the ailments and the diseases of mankind. The iniquities of everyone fell on him who carried them in silence. After he was apprehended and judged he was condemned to die, although he never committed any violence, nor was any deceit in his words. Thus that innocent died...

But the Earth, the skies and all the creation cried out and they shook before such a tremendous injustice. The sun was darkened and the Earth shook in violent cataclysms and earthquakes and immense smoke clouds ascended from the Earth."

"Father Carlos related that what seemed a defeat turned out to be a triumph and a great victory; that at the third day, Christ arose again with great power and glory, because death could not dominate him. That the Christ came as servant and redeemer and now reigns as King and Lord and that one day He will return as a glorious King and before Him all men will bow and confess that He is truly the King of kings and The Lord of lords, worthy of all glory and honor."

"In this manner Father Carlos has been our guide and teacher" continued Bachu. "It is he who protected many of our natives in these lands. With his great persistence and tenacity he managed to rescue many from slavery and from ill treatment of violent European conquistadores and in many instances even saved them from certain death. Now, it is with great pride and reverence that I present to you Padre Carlos."

Father Carlos rose and giving a glance around the

table he saluted in silence with a friendly smile on his face. He appeared to be about thirty years old. His humble manners made a clear contrast with his young, athletic and agile body, the consequence perhaps of a rigid discipline.

Clearing his throat, he directed his attention to Juan and Chepe:

"Welcome my children. For about five hundred years I have been waiting for this special and prophetic moment. As you already know, a special mission awaits you, which none of us who have been here for such a long time can carry out. No one who has drunk from the water of the fountain can leave this palace or have direct contact with the mortals outside this place, because it is eternal and it has prodigious powers."

"There lays the great mystery! The water used for the daily necessities of this place comes from the lagoon located exactly above us, but it is not possible for that water to be mixed with the water of the fountain. You will have the privilege to drink of the water of the fountain but not before completing your final mission, not before accomplishing the purpose of your visit; the same for those that will accompany you. My children: the mission is difficult and dangerous and because of that, initially you will receive the instructions with the required discipline. At the end of this stage you will also receive special powers and the necessary equipment for each mission."

"Each mission?" Chepe asked suddenly, interrupting the Father almost without realizing it. Father Carlos looked a Chepe and paused for a moment. "Yes, my son?" asked Padre Carlos.

"Forgive me Father; I had understood that our mission was to find *"El Dorado"*.

"That will be your mission but there will be others as well. In reality your mission will be done in stages. This was designed by the King. I am only his spokesman and my task is to train you and to prepare you well for a successful undertaking. The next days will be of intense work, which will take place in the hall of arms. During this time you will also be tested so that you yourself can be assured of your success when the moment arrives to facing the enemy."

"About this King, when will we be able to see and to meet this King that you speak about?" interrupted again Chepe. "At this point it will not be possible to meet him in person, but you will know him through his voice and by means of the sacred book during the training phase."

"Also I want to introduce Joaquin to you; he is my assistant. We call him affectionately Chiqui. He will help you throughout the whole process, so you will have the opportunity to know him well."

At five in the morning the following Monday Juan and Chepe woke up to the sound of trumpets that indicated to them that it was time to begin the training. They were still very tired and additionally, they were not accustomed to get up this early yet. Chiqui passed by their room to take them to the room where they hoping to find the necessary equipment for physical warm-up. To their surprise, all they found was a solemn and quiet atmosphere. Father Carlos was seated on the floor meditating. Chiqui invited them to follow his example. After an hour, Father Carlos led them to a room located behind the main hall where they received instructions for another hour; later, he took them to a small room. In this place there was only a small table with a great open book. The white gold cover and its pages shone under a light that descended from the top. Leaning on the book, Father Carlos began to page through it carefully. Then he spoke to his students:

"A large part of the time in this room will be used to study and to search this Sacred Book, which contains the great mysteries of life and the power as well as the secrets of the King and Lord. Little by little it will be revealed to you. These mysteries and knowledge must be studied with great diligence and searched for many days as part of a deep training.

You will learn its principles in which you must meditate constantly; when you lie down and when you rise. These will be of great importance for the success of your mission. Write these principles and these words in your heart, in your soul and your mind; because if you are careful to remember and keep these precepts from the Sacred Book, the Lord will take you to the success of your mission and your purpose, and He will defeat the enemy before you. The places you step on will be protected. No evil will be able to stand before you because the Lord will instill fright and fear to all who come before you."

There they were for a long time with Father Carlos who directed them with great skill in their preparation, in the principles and mysteries of Sacred Book. The physical training was directed mostly by Bachu, who for the first period of warm-up demonstrated the best way to do it, step by step: "Move your body, breath deeply, relax and feel the circulation of a new energy so that it can become a flexible and dynamic structure, with optimum and free operation of the joints, allowing movement free from any pain.

Why should we train the physical and the spiritual simultaneously?" asked Bachu rhetorically. "For a simple reason: because man is formed of both and it works better if these components work in a synchronous way. The objective is to develop at the same time and to improve all the required conditions. Training is a process and as such it requires time, hard work and maturation in order to obtain good results. The time is relatively short but very intense, with daily sessions during several months, which include specific exercises: skill, coordination with elements, flexibility and power. At the end of this period you will have two tests to measure your level of learning and development. An evaluation will be taken to empower you to improve the weak areas. Regarding your attitude, although you may arrive to the high objectives, you must always train with the same persistence and humility of a beginner. Keep your enthusiasm and willingness to learn and to improve" he concluded.

After two hours of exercise they went to take a nutritious breakfast, to regain the necessary energies for the rest of the day that they already had a feeling, would be arduous. The first physical tests were designed to develop agility, skill and flexibility. The execution of this variety throughout the day left them exhausted.

The regime of this routine continued for a week. The following Monday already their bodies and their minds were a little more accustomed to the new physical requirements. Now they felt a great pleasure when rising in the mornings for their training. The music used during the demanding routine of preparation inspired them to give the maximum, to exert the maximum, to push themselves beyond what their bodies could endure.

After the workout on Friday of the second week Father Carlos made a short demonstration of how a body in good physical conditions can accomplish much. Agile as the tiger and graceful as a gazelle, he moved perfectly through the room performing coordinated movements well choreographed.

Astonished, Juan and Chepe observed this man, known for his humility, modesty, spirit of patience and mild manners, now he demonstrated almost the opposite qualities of high energy and pride, and indomitable spirit. At the end of his demonstration, he was transformed again into a docile and humble person. He approached his disciples to greet them and to congratulate them for the progress obtained, saying to them:

"My Children, the secret to the personal power is in having control of the body in a careful balance with the mind and the spirit. That is the reason why the day must begin and end with exercising the mind. It says in the Great Book: "Those who honor me I will also honor".

This is the reason why the first stage must be concentrated in the synchronous exercise of the mind, the spirit and the body. This is the center, the fundamental axis for success or failure. The rests are only tools to help you develop the work. The secret is here and here, he said indicating with his forefinger, to his head and his heart."

"Father" asked Juan, now very interested. "When will we be ready for our mission?"

"My son, the mission will come to you when you are ready, neither earlier nor later." Saying this he retired in the direction of his study.

For their part Juan and Chepe continued with their training, every time forcing their muscles to improve, acting with more force, more consecration and perseverance. Their objective now was to be like their teacher, Father Carlos, who day after day inspired them in an extraordinary way.

This went on for a period of three months. Every day with new objectives; one of being better than the previous day; of reaching new goals; faster, stronger, more capable. The challenge was personal and seemed not to have a limit. Both young lads began to feel in their body and their spirit their progress towards the high goals.

The following morning as Father Carlos had indicated, was the training for physical and mental agility. Father Carlos and Bachu were active participants, not as instructors but as the test instruments. This was done one on one. In the first period Chepe and Father Carlos; then Juan and Bachu. The test began with both contenders bowing to each other as a sign of respect and mutual admiration.

During one hour the four fought in that room with the agility of a wild tiger and the gentleness and the grace of a dancer. At the end Juan and Chepe were tired although this was only the first half of the encounter. In the second period, the confrontation would be between Chepe and Bachu on one side of the room while Father Carlos and Juan in were in the other side.

"It is impossible! I cannot continue; I am tired!" protested Juan.

Father Carlos approached the two young lads and as an understanding teacher said to them:

"Where do the strength, the energy and perseverance come from? They come from within, from the soul and from the heart... do you not know that? The Lord, the creator of the universe does not get tired; His intelligence is infinite. He gives strength to the exhausted and to the weak, increasing his vigor. Remember, the energy that prevails comes from within, from the spirit. The young athletes can get tired and the strong man can fall, but those who trust in the Lord will always have new strength to accomplish their purpose."

Those encouraging words provided new strength to the two cousins who with renewed spirits, continued the second part of the test. This was as intense at first, but with a remarkable difference: the force and the energy now seemed to come forth from within with a determination and passion worthy of the students of Father Carlos and the native Bachu.

As they finished, the athletes bowed to each other with respect and they shook hands as a sign of friendship. The four of them had an aspect of tired athletes but their faces shone radiating with success. After a brief rest, Father Carlos went to Juan and Chepe to congratulate them for the wonderful performance. The scores they had obtained were worthy of celebration.

"As you know, all those who compete in the games, all run in the race, but only one gets the prize; and all that fight abstain from everything with great discipline and austerity. In this opportunity both of you have demonstrated a worthy spirit of admiration and respect. You have been able to obtain the prize. All the athletes train with the purpose of obtaining an award that soon disappears, but you on the other hand have a purpose, a mission of eternal impact." "I congratulate you for competing with conviction, to reach a noble and worthy goal, Father Carlos concluded enthusiastically."

CHAPTER 7

The following week, it was Bachu's turn to start the new training phase of the two cousins. He entered the training room dressed in the same manner as the first moment they met: a skin tied to his waist covering his body to half his leg; a belt also of skin which kept a sword on his left side and something that seemed like a blowpipe to his right side. He stopped at the center of the room and saluted with brief bow. The training took place in the room adjacent to the one they used during the previous three months.

"Father Carlos is very satisfied and proud of your progress and accomplishments" said Bachu before beginning his session." I also congratulate you! Now we will have one week for the training on the handling of a weapon."

"One week?" Interrupted Chepe". We have been through an intense physical training of three months and now the training of arms will be of only one week?"

Fixing his glance on both apprentices Bachu responded with the great serenity and gentleness:

"The most important is not the control of weapons but control of one's self. Although we lived in this world, we did not fight the battles like the other mortals. The weapons with which we fight have the divine power to demolish spiritual strongholds. The greatest battles are fought in the human mind before they are fought in the physical world."

"The sword is an individual weapon for battle which is used to reach to the adversary" he continued explaining. This sword contains in itself great powers. As you develop your skill with this weapon, its power will begin to be increased" added Bachu. "This power must be used solely for a good cause, or a good purpose, to make justice, to defend the innocent and to release those who are under unjust dominion."

Bachu, pulling out the sword from its sheath, raised it in his right hand. This position made him seem taller and defiant. The sword was of a transparent and brilliant crystal like a diamond. The handle was golden, like of pure gold, seemingly custom-made to match his hand perfectly.

"This is a weapon of great power; it depends on the hand that uses it" said Bachu to them, as he moved swiftly with his arm and his body in attitude of battle. Initially the sword gave the impression of being transparent, but suddenly it changed to a combination of beautiful colors simulating a flame in his hand; red, yellow and blue. When static, it returned to its original state, a beautiful crystal sword. "This is a simple training but it requires much discipline and skill. Sword and fighter become one" continued Bachu.

Next he went on to explain the movements and the fundamental bases for its handling. His body, his arms and his sword, moved at the same time with movements well calculated and artistically executed.

After the first demonstration, he requested Juan and Chepe to follow his instructions, imitating him without the weapon in hand. This seemed as an advanced class of choreography. The training continued during a week of intense work. The two cousins practiced daily the exercises and strategies of defense and attack that Bachu taught them; each time with higher skill and dexterity. The instructor at every moment followed the movement of his students with great interest and enthusiasm, making sure, that they worked towards the desired perfection. In the end he congratulated them for their progress, informing them that in this manner they could obtain their own weapons with the corresponding powers, but only when they were ready.

"The time has come to celebrate your progress and accomplishments" Bachu said to them.

"Tomorrow we will have a special ceremony to formally transfer the arms to you which you will need during your mission." Finishing their conversation, they retired to their respective rooms for a deserved rest. Before entering, Chepe approached Bachu to request a special favor.

"The place where I will return in few days is full of suffering and pain. So I want to ask if in my return I could take with me the miraculous water of the Fountain of Youth, to alleviate the suffering and the pain of some."

Bachu thought for a moment considering the repercussions that this could have for his friend Chepe and finally responded.

"I do not have the power to give you this water nor

the powers that it has. This belongs to the King and only He can offer them. This request will be possible solely with His consent."

Chepe was left a little sad by that answer. His heart could not understand how this could be, and the remote possibility that the King could allow such a high privilege to him. That night he was wide-awake in his bed for a long time thinking about the great benefit that this would be during his mission. He loved his people and was very sad to see them suffer from diseases and incurable ailments. That same night the King and Lord appeared to him in a dream, and said to him:

"Ask me what you want." Chepe responded:

"You have reaffirmed your great love and mercy when granting me to know this admirable and sacred place and to allow me to participate in this special mission. Now, my Lord, you have chosen me for a very high purpose, but I am not more than a poor farmer's son, a fragile boy and without experience. Nevertheless, I am here, I am your servant, ready to serve you. I request to you that additionally you grant me the privilege to use the water of the fountain to alleviate the pain they suffer, because there is much disease and sickness in the world."

The King was pleased with Chepe's request in favor of his people and not for himself, so He responded:

"Since you have asked to be able to alleviate the pain and suffering of your fellow men and not power or wealth for yourself, I will grant you this and even more. You will have the privilege to use the water from the fountain and the ability to alleviate human sufferings as nobody before you. In addition, although you have not asked for it, I will give you a long life."

When Chepe woke up the following day and remembered the dream, he returned to the chapel with great joy to share it with Bachu. Minutes later he met with Father Carlos, who shared the joy of the young man as he received such a distinguished honor from the King. He promised to offer a banquet in the Palace to celebrate with the graduation.

The day they have been looking forward finally arrived. From that moment they would have to assume the great responsibilities and obligations of having the privilege to be the chosen ones to fulfill the transcendental mission.

"A few hours after breakfast the official ceremony will begin," Chepe reminded Juan.

"I am not sure yet if I am ready for this. Still feels like a dream" responded Juan. "This reminds me of stories of legendary characters I read during my last year at school: the legend of caballeros, those young people who at seven years of age were sent to the house of a great lord who would turn them into Caballeros. The women taught them manners, the men trained them in the use of arms and horse riding."

"When they learned to defend themselves, approximately between the fourteen and sixteen years, they became squires of caballeros, their assistants, and at the same time their disciples. While they completed their education, the squires dedicated themselves to work to take care of their properties and even to guard their door at night."

"In battle they attended the caballeros in whatever they would need," Juan continued, "for example, attending the horses and the arms. In many instances, they accompanied them to the battle and they fought at their side. When becoming twenty one years of age, if the young men were considered worthy to become caballeros, a ceremony was arranged to receive this honor from the hand of a caballero or a high ranking warrior."

The cavalry was the force of the armies, the elite that became a form of life with strict rules that talked about not only the behavior of their members, but also the morals and the type of creed of the horsemen. The minimum norms could be summarized in this manner: The protection of the women and the weak; the search for justice, and the love of ones own land and country.

Chepe listened to the story with great patience and moving his head with incredulity he responded to Juan: "This is not a fantasy. Great events of dangers and adventure are ahead of us. I have been prepared for this day and am ready for this extraordinary occasion" said Chepe in a more serious and solemn tone.

The event started at ten in the morning. The imperial music of trumpets sounded majestically announcing the occasion, with Father Carlos as a master of ceremonies. Bachu, his sister and other guests of honor already were present in the main chapel.

Juan and Chepe, with white linen uniforms, their heads covered with a mantle of the same color, bare feet, marched in solemnly at the tone of martial music, towards the chapel. The moment was very solemn.

They approached Father Carlos in silence, who was waiting for them; they knelt reverentially before him. Father Carlos directed his eyes to his students and to the guests inviting them to kneel down in the same way to begin such special ceremony. After the blessing, all the audience took their seats while Juan and Chepe remained on their knees.

Father Carlos proceeded with the ceremony; then he asked that the two young students move closer to the altar; he placed a white tunic embroidered with gold borders on Chepe; he fit a belt around him and then he placed a turban on his head and on his chest a gold plate that consecrated him for a special mission. Later the assistant took a lamp of incense and with a ceremonial step he took a walk around the chapel. This did he did seven times, while the aroma filled that room to consecrate it.

Following, Father Carlos requested a small gold jar with water from the Fountain of Youth. Next he took a few drops from it and applied it the lobe of Chepe's right ear, the thumb of his right hand and the big toe of his right foot. Then he asked Juan to approach the altar and proceeded to do the same with him. Later he sprinkled some water on the altar.

"Now you can follow the voice of the Lord" said Father Carlos "and see the purpose of His creation just as He has established it. Now you can speak as His emissaries."

Fixing his gaze on Chepe he spoke in this manner:

"Today, I confer to you the same power that I have received from the Lord; with it you will dominate your enemies and you will release the oppressed. The power will not depart from you until you fulfill the purpose of your mission as ordered by the Lord who deserves the obedience and the reverence of men forever."

Then he took one step back and addressed the two cousins:

"My Children, you have been called for a special mission, hard and difficult, but you do not have need for great weapons. You already have them in your mind and your heart. You do not need the image of a soldier covered with armaments, with a Red Cross stamped on a battle suit. You do not have the mission to save beautiful princess from fortified castles of stone walls and pits with dragons. In reality you have now the standard of a royal lineage that with the required training confers you the power for assured victory. You will prevail in the name of the Lord."

"In the same manner you have this from the King: you must be worthy of the calling, kind, of irreproachable conduct, sober and prudent; you must not be given to drink, nor loving of dishonest gains, and always act with a clean conscience."

He then ordered them to bring the sword and addressing Chepe, who still remained on his knees next to his cousin, he read from his manual, like reciting a devoted prayer; in the middle of his reading he raised his hand and gave a slight touch on the right shoulder and then on his left shoulder in the same manner, murmuring some words dedicated to the act. Then he requested one of his assistants to fit the sword around

Chepe's waist. This was done with great ceremony.

Then Father Carlos said:

"May the power of the King be with you; with this sword you will overcome any difficulty. In His name I declare you a suitable servant of his kingdom, fit for the mission that awaits you and that will be revealed to you at the proper time."

"May the power and the wisdom of the King be always with you in every circumstance of your life. As the King has promised, your sword is equipped with the power of life from the Fountain of Youth. The holy water in your sword will never be exhausted while you live.

Finally he went to Juan who also remained on his knees. He proceeded to ordain him as an assistant and support of Chepe, in a royal ceremony as done for Chepe. As he finished, Father Carlos indicated to everyone in the audience to rise as the royal music from the trumpets returned once again while they left in a solemn march. At the sound of the music, the two cousins, now transformed, marched with much elegance. Chepe displayed the powerful sword in his waist, ready for the great adventures that awaited them. They were now prepared for their future mission.

All the assistants of the ceremony came over to congratulate them. That evening was of the great rejoicing; with varied and abundant food and drinks. Jokes, stories, and resounding outbursts of laughter filled the environment, intermingled with dances, music and songs.

During the celebration that extended until late hours

of the night, the presence of Tachia was especially note worthy. She was dressed in a beautiful white blouse with embroidery and gold buttons across her back. The skirt was highlighted with satin of bright colors, decorated with flowers, matched well with the blouse, covering her body down to her feet. Her hair was adorned with pretty flowers.

The suits of the men were more plain; a white hat with a black ribbon, a white shirt decorated with ruffles and with open neck. The pleated pants of the same color were well pressed; a silk red handkerchief and a leather belt.

The two cousins and their friends enjoyed the celebration with folk music and melodies: the sounds of the guacharaca, the maracas, the drums and the accordion offered a good repertoire of dancing music; porros, cumbias, and vallenatos; the traditional music of Colombia.

To this celebration also were added the string instruments; the harp, requinto, tiple and the guitar with festive sounds like the joropo llanero. Happy and delightful music ran in the blood and the spirit of those people celebrating this occasion.

At a certain time, Bachu interrupted, calling the attention to everyone present for the purpose of rendering tribute to the King and congratulating the special guess of the day: Chepe and Juan. He asked everyone to participate in songs, with any instrument available; each one of the assistants immediately accepted the invitation enthusiastically. It started with a lively and cheerful heavenly cumbia, interpreted by Bachu as a special tribute for that moment in the middle of the shouts of joy and enthusiasm from everyone present there:

Long live the great King!
Sing songs of great joy!
Sing of His wonderful works!
Let the faithful be glad!
And remember the wonders He has done,
For the King is our Lord,
His judgments govern the land.
The King does not allow them to be oppressed;
Because of His love He warned the adversary:
Do not touch my people!
Do not mistreat my nation!
Let everybody sing to the King!
Proclaim His power every day!
Speak of His glory among His people,
and of His wonders to all the nations.
Because our King is great,
worthy of all honors;
Splendor and Majesty are in His presence;
Power and glory are in His sanctuary.
Let the heavens be glad, let the earth rejoice,
Let the nations say: The King is Lord!

An every one joined in:
Long live the King!
Long live the King!
And long live His emissaries!

CHAPTER 8

At breakfast time, the following day it was time to say goodbye. Father Carlos, Bachu, and his sister Tachia were present there to share the last moments with their special guests before they wished them farewell. The atmosphere, although solemn, was festive. There was an exchange of stories and jokes.

After breakfast Chepe and Juan packed small bags with provisions for the trip. It was not much, but sufficient for a day of travel. Chepe wore the new sword in his waist, ready for a new life of adventure that awaited them.

At the last minute Bachu, his sister Tachia and Father Carlos accompanied them to the garden entrance. There they gave each other a warm and brotherly farewell hug and Father Carlos gave them a final blessing:

"*May the King bless you and honor you;*
may the King watch over you with satisfaction and delight;
may His generosity be with you
and may He grant you great victories
in all your ventures and accomplishments... "

"... May the presence of the King be always with you, may the victory always shine in your sword; may the light of hope, certainty and faithfulness be always with you."

Bachu showed them a trail through the garden that disappeared at the distance, in the other side of the hills, instructing them to follow it all the way to the exit. Then he said to them:
"There you will find the entrance to your new world."
The two cousins started down the trail but before they went too far, they turned around to observe one last time their friends and hosts. Father Carlos and Tachia raised their hand as a farewell. Bachu on the other hand gave them a one last farewell in the same manner as he had welcomed them sometime back: taking his right hand to his chest, then to his lips and finally extending it in the direction of the travelers, he bowed to them. Juan and Chepe in turn bowed to them from the distance and then continued on the trail to the other side of the garden.
The trail led them to a large tunnel and without thinking much about it they entered it. Suddenly, as if by magic they found themselves in a new and strange place. They looked carefully at their surroundings for a few minutes and then they looked at each other. Although they did not observe any physical change, both knew with certainty that their lives had changed forever. In their minds and hearts now they had a purpose and a destiny, and the power and the determination necessary to make it come to pass.

The Power Of The Relic

The roar of great torrential waters surrounded them. The humidity of the fog made the ambient a little cold. Initially Chepe thought that they were elsewhere in a strange place but after a few moments he exclaimed: "It is the Tequendama waterfalls! We came out at the Tequendama waterfalls!" he repeated with great emotion, when he realized that they were suddenly again in familiar grounds.

Indeed they had come out at the base of this majestic natural wonder. From down there, at the base of the water fall, the water of the Bogota River could be observed becoming the imposing waterfalls that look like large cotton balls descending into the deep abyss. The surroundings were covered by beautiful tropical vegetation which complemented the natural beauty of this place. The path downhill was quite slippery and dangerous, since the ground was humid due to the fog that rose from the waterfall giving it a beautiful and amazing aspect. The sound of the waters made it difficult to hear each other. They had to speak quite loud, almost shouting in order to be able to hear each other.

The water from the river fell vertically near the wall. In the upper part, you could see the falling water as if splitting into silver plated threads forming fine pearl necklaces. The mist produced by the evaporation and the foam, offered a spectacle of great beauty. The water almost disappeared in the air and the foam that ran downwards extended gradually to loose themselves in dense rays that hurried into the abyss. From the place where the two cousins were, the waterfall seemed to be a silver carpet which in a smooth and subtle way, touched the ground as it reached the bottom.

The prodigious Tequendama waterfall, was not a source of fear for these youths. On the contrary, the spectacular vegetation that surrounded it, in addition to the humidity and the fog in the air made it a pleasant and idyllic site. It was a great delight to observe the orchids, the ferns and tall palm trees, as well as the butterflies and birds of pretty colors.

As if waking up from a deep dream, Chepe reminded Juan that they had to cross to the other side of the river, where new adventures awaited them. They walked down with extreme care to the base of the waterfall where the river formed once again. It was wide and deep there which prevented them from crossing easily.

"We cannot cross the river here," pointed out Juan. "It is very deep and dangerous."

Chepe studied the situation looking in both directions and after thinking it over for a few minutes he said:

"We will cross here."

"But is deep and dangerous," insisted Juan.

"Do not worry." Remember: "everything is possible with the power of the sword."

Saying this, Chepe pulled out his sword and grasping it in its right hand, it shone as a sparkling flame of red, yellow and blue tones, just as it did before in Bachu's hand. He approached the river and immersed the end of the sword in the water and right away appeared something similar to a crystal bridge, almost invisible. It joined one side of the river with the other. The water followed its course underneath, running its course, down to the valley.

"Let's go to the other side," ordered Chepe.

Indeed both of them crossed the bridge. Once at the other side, Juan still astonished by the miraculous act that had allowed them to do it, looked back with incredulity but the bridge had disappeared.

When looking for Chepe, he noticed that he was already climbing up the steep mountain towards the top of the waterfall. The ascent was difficult due to the humidity and the moss covering the rocks making it slippery and dangerous.

"Be very careful! It is very slippery and a fall from here could be deadly," said Chepe to Juan.

While they continued climbing, they looked for solid rocks and branches of shrubs to hold onto. From time to time they took a few minutes to rest and to enjoy the magnificent waterfall from different angles on the way up.

Already at the mountain top Chepe took a deep breath and looked at the distance into the valley, while he waited for Juan. At the right hand side of the river, was a plain of warmer lands belonging to the town of La Mesa. On the left hand side was the village of *Mesitas*.

When looking downwards in the narrow abyss that formed the waterfall, the fog formed silver clouds. The abyss was a panorama of rocks and moss that, like silent witnesses of the history of this place forming the bed of the lower river. Alongside, a rocky wall rose which seemed to be designed by the hands of an artist. The naked profile of this rocky wall contrasted wonderfully with the thick vegetation at the base of the mountain. There the palms between trees and shrubs stood out giving the surroundings an extraordinary beauty.

At the top of the waterfall there were always clouds, formed by the mist that rose from the bottom. They were best viewed from the mountain top. Today the fog was a bit light and less dense, almost transparent, which allowed Chepe and Juan to observe a beautiful rainbow, which changed according to the position of the sun, adding new colors to the panorama, turning the waterfall into something admirable grandiose and charming.

"It says in a legend," said Juan, "that Bochica, a type of prophet who had come a long time ago to teach moral principles and good habits to the Chibcha Indians, as well as to work and cultivate the ground, one day disappeared in the direction of the rising sun, leaving a footprint marked on a large rock. Years later a terrible flood took place which destroyed many towns and killed many people.

"After this tragedy and misfortune," Juan continued, "the natives cried to their hero and protector, who appeared on the rainbow and with his gold scepter struck the rocks, dividing them in the middle of a great roar. The water, that already formed a lake in the savannah, broke out becoming a gigantic cascade of white foam. It was this way that Bochica created the Tequendama waterfalls.

"The guilty party which had caused this destructive flood was Huitaca, a beautiful and evil woman. She and Chibchacum, the god protector of the farmers were punished; she was turned into a night bird and he was forced to carry the earth on his shoulders. For that reason, whenever he gets tired and switches shoulders, there are earthquakes."

"Very interesting," commented Chepe with a slight smile, "Now we must continue our trip."

The green and peaceful territory of the Tequendama region to the south of the waterfall and east of the central mountain range of the Andes is the home of hardworking farmers. These territories are divided in two main regions located at each side of the Bogota River, which forms the majestic waterfalls.

The modest traditions of these farmers adapted well to these fertile lands. In their small farms and with hard work they had prospered well by growing coffee and large variety of fruits. This zone has been traditionally very pacific and their inhabitants have tried hard to maintain this region as a peaceful, tranquil and hospitable place. Up on a hill near the small village of Mesitas, and about an hour walk was the Santa Barbara farm of Don Heliodoro. Chepe and Juan found the way that according to Father Carlos would take them to Don Heliodoro's farm. This was located among beautiful green rolling hills. At their arrival they were met by Don Heliodoro, who was waiting for them just as

Father Carlos had mentioned. He was quite happy to see them and offered them the special attention worthy of these emissaries. After an enjoyable and delicious supper they offered them night accommodations so that they could rest and be prepared for the following day.

Before the dawn everybody in the farm was wide-awake and making preparations for a day of work. Don Heliodoro gave orders to provide any food or supplies that the two cousins may need on the way to their next destination. When everything was ready for the trip, they were quite grateful to find that everything had been taken care of for their stay in the capital city of Bogotá.

At eight in the morning, once all the pertinent details about the trip for Chepe and Juan were taken care of, Don Heliodoro invited them to move to the dining room where a succulent breakfast awaited them, prepared specially for the occasion by his diligent wife. The aroma of food invited the visitors to participate in the delicious feast.

The day was splendid. The sun rays caressed the mountains and the hills of the surroundings; the fresh air and the sweet fragrance of orange and coffee flowers gave the morning a sense of new life. The conversation was friendly. Soon, Don Heliodoro gave them precise instructions as to what to do in route to the capital, their next destination, warning them that their first task would be to find additional information as to the location of the magic *balsilla*. "Part of the information can be obtained in the gold museum downtown Bogota" he told them. "This information has been kept secret for many years to assure its safety and that only the proper person can obtain and solve the mysterious enigma. A friend of mine can help you." added Don Heliodoro. There you will find only part of the information as to the whereabouts of the magic *balsilla*. My contact in the capital will let you know where you can obtain the rest of the information."

"The task that has been assigned to you is of extreme importance and the dangers that await you are considerable. Astuteness, wisdom and talent will be required for your future success," he said to them with words of encouragement but then he also warned them:

"You will have opportunities to use your special powers but the enemy will not allow you to accomplish your purpose easily. Never be dismayed nor become weak! Success is imperative! Success is possible! Not everyone in your path will be glad to see you come, but those that know your mission, will be waiting for you and will be your main allies," said Don Heliodoro finally.

About half way through the morning they started their way towards the village of *Mesitas* where they hoped to find a bus that would take them to Bogota. On the way there was an exchange of a few words but there was much silence. Little by little Chepe began to understand the importance and seriousness of their mission. The path to the highway was not very long, the climate was fresh and humid and the surrounding fields shone their color of different green tones.

Suddenly, the sun rays stroked Chepe's sword making it shine as if made of fine diamonds. Its presence seemed to give the two cousins new energy and purpose.

After a few minutes delay the bus appeared in the distance. The two cousins thanked Don Heliodoro once more, not only for his attention and hospitality, but also for his Fatherly advice. Don Heliodoro for his part gave them one last good bye with a hug and wished them great successes.

Although the trip was not very long, the highway was a winding dirt road which did not allow driving at great speeds. The bus was old and the seats were covered with dust, indicating the difficult trails this vehicle had to travel. But Chepe and Juan were very interested in discovering and enjoying any novelties to be found on the way. At the same time, they look around the bus with curiosity. The passengers were not many; the majority were humble farmers taking fruits and chickens to sell in the market at the capital. Among the travelers Juan noticed somebody with characteristics different from the rest. It was a man of medium stature with racially mixed features with a black hat which he used to cover his eyes. In spite of this, their glances crossed several times in mutual distrust. In low voice and trying not to draw attention, Juan announced to Chepe the presence of that strange person. Without paying much attention, Chepe suggested they enjoy the beautiful landscape of the Savannah as if it was the first time they had seen it. The two cousins had previously visited the capital, but this was a very special occasion.

CHAPTER 9

The Savannah of Bogotá is a large plain where Colombia's capital is located. The climate is cold and a little humid. As the sun shines, it accentuates its beauty and serene atmosphere. The country was covered with bright colors and smooth green and brown tones from crops of barley, potatoes, corn, vegetables, a large variety of flowers and large fields of grass for the cattle ranchers or dairy farms. The gigantic eucalyptuses stand out as the most vigorous among the trees of this region. The landscape around the capital offers a thousand different shades. It is quite different from the hot tropical areas of the lower lands of most of the country, which contrasts with the diverse deep green of the forests, or with the Andean slopes covered by coffee plantations, bananas and fruit trees, or with valleys and plains. It is truly a country of great diversity.

It was in this land where the conquistador Gonzalo Jiménez de Quesada and his companions found a few muisca villages, whose natives were dedicated to the cultivation of corn, beans and a large variety of potatoes, under a system of communal property. There was also commerce of salt which they extracted from the mines of Zipaquirá and Nemocón. These ancestors inhabited the Savannahs over two thousand years ago. The city of Bogotá occupies the main part of this plain, and lays on the Eastern mountain range that flanks the

The Power Of The Relic

imposing mountains of Monserrate and Guadalupe, emblems of the beautiful landscape. The main one is Monserrate. This is the most traditional for the natives of Bogota and it has a Sanctuary of peregrination that looks quietly over the city and it is also the best lookout point over the city.

   The bus took Chepe and Juan to the central station which was located near the colonial sector of the city, built by the Spaniards many years ago. The day was clear but a little cold for them who were not yet accustomed to these heights. Just as Don Heliodoro had indicated, one of his friends had come to meet them. He was a man of friendly appearance who apparently had grown in the Savannah. This was easy to notice due to the color and texture of the facial skin. With a pleasant gesture, he introduced himself as Don Francisco; after an affectionate greeting, he helped them with their luggage which was not much. They had only brought the necessary supplies for a couple of days in the capital.

   The trip to the residence of Don Francisco was short; it was in a public mini-bus which quickly took them through the narrow streets of the city. His apartment was located in the district of Chico, not very far from the city center. It was located on the fifth floor of a building with a private and secure entrance. Upon arrival, Don Francisco's wife was waiting for the new guests, and immediately she led them to their room, their temporary residence. Once they made themselves at home, they were invited to come to the dining room to share in the afternoon refreshments: a delicious hot chocolate with bread and cheese. Don Francisco's wife was a beautiful woman of white features, maybe of German ancestry.

"My name is Helena, it is my pleasure to have you with us" she said in a friendly and hospitable tone. "I understand your visit is short, but I hope to see you again with more time." Immediately she retired to her room knowing that the young cousins needed time to get ready for the next day.

At eight in the morning the next day, Don Francisco took them to the city center by the same means of transportation as the previous day. The historical city center was a well preserved district called *La Candelaria.* This is a place where you can still smell and feel the ambient of the Spanish Colony and the beginnings of the Republic of Colombia. There you can find the best of the religious architecture of those times. It is actually a mixture of the epochs of the Spanish colony, the Independence, the civil wars of the last centuries, and the advances and the modernization of the city in recent years.

In this district it is possible to enjoy the best tourist and cultural attractions, in the middle of colonial churches, historical monuments, museums, theaters, art galleries, and concert halls. In many of these places, history seems to have had stopped in time. Walking through the narrow streets and up the hills steep hills of *La Candelaria*, Chepe and Juan found it hard to believe that they were actually in the middle of a metropolis of several million inhabitants. In this area of calm town squares, with a great view to green mountains, Bogota resembled an Andaluz, with its balconies of carved wood, austere vestibules and patios richly adorned with flowerpots of bright and lively colors. In this fresh atmosphere of rare tranquility, the aroma of the freshly made bread combined with the scent of the fresh coffee was an irresistible temptation to the passers by. Chepe and Juan yielded to the temptation, finding a small establishment; they went in to enjoy a delicious *café con leche* with mouth-watering hot pastries.

A few blocks from there they found the *Plaza Monumental*, the historical city square framed by great architectural works: to the east the *Cathedral Primada* , the chapel of *El Sagrario* and the Arch-bishop's palace; to the south the National Capitol; to the West the Liévano Building, the city mayor's office; to the north, the modern Palace of Justice. In the center of the main square is a statue of the *"Liberator of America"* Simón Bolivar whose name is given to this square as a tribute to his triumphal entrance to the capital in August of 1819, after his victory in the War of Independence against Spain, which lasted almost ten years. Without a doubt, this was one of the high moments in the life of the charismatic Venezuelan Commander who soon would be declared president of the Great Colombia.

"This is a place of great historical importance for the country," said Juan while they walked through the square enjoying the surrounding beauty. After being a silent witness to so many transcendental events, it now offers a sober and peaceful feeling."

"Note that the religious aspect also played an important role in the development and promotion of education and culture of the city" said Chepe. "As in other important cities of Latin America, in Bogota the religious orders of the Franciscans, Dominicans and the Jesuits not only were dedicated to the mission of evangelizing the natives and trying to save the lost souls of the conquistadores, they also dominated in a special way the cultural life. They founded schools and universities and they exerted great influence in sciences and the academic and technical education and wholesome formation of the people. Those three orders also contributed to the architecture of the city, constructing sumptuous churches and immense convents that occupied whole city blocks.

"For example," added Chepe, "in the Palace of *San Carlos*, right in-front of us, the Jesuits inaugurated in the 18th century the first public library of America."

Around noon, Chepe and Juan decided to look for a restaurant that would offer some typical Bogotá dishes. They wanted to savor a real delicious *sancocho* with chicken. Two blocks from the *Plaza de Bolivar* and in direction to the sanctuary of Monserrate they found what they were looking for: a restaurant of rustic and pleasant atmosphere. Minutes after ordering lunch the desired *sancocho* was brought to them: a wonderful broth with prey of hen, potatoes, plantain, yucca, corn, onion, condiment with pepper, cumin and sprinkled with coriander. This dish came accompanied with avocado and sharp red pepper... a true delight of the Bogota culinary!

After lunch, Chepe and Juan went to the famous Gold Museum located in the heart of the city. This was the moment they were long wanting for. Once they entered the building, along with a group of tourists from Japan and the United States, a friendly and quite knowledgeable guide from the museum explained with great detail the meaning, the history and the importance of each one of the objects in the museum's collection. He began with a brief introduction:

"The Gold Museum is an irrefutable example of the great ability and skill of the indigenous inhabitants of this region who skillfully dominated the art of gold working before the Spanish conquest. With this visit you will see for yourselves the exquisite and impressive way the natives worked the gold, the silver and other precious materials. This museum is recognized as the richest museum in golden works of Latin America. Several collections of pre-Columbian pieces are preserved here. Nevertheless, one of the most valuable, the denominated *"Tesoro Quimbaya"*, that was found several years ago, was given to Maria Cristina, Queen of Spain."

"In 1939," continued the guide, "the Bank of the Republic of Colombia bought a gold object of 777.7 grams of weight and 23.5 centimeters of height that gave origin to the Gold Museum. It is the famous and beautiful *poporo Quimbaya*, a pre-Hispanic masterpiece of gold working; a round belly with its neck crowned by four spherical bodies on a fused filigree base. Anyone who contemplates that piece cannot, but be astonished with admiration about the skill and creativity of its creators.

Upon their arrival, the Spaniards found these metals in abundance, hidden in rich mines, covering the walls of old temples, or used as ornaments by the Indian chiefs or as decorations of the indigenous towns, hanging from trees or from the ceilings of their huts to shine under the tropical sun. Many of these objects, as well as ceramic containers, true works of art were buried with human remains in tombs and cemeteries.

But the Spanish Crown needed those treasures to maintain its great empire. They ordered to take whatever could be found. The result was the disappearance of a considerable part of our treasures. It is impossible to calculate the actual cost of the valuable booty! Not quite satisfied with the sacking of the precious relics and jewels which adorned the natives and their villages, and not wanting to look for gold in natural surroundings the conquistadores plundered the tombs from which they removed immense amounts of the precious metal and jewelry of the finest and delicate work.

More than three centuries have passed, but we know that there are still left a considerable number of tombs that have not been found. For that reason, the looting continues even with the *"guaquería"*, or search of treasures in the indigenous tombs on the part of farmers and treasure hunters who make these searches their way of life."

"As I said at the beginning," continued the guide,

"the most famous collection among those that left the country is the one that is known as the "Tesoro Quimbaya", donated in 1892 by the government of President Carlos Holguín to the queen of Spain in gratitude for a favorable arbitration to Colombia. In that year, Spain had organized a historical exhibition of the American countries to celebrate the fourth centenary of the Discovery of America. Ironically, the one that most captivated the attention among the objects from Colombia was indeed that invaluable treasure.

It is almost a miracle that so many pieces of this gold working have been able to survive" he added.

"Nevertheless many are still preserved, partly due to the vast volume of pre-Hispanic fine metallurgical production and partly by the fact that many of the burial places and places of rituals were well hidden."

The guide stopped for a few minutes to make sure everyone was paying full attention. Then with a proud and patriotic tone, he added:

"The Gold Museum is, without a doubt, the most extraordinary attraction of cultural character that Bogotá can offer and very particularly to tourists and visitors who come from distant lands to visit us hoping to find here new and exotic things that other parts of the world cannot enjoy.

This demonstrates, for satisfaction of the Colombians, that in those same fields where now reigns violence, were also inhabited thousands of years ago by communities that left amazing works of beauty and perfection. As you can see here, Colombia is not only a country of violence, but also a country of wealth and creativity. It is a positive reaffirmation of our national heritage and for that reason we show it with pride to our foreign visitors.

If at some time the *poporos, pectorals, and narigueras* of the native inhabitants of these land started to become symbols of national identity: of a rich, complex and sometimes contradictory identity, that moment is now," ended the guide.

In the display glass cabinets of the first floor of the museum were objects and figures organized by their form and function mainly: Poporos of the Quimbaya culture, head bands of the Calima, pectoral pendants and of the Tolima, and tunjos of the muiscas.

With the assistance of the guide, the visitors could learn about life, the economic and social organization, the religious and mortuary practices and the metallurgical techniques of the Pre-Hispanic societies. The ceramics, which had a special presence in this place, showed examples that these were not static communities but that they evolved permanently throughout time. As a result there were different styles in the figures and containers and a great variety of stone tools, precious metals and objects of shell, bone, and wood.

In the third floor was a "the vault", a type of fort that contained a great number of gold pieces worked by the Indians, selected pieces of the different styles corresponding to the different geographic zones of the country. This is a very important one about the exhibition. All of this, nevertheless, is a miniscule amount, compared to the immense treasure that was taken by the Conquistadores. The place is constructed with walls of reinforced concrete, without windows and with a unique bank vault, necessary to the safekeeping of such valuable treasures.

    The exhibition begins with the samples of *Tumaco* and *Calima*, the most remote in time, to continue with objects coming from *Malaga, San Agustín, Tierradentro*, the *Cauca, Tolima, Quimbaya, Urabá, Zenú* and *Nariño* and finishes with pieces of the *Tayrona* and *Muisca*, the cultures of native societies of Indians which survived shortly after the Spanish conquest.

    In order to produce a yet more impressive sensation, at the end, the visitors were taken to a room completely in darkness. After a few seconds, the intensity of the light gradually increased, transporting them magically to a place surrounded by display cabinets that contain a great number of masks, pectorals, hangings, command batons, nose pieces … thousands of shining pieces that pleased the vision. "It is the "Salon Dorado" or golden room. "To have in their hands a similar treasure, would have been the culmination of the dream for the European conquistadores" affirmed the guide.

    In this hall, finally the two cousins found for the first time the figure they had come to see: The famous *Balsilla Muisca*. It is fantastic! It appears as if it was floating with its tiny people under a great show of lights and sound, as if reliving the legend of the ceremony of "El Dorado".

"This piece is something exceptional. It is a unique treasure and the only one of its kind in the world at this moment" explained the guide. "Traditionally it has been interpreted as the representation of a ceremonial ritual of the Indian chief from the region of Guatavita. From stories of the conquistadores we know, that when the Indian Chief of the Muiscas would die, his successor was recognized through a special ceremony that took place at the lagoon of the same name while sailing in a raft of logs, offering pieces of gold and emeralds to its waters. The "Balsilla Muisca" or golden raft was found inside a ceramic container in a small cave by three farmers to the south of the city of Bogota. It has not been possible to accurately determine the date of its manufacture, although probably belongs to the last period of the Muisca culture. But it is known that it was made using a single piece, by means of a technique of wax in a clay mold. The metal is gold with a silver alloy" said the guide.

"In center of the raft" he continued saying "is a person of great importance that is believed to be the Indian Chief, richly adorned and surrounded by twelve smaller people. Some carry standards and canes, those of the front wear two masks of jaguar and the smaller ones on the side are recognized as the rowers.

"Colombia has not been object of great international scientific expeditions as in other South American countries. Here there are no enormous pyramids, neither monumental constructions, nor fabulous prehistoric temples. The works of art made of gold did not show much interest in the past. The main concern was its weight and its purity, to sell it in the market turned into ingots.

But the day has come in which a great finding has taken place and the works of perfection of these pre-Columbian objects are now recognized; beautiful, amazing and enigmatic, which demonstrates that the monumental factor is not a question of dimensions but of creativity and skill. These pieces are great masterpieces in miniature."

To finalize his presentation the guide said to the visitors:

"There is no doubt that in Colombia exists a seed of authentic appreciation for the pre-Hispanic roots, but this has only began to developed with material evidence of the wonderful works left by the old inhabitants of this land. In this way we see as a good thing, and not as a dishonor, the indigenous element of our heritage. It is for that reason, that the Gold Museum has a special meaning for the Colombians, because it keeps among its collections some of the most representative symbols from our culture."

CHAPTER 10

The following day they took advantage of their free time to make a trip to Monserrate. It was about nine in the morning when they went out looking for transportation to go to the station where they could take the cable car or funicular that would take them to the top of the mountain.

"People say that the view of the city is spectacular from that place" observed Juan.

"We have all day to enjoy the beauty and the cold of the heights" answered Chepe in joking tone.

Monserrate is the sacred mountain located in center of Colombia almost three thousand two hundred meters high. On its summit a church stands out, of shinning white color, overlooking the city of Bogota like a crown. Great numbers of pilgrims climb up on foot thought the steep mountain side until they arrive at the sanctuary doing penance for sins committed in the past or requesting divine favors for the future. Other less devoted visitors simply want to enjoy the beautiful view from the mountain top using a much more comfortable alternative to arrive at the summit: the funicular or the cable car.

The day was perfect for the trip with a sun that shone on the mountains to emphasize its dark green color that contrasted well with intense blue sky free from clouds. The street traffic was not as busy as in the earlier hours. The two cousins crossed the street and after a minute of waiting, they found a bus that would take them to their destination. They went in through the front door, they paid the fee and they passed the register in search of seat.

Two blocks ahead, a little street boy boarded the bus behind a passenger and went under the register in order not to pay the bus fee. This displeased the driver of the bus who shouted to him immediately:

"You pay or get off the bus, little fellow!"

The street boy ignored the order and proceeded to request the attention of the passengers:

"Ladies and gentlemen! I want to sing a pretty song to you so that you that can help me with a few coins to buy something to eat."

Juan rose of his chair and offered to pay the bus fee for the street boy, which the conductor accepted with a bad mood.

Without his audience approval, the small boy proceeded to sing a popular country song. He was dressed with short pants and an old shirt that was too large for him. By the looks of his face and hair one could guess that he had not bathed for a very long time.

The song lasted about two or three minutes. Juan remained standing up until the end of this unexpected performance studying carefully the spontaneous artist. Once he had finished his performance, he moved though the bus in search of his payment. Some people gave him some coins. After getting the coins he would bow and thank them for it. Others looked in the opposite direction trying to ignore to him. When coming to Chepe and Juan, he said to them with very good manners:

"Sirs, can you help me with a few coins for my breakfast?"

Chepe did not even make an attempt to search for the requested coins but looking at him he asked:

"What is your name?"

"My name is Pablo, but my friends call me Paco."

"And where is your mother?"

"I do not have mother" was the answer.

"Very well Paco, I am not going to give you money but we want to buy breakfast for you."

The eyes of the boy shone of joy at such an offer and he responded immediately:

"Yes Sir! Thank you Sir! Thank you very much Sir!"

Accompanied by the boy, they got off the bus in front of a restaurant, few blocks from the cable car that would take them to Monserrate. But first they would have to fulfill their promise. They entered the restaurant, found a table and then Chepe requested two coffees one for him and another one for Juan and a breakfast for Paco, who devoured everything they served without saying word. Chepe and Juan observed him carefully without daring to interrupt him. After finishing his breakfast Paco rose satisfied from the table.

"Thank you very much Sirs! Thank you very much Sirs!" he said as he bowed with gratefulness. His good manners caused curiosity to Chepe and Juan. They did not know if they were part of his education or he had learned them as a tool to survive. Then Chepe decided to ask to him:

"Where did you learn your good manners?"

"My mom, Sir. My mom taught to me to have good manners and to respect my elders" was the answer from Paco.

"How old are you?" asked Juan.

"I am only eight years old. I was born in misery... in the cold and nakedness. My mom loved me... but ever since she died, I must sleep in the streets and live on what people give me, Sir. Sometimes, I must eat what I find in the trash and my blanket is a newspaper. My mom loved me but people do not want me because I am a street boy. The coldness and the lack of affection from people hurts deeper in the soul than in the body. I do not say this because of you... because you are good people, Sirs..."

"The gamines are like that" he added. "They always walk the streets trying to survive with handouts or looking for things in the trash, stealing, or living on what they can make shining shoes, selling cans, bottles or newspapers. Many of us slept in the sewer system" concluded Paco, as he exited the door, but Chepe stopped him and asked him:

"Would you like to go with us to Monserrate?"

The boy thought for a moment and answered:

"Yes, thank you Sir...! Nobody has taken me to Monserrate before... thank you Sir!"

They went to the station of the cable car where they bought three tickets. Minutes later it descended from the mountain, unloaded the passengers who were coming down from the mountain and loaded the new visitors. To the surprise not only of Chepe and Juan, but also of all the passengers, Paco got ready for his next performance:

"Ladies and gentlemen...! I want to sing a beautiful song so that you may help me with few coins for something to eat."

Chepe and Juan burst out in laughter upon seeing Paco's ingenuity and persistence.

"This boy does not waste an opportunity" said Chepe with a smile of complicity.

The song, happy and filled with life was compensated with some coins.

The avenues and buildings of Bogota got smaller and smaller as the cable car went up higher and higher towards the mountain summit. Chepe and Juan were astonished at the beauty of the panorama; the view of the entire city was spectacular. While they were getting accustomed to the air at the altitude, Paco ran with great enthusiasm recognizing each new place.

Soon they found the first group of sculptures of the famous Via Crucis of Monserrate which were in the beginning of the stairs that would take them from the cable car station to the vestibule of the church. Each one of the Stations of the Cross Route was decorated with different species of plants, flowers and small shrubs coming from different regions of Colombia: the desert, the high lands, and the tropic.

It seems incredible that at more than three thousand meters of height, they can grow simultaneously, next to trees thirty meters high, which in other places of the Savannah is not possible to cultivate. This showed a splendid harmony between the magnificence of the nature created by God and the works of art created by the hand of the man.

From the summit one could enjoy and admire an

incomparable landscape with thousand shades of green from the forests that covers the mountain. One could also notice to the one side one hundred meters higher, the mountain of Guadalupe with its small church and the image of the Virgin from whom it took its name. This is the other sacred mount that looks over Bogotá.

Monserrate, on the other hand, is the Hispanic form of the name of the Catalan sanctuary Montserrat, which is located near Barcelona. While Chepe, Juan and Paco contemplated the city and the surrounding hills, dark clouds covered the summit of Guadalupe, where it already began to rain. Almost immediately a dense fog surrounded the mountains turning the bright colors observed before into fading tones of gray. The trees transformed themselves into outlandish shadows that little by little disappeared in the dense fog.

Unexpectedly, the two cousins saw in the middle of this fog, the mysterious man of medium stature, racially mixed features and a black hat they had seen in the bus on the way to Bogotá. They tried to follow him on order to find out his identity but he disappeared in the direction of the Church. Forgetting that incident and before it started raining on them, they searched for a refuge inside a restaurant. After the rain stopped, the fog disappeared and slowly everything returned to normal. During the time they were there, Paco sang to the visitors in three occasions, with relative good luck, because many people who listened to him gave him some coins. When they left the restaurant, the sky was already totally clear.

"This boy is a good entrepreneur" exclaimed Chepe jokingly, and then adding with more seriousness:

"For being such an unfortunate boy and without anything in the life, he is very content and offers more joy to the others, than many that have great fortunes."

"I hope that this is a good example for you" he said again jokingly to Juan and going to Paco, he asked him if he was hungry and if he wanted something to eat, because it was already time for lunch.

"Yes Sir! Thank you very much Sir! Thank you very much Sir!" was Paco's answer.

The three tourists approached a small food stand and Chepe requested three *empanadas* and three *arepas* with hot chocolate. This would be sufficient to hold them at least until supper, which he hoped to have once they returned to the City. Paco sat at the table and, just like breakfast, he devoured his portion without saying word. Chepe observed him and then said to Juan:

"This boy to be so loquacious in public is quite timid. He does not say more than what he must say."

After this delicious snack, Paco thanked as customary Chepe and continued his way.

The climate had changed again. The rays of the sun penetrated the fog, illuminating the streets and the skyscrapers of Bogotá still wet from the rain, flooding everything with a shining light. The visitors could observe the incredible contrasts that the city offers from Monserrate: to the West, an immense gray spot that corresponds to a large number of districts which disappear in the horizon. The noise of the traffic of the capital with so many vehicles transporting several million inhabitants seemed to come up even to these

The Power Of The Relic

heights. In the east, the panorama was that of an almost total solitude. The green and majestic forests of the Eastern Mountain range appeared in the distance. This was a quiet and tranquil scene with no buildings in sight.

The two cousins now wanted to explore the solitude of the surroundings while the preoccupation of Paco was to be able to approach the visitors, looking for the opportune moment to offer a song.

From the height summit of Monserrate, Chepe and Juan fixed their glance one last time over the noisy city of many contrasts. It seemed to move in a great disorder although its houses and buildings gave the impression of a harmony and peacefulness. In the quietness of this place, next to the church and among the clouds these two young fellows from La Mesa felt a vivid desire to pray for the peace in this place and peace in the rest of the world. "Perhaps Paco is right" said Chepe, "it is better to sing a beautiful song."

At dusk, when the sun descended on the horizon offering a spectacular view of the mountains, the three friends started their way back to Bogotá. Once back in the noisy city, they went in search of a place to have supper. Not very far from the cable car station, they found a small family restaurant. As they had done previously, they ordered three meals, while Paco's eyes shone of joy and expectation. He had never had a day like this, a day with three delicious meals.

The restaurant was plain but the service was very good and the food well prepared and delicious. At the end, already satisfied, Juan and Chepe asked for two coffees to take the time to chat about their trip to Monserrate. Only a few minutes had passed when suddenly the tranquility of the moment was interrupted by the sudden flight of Paco who taking advantage of the distraction of his benefactors, he took Chepe's wallet and started running among the crowd and the heavy traffic. Still shaken by the unexpected surprise, Juan offered to go in search of the young thief but Chepe dissuaded him. Grasping his arm he asked him to have a seat as he said: "Let's be calm... I have a feeling that this is not going to be our last encounter with Paco. In addition, you have enough money to be able to return to our home."

When they were again in the street, they observed with astonishment how the shining lights of the city had transformed the surroundings. The extended and pointed shadows of the buildings in the city center stuck out looking mysterious. Darkness covered the flanks of the mountains that guarded the city on the east and on the summit of the high mountain stood, majestic, white and brilliant, the sanctuary of Monserrate watching in silence over the large city.
"Let's go home, we still have a long way to go ..." said Chepe, who was already tired.
They went through the noisy streets in search of transportation that would take them back to the home of Don Francisco. Upon arriving, they found him anxious and worried about them being so late. They spent some time in the living room talking about the events of the past two days while enjoying a delicious cup of coffee.

They shared their experiences of the trip to Monserrate, and their visit to the Gold Museum where they had been able to observe for the first time the wonderful and enigmatic *balsilla muisca*.

"This is a wonder of the indigenous culture" added Don Francisco. "But the location of *balsilla of the power*, coming from the Middle East, is yet unknown; Father Nicanor has more details of its location. But lets' not speak of that now. Tonight you must rest because you have a long trip awaiting you tomorrow. For now you still have a night of peace and tranquility."

CHAPTER 11

They got up early the next day to get ready for their trip to Santander, a province in the northern part of the country as Don Heliodoro had told them. In the dining room, breakfast was waiting for them: corn bread, fried eggs and hot chocolate. They were at the table delighting their eyes, when Don Francisco entered the room to join them for breakfast, to provide more details about the trip and to advise them to be extremely careful in the days ahead.

"Father Nicanor will be waiting for you in San Gil and he will provide additional information related to your mission" said Don Francisco with the authority, the compassion and the gentleness of a Father.

At mid-morning they undertook the way towards the bus station at the city center. When arriving they went to the window where they could buy the tickets for the trip. Suddenly a noisy crowd of people gathering in the opposite side of the street caught their attention. A smaller crowd of curious people were giving shouts and making a big uproar. Chepe, having a feeling that something strange was happening, broke through the crow to observe more closely. At this moment he saw that a young kid of about fifteen years of age and dressed in ragged clothes took off running with a stick in his hand. Nobody dared to go after him. Lying on the ground was another young kid covered with blood and crying out in pain to an indifferent crowd of passers-by.

"It is Paco!" exclaimed Juan with much emotion and eyes of incredulity.

Chepe came closer and watched him carefully. The crowd of onlooker curious moved back to a prudent distance while Chepe knelt down in the cold pavement, bending over the boy to examine his condition. Paco's face was covered with a mixture with tears, blood and dirt and his expression was that of an unbearable pain. His body, partially naked, also was covered with blood and dirt, as a result of an unequal and ferocious dispute with his aggressor who had managed to escape.

While examining him in detail he discovered with horror that both arms had been broken by his attacker. At this moment, Paco opened his eyes and saw the figure of the person watching over him, he was terrified to recognized Chepe, the person he had robbed the night before. He tried to rise up and flee but his legs did not obey him. To his pain and agony also added the anguish and the shame of the malicious act committed the previous night, knowing that he had no choice but to wait for his deserved punishment.

The group of by-standers did not understand what was happening. Chepe touched tenderly with his hands the weak body of the boy trying to calm him but had no results. Still on his knees, he leaned back and reached under his jacket to grab his sword which shone in his hand; seeing this Paco gave a cry of panic:

"Please Sir, do not kill me! I will pay everything I stole from you! Please do not kill me!" He implored again in the middle of tears.

Chepe kept calm and slowly opened the handle of

his sword to obtain a few drops of the water from the fountain of youth which he placed in the palm of his hand, passing it over Paco's body and over his dirty face, keeping it there for a few seconds. He moved his hand from Paco's body and gave him a tender look, and then extended his hand to help him get up, then he gave him a strong hug which lasted for several minutes. Paco did not want to move, feeling the strength and security he had never known before.

When finally they separated, Paco began to examine himself all over with incredulity. The pain had disappeared and his broken arms were in perfect condition as was all his body. Moving his arms and legs he started jumping from joy, trying to make sure that all of this was true. It did not take long for him to realize that what had happened was a true miracle. He felt like new, as he had never felt before. Chepe remained in the center of the street standing up; smiling with satisfaction as he saw Paco's happiness. Paco ran towards him, knelt down at his feet and put his arms around Chepe's legs and in the middle of tears of happiness he began to cry out:

"Thank you Sir! Thank you very much Sir!" were the only words that he could stutter.

Chepe observed him for a few moments and then he knelt down in the pavement in front of Paco and surrounded him with his arms for a long while and then finally said to him:

"The Lord has great plans and a great purpose for your life... you are very special..."

Chepe pondered with a smile of compassion Paco's

fragile figure. He could now imagine a better future for the boy.

"Can I go with you?" begged Paco with eyes full of tears. I do not want to live in the streets. I do not want to be a street kid, Sir! Please take me with you!" he begged again.

Meanwhile Juan, who had witnessed this miraculous sight, was trying not to miss any small detail. His glance was fixed in Chepe and Paco as he listened to the request of the poor kid. Tears of compassion rolled over his cheeks knowing that his request would be impossible.

"Where we are going you cannot go" answered Chepe. He studied the situation for a few minutes as he stood in silence considering the alternatives. Suddenly Juan approached him.

"Don Francisco! Don Francisco! He could surely share his home with Paco! It is perfect... they do not have any children at their home!" exclaimed Juan, convinced that this could be the best solution.

Chepe remained thinking it over and after awhile he turned his head and answered:

"Is a good possibility, but I must talk it over with him first."

Saying this, he went to a telephone booth leaving Paco under Juan´s care.

Chepe briefly explained to Don Francisco all that had happened and asked if he and his wife could take care of the boy. His answer was immediately positive and full of enthusiasm.

While they waited for Don Francisco´s arrival,

Chepe took the time to explain to Paco many details about the life and of the family of this friendly couple that so generously had accepted to take care of him. The happiness of the little boy was beyond compare at the possibility of having the home he had never had.

After almost two long hours of delay Don Francisco finally arrived. As soon as they saw each other, almost like a miracle, they established a strong bond, just like a Father and son, as if they had been always known each other. After a while they were ready to go home. Chepe and Juan saw them walk away, holding hands, as they went towards the bus stop.

"This is a perfect picture" said Juan as he saw them walking away as Father and son. They remained there for some time, observing them. At the distance, Don Francisco and Paco turn around one last time to wave their hands as a farewell.

Early in the afternoon, the two cousins took a bus that would take them to Santander, a northern province of Colombia, eager and with plenty of optimism for their new adventures. The first part of the road took them through savannahs, lagoons, small farms and beautiful fields of the Andean region. Little by little, through a very long and winding highway they entered the steep mountain range with its spectacular landscapes. The second part of the trip was through a quiet extension of several kilometers, flanked by gigantic rocky walls with waterfalls and covered by intertwined species of green vines and shrubs. From the mountains came down rivers and water streams born in the upper cold peaks and deserts forming beautiful cascades that unfolded along the way. All this resulted in wonderful and picturesque landscapes.

After a few hours during the trip, Juan reminded Chepe how the natives who lived in the past in this region, had left behind an agricultural culture that is still preserved today, thanks to the people of this region, peaceful and hard working, who dedicate themselves to farming these productive fields: potatoes, corn and cereals, in a similar manner to their native ancestors.

Farther down the road, as the bus entered the mountains where the famous condor of the Andes has its dominions, the mysterious bird of the heights, that Chepe and Juan never had seen, the landscape became steeper and the vegetation more rare; from here to Santander the land was mostly desert. The two cousins were now anxious to arrive at their destination, the small and historical village of San Gil. They arrived there late into the night.

Many of the streets in this village were paved with stones and lined with beautiful churches and houses with balconies characteristic of the colonial times. Their inhabitants were the typical mestizo, the result of the mixture of the Guanes Indians and Spanish conquerors who populated this province. The liberation army passed through this charming city on the way to the capital making it part of the historical cradle of the independence.

After finding lodging in a hotel not far from the cathedral, Juan and Chepe ventured into the streets ready to enjoy the historical past of the city, its cheerful and musical spirit. Here people dance to the tune of *bambucos, torbellinos, guabinas and pasillos*. The dances are a natural expression of the region. In this festive atmosphere frequently there are men and women, adorned with hats, ponchos, machetes and long skirts of bright colors, giving loose rein to their joy to the tune of music, remembering the times in which the farmers conquered the night and the hostile nature.

"These are territories of exotic fruits," said Juan as they walked down the streets paved with stones in search of typical food of this region. "I have heard that the santanderean cooking is quite famous for its quality, its preparation and most of all for its flavor. The traditional dish is mute, but what the visitors enjoy most are goat, *sancocho, arepa* and fried yucca."

Chepe scratching his head added:

"Do not forget that this region is famous for the fried ants, which are called *hormigas culonas*. They say that they are delicious; the truth is that I have never tasted them, but I would like to. Also they say that the Guanes Indians, the old inhabitants of the region, attributed their height and strength to the diet of fruits, little meat and much fish. They also discovered that the ants not only were exquisite but also had aphrodisiac properties; for that reason fried ants are so famous.

Juan smiling at this explanation, said:

"Tonight I prefer something more typical and conventional like a delicious *sancocho*."

Moments later they found an elegant and traditional restaurant, located in the middle of a beautiful landscape with waterfalls and wild vegetation. The

The Power Of The Relic

atmosphere here makes the visitors feel in contact with nature. The two cousins enjoyed a delicious supper brightened by a happy group of string musicians.

Chepe and Juan returned satisfied to their hotel for a good rest after a long and exciting day. They planned to visit the famous park of El Gallineral, early the next day. This is one of the most important tourist places in this region.

When they rose up next morning, they started towards the park, located a short distance. The air in the morning was pure and refreshing. They were walking calmly through the park when suddenly a tree branch fell noisily behind them. In front of them were immense trees covered with moss, interlaced with each other giving this beautiful place a somewhat mysterious appearance.

"Perhaps they do not like strangers so early in the day" said Juan jokingly, trying to disguise his anxiety. Chepe did not say anything, but he was a little worried, having a feeling that something strange was about to happen. He was almost determined to stop and go back but he did not want to show any fear to his cousin.

El Gallineral is located on an island formed by two rivers. Within the abundant variety of trees in this park, the *gallinero* trees stand out from which the park gets its name. Their branches are covered with dark-brown moss that extends down, forming a type of long and elegant curtain. Leafy *ceibas*, the *anacos* and other species add to great diversity of trees and shrubs shading the paths where visitors walk placidly through footpaths surrounded by beautiful gardens.

The main path of this peculiar and fascinating park begins in the small square of The Fame where there are different monuments carved in stone. The most representative is the *Opened Paper*, a tribute to the musicians who will always be remembered here.

Continuing towards the center, the dark trees seem to move aside as to let you see straight ahead. At the other side of the island, a green hill without trees rises over the forest and the path seems to take you magically directly towards the hill. Both cousins followed the trail to the center where they stopped to look around. The landscape was dazzling, illuminated by the light of the sun, although still a little dimmed by the cold fog in the morning that did not allow them to see at long distances.

"Look there," said Juan, indicating towards the front of where they were: "it is the Small square of Count *Cuchicute*. This was a very well known person in the region whose name was Jose Maria of the Passion. The legend says that he was an eccentric man who thought himself to be perfect, and to get the attention of the people of the region, who were given to outlandish things, he removed his right eye and replaced it by one of glass. He used to ride his horse naked and come out to his balcony without clothes to give candy to the children. He liked women very much and had three daughters although he never married."

"They say" continued Juan, "that his own butler killed him. He was taken to the hospital still alive but he did not survive. His last wish was to be buried standing up, because according to him, this way he could get to heaven running. But instead he was buried head down so that he could not come out of his grave."

"Why don't we go there!" proposed Chepe. "They say that it is the strangest site of the park; the center of attraction and mystery where all these fables come from."

But when he looked in the direction Juan had indicated, he noticed only the fog that slowly extended over the small square making it impossible to see anything in that direction.

It was almost seven in the morning and the sun began to raise the temperature, so they decided to sit down near the small plaza, in that lost island, in the middle of a sea of trees, where hanging moss intertwined like a dense curtain.

After a while they continued their way. The trail that had taken them there reappeared at the other side; they had not advanced much when they noticed that it was turning to the left, towards some thick scrubs. They exchanged a few words and then decided to leave the trail and turn to the right, where the soil seemed drier and the trees thinner and less loaded with moss.

At the beginning, the selection seemed to be good. They were walking with firm steps, when suddenly the trees, with their branches covered with moss began to close in, leaving open an unexpected and steep trail going down. As they advanced, the woods were more intense and dark, making it more and more difficult to break through.

CHAPTER 12

After two hours on this trail, they realized that they had lost all sense of direction and that they were now in a strange and unknown place. They marched without course, apparently following a path somebody else had chosen for them. All they could do at this point was continue down the narrow path, which was becoming softer and in some places marshy.

Minutes latter they found themselves by a water stream that murmured along a bed of wild grass. But as they began to descend, quickly, jumping down the slope, the stream became more loud and mighty. They were in a deep and dark depression, covered by a high vault of great leafy trees, very different from those of El Gallineral.

They advanced for a while following the stream. Suddenly they left the darkness as if going through a curtain and saw in front of them a shining light. In the middle a clear and sluggish river wound bordering gardens with beautiful flowers and shrubs. A fresh breeze blew and the sound of the branches of the old trees seemed to sing a lullaby to them.

"Good, at least now I have an idea of where we are!" said Chepe. "This is completely different from El Gallineral. It seems that there is a trail that follows along this water. If we go to the left and then follow it, I believe that we will get to the other side of the forest, but I am not very sure."

"I agree" said Juan. "Who could have drawn up this trail and why? I am sure it was not for our benefit. Do you have any idea of the distance that we must cross in this place?"

"No," said Chepe, "I do not know."

Now they heard a very soft whisper, as if somebody was singing and it seemed to come from the middle of the dense foliage of the trees. Chepe raised his glance and saw an old and enormous tree covered by its branches that seemed to reach down to them with its extended arms. In the meantime, Juan, worried, sat down scratching his head. He felt discouraged and lost; it was late in the afternoon and everything was still unknown to them.

Suddenly they heard something strange that made them turn around. There was no doubt; they had heard a deep and mysterious voice that sang a song with a sad message that spoke of death, distress and desperation.

Chepe and Juan seemed charmed; the fresh air blew smoothly. The song sounded again and suddenly they saw a young man walking towards them on the same trail. He came closer to them who watched him bewildered, without saying word. Chepe shook his head to make sure he was not dreaming. The young man had the typical characteristics of a mestizo, the perfect characteristics of the mixture the white and the aborigine races; his skin color was like cinnamon, his eyes black and shiny; his hair, well cared for was black and short. He was dressed with an animal skin.

The Power Of The Relic

The two cousins remained still, as if paralyzed, not understanding what was happening around them.

"Welcome!" said young man as he raised his hand. "We would like for you to tell us everything!"

"What do you mean?" asked Chepe a bit confused. "You mean to tell me that you know who we are?"

"We have been waiting for you for a very long time. According to the legend you would come to us with the good news for our people."

"Our people?" interrupted Juan, surprised.

The young man started laughing with an attitude of joviality and good humor, without answering the question he continued:

"Come to my home. There is good food to share on our table. There will enough time for questions while we have supper. Follow me please!"

Without thinking much about it, they followed him through a beautiful trail surrounded by trees whose branches came down touching the ground. A white fog began to cover the surface of the river penetrating between the roots of the trees that grew at the borders. The cousins began to think that that this was only a dream.

They slowed down as they approached their destination, when they heard the sound of a waterfall nearby. The grass was smooth and not very tall, as if it were cut recently. The trail was now flat and well cared for, surrounded by pretty flowers; then it went up to the top of a hill covered with small shrubs. The lights of a house there blinked. Upon arrival, the door was opened to them radiating a yellowish light. It was the house of the young man who took them there.

Chepe and Juan stopped in the threshold. The room in front of them in spite of being spacious was not very high. It was illuminated by lamps that hung from the beams of the ceiling. A wood table located in the center of the room had two candles with shining flames. In the opposite end, looking towards the entrance was a woman sitting. Her straight black hair covered her shoulders. She was dressed with a long brown dress with a golden belt with precious stone incrustations. An emerald necklace around her neck accentuated the rare beauty of her face. Her black eyes gave a brief look at the visitors.

"Come in, my special guests!" she said.

The two cousins approached the table timidly, bowing briefly as a greeting but still surprised not knowing exactly what was happening. They did not know who this beautiful lady before them was. Before they could say a word, the beautiful lady addressed them again:

"Come in my dear friends!" She said, inviting them in again. "I am Sinú, daughter and princess of the Guanes Indians."

Immediately she passed by them to close the door. Turning around she said:

"This is your house! Tonight you are under the roof of Count *Cuchicute*".

Chepe and Juan looked at each other in astonishment as she observed them with a smile on her lips. Chepe remained still, so captivated as he was when he met Tachia for the first time.

"Beautiful princess of the Guanes!" said Chepe

finally, as Sinú continued to smile.

"I hope that you will tell us everything!" said the young princess. "I understand that you are the special emissaries sent to bring good news which we have been expecting for many years. Please have a seat and let's wait for the man of the house. He will come soon."

The two cousins sat down in the small chairs; they followed with their eyes the attractive movements of the young native princess. In the meantime, Sinú took care of setting the table.

"Who is the man of the house?" asked Chepe.

"He is our Father. Just like us, he has been awaiting your visit for many years. The legend says that two men just like you would come from the high savannahs with a message filled of hope."

All of a sudden the door opened and a man of medium stature and white complexion came in. He took off his hat and placed on the table, leaving in plain sight his hair sprinkled with white which indicated his mature age. He smiled and going to Sinú he took her hand.

"Here is my beautiful daughter!" He said with a brief bow towards Chepe and Juan. "I present to you my Sinú of the Guanes!"

Then he asked:

"Is the table ready?"

"Yes, it is ready" answered Sinu as her young brother entered the room to greet his Father.

After awhile, all sat around the table. It was a great banquet, quite cheerful, lacking nothing. The drink seemed to be simply fresh water, but it had a delicious wine flavor that cheered their heart and comforted their spirit. All sang and shared histories enthusiastically. The man of the house told them stories of his family, the good old times, of his European heritage and how he got to know the most beautiful woman of that region, the princess of the Guanes.

"Fruit of our great love are these... my treasures" he said affectionately embracing his two children.

Although the young man had racially mixed features, Sinú conserved her purely indigenous appearance.

"Unfortunately the beautiful mother passed away many years ago and now we are only three in the family" he said with sad voice.

He spoke of the native ancestors and their customs and traditions; he spoke of the history of that village; he spoke of evil and cruel things but also of pleasant and positive ones; he spoke of his friends and his enemies; he spoke of the secrets that were hidden in that mysterious and unexplored place.

Astonished, Chepe and Juan listened to him with much attention. As he was speaking, they began to understand the lives of those people and to feel like true foreigners in that place.

"Our ancestors always have wanted to know the purpose and the reason for life... For thousands of years they have incessantly searched for identity and for a destiny. The legend says that long ago, they received a promise that they would obtain the answer to their quest during these times and finally they could know the answer to their quest.

"For that reason they all hope to see you tomorrow;

we all have been yearning for the arrival of this moment" said the man of the house.

The two cousins rose from the table without saying a word, Chepe now felt the weight of this responsibility in his heart. They proceeded to explore the room; their host, as he saw them contemplating the fine blankets and ceramics of beautiful colors that adorned the walls, explained to them:

"These are objects from our ancestors; they exchanged them with the Chibcha Indians for gold, emeralds, salt and other products."

Then, they stopped in front of other ornaments made of a mixture of copper and gold, pectorals and wood needles used to weave blankets.

"The tribe of the Guanes is counted as the best weavers of the region" said the very proud man about his ancestors.

Finally they extinguished the lights of the living room, except a lamp and two candles that were at the ends. All were seated again to enjoy moments of silence before retiring to their rooms. The host, with a candle in his hand, approached each one and wished them a good night and a good rest.

"See you tomorrow!" were his words of goodbye. Saying this he lowered the lamp and extinguished it with a blow.

The beds were prepared with special care; with soft pillows and white wool blankets, they soon went to sleep.

When waking up with the first light of the day they felt renewed. Chepe went to the window of his room and observed a beautiful orchard, covered with fresh dew. It was a splendid morning; the yellow and red flowers and of the garden stood out between the wet green leaves.

"Good morning, my friends!" greeted the man of the house as he opened the other window. The fresh air flooded the room, bringing with it the aroma of the garden.

"It is breakfast time!" he said, as he disappeared through the kitchen door.

Minutes later he returned with a full tray of food which he placed on the table. Immediately Sinú and her brother entered the room and all sat down at the table.

"Breakfast is served!" announced Sinú.

The food was diligently served by the beautiful lady as the light that entered trough the windows reflected on plates and other utensils.

Chepe and Juan were delighted as they observed the beautiful white dress and the skin sandals Sinú was wearing. She had the beauty and the sparkle of a woman at the height of her youth.

During breakfast they did not speak much as all were enjoying the wonderful foods, but after a while their voices and their laughter resounded gladly in the dining room. After breakfast the five of them left the house and started towards a large hill nearby where the rest of the people waited for them impatiently.

The trail went across lands covered with shrubs and green meadows with wild flowers; there were also large stone circles which were used as corrals for the sheep flocks. Some ewes dispersed in the prairies broke the silence with their bleats.

After two hours of walking, the two cousins stopped for a moment; although they did not feel tired, they were astonished by what appeared before their eyes: a somewhat unknown, strange and mysterious place.

Suddenly, just in front of them appeared an extensive hill covered with rocks organized in concentric circles. Many people were already there congregated and a large number of men, women and children continued to approach from different directions. It looked like a large pilgrimage.

The beautiful sun rise and the morning air renewed the spirit of the travelers. The cousins and their three companions remained in silence, waiting for everyone's arrival. Finally, the host took them to the top of the hill. Chepe looked around the multitude and raised his hand; the man of the house requested attention and silence. In the faces of everyone present there you could notice anxiety and expectation.

Juan sat in silence next to Chepe. Chepe stood up and observed the crowd for a few moments and then he started talking; after a brief introduction he related his history to them: Of how, providentially he and his cousin had discovered the Fountain of Youth; of that wonderful place in mountains near the village of La Mesa; of their encounter with Bachu, his sister Tachia and Father Carlos. He spoke to them in great details about everything they had learned there from Father Carlos and the great sacred book; the miraculous Fountain of Youth and its relationship to the death of an innocent man called the Christ, who had come as a servant but at the same time as a redeemer, doing great and noble works and miracles and performing great signs among men. He told them that the Christ, in spite of his innocence, had been condemned to death on a cross between two evil men; that the Christ in this manner had assumed the faults of all mankind and carried with him the ailments and the diseases of the men; he had to suffer for the iniquities of his contemporaries, who despised him, rejected, humiliated and mistreated Him. He was hurt and stricken without compassion, but in spite of so many tortures and degradation he did not open his mouth to complain. After apprehending and judging Him, they punished him by nailing Him to a cross, even though He never committed any violent act, nor deceived anybody, neither in His mind nor in His works. Thus that innocent died...

    Chepe also emphasized, that what seemed a defeat became a true success, a total victory... that on the third day the Christ had resurrected with power and glory, because death could not dominate He who came as a servant and a redeemer; that now He reigns as King and Lord and that one day He will return and before Him everyone will bow down recognizing that He is the true King of kings and Lord of lords, worthy of all glory and all honor...

    Then he made a long pause. Chepe looked over the crowd at each face present there and then concluded saying:

"He will reign in an ideal and marvelous place.

There he will live with his people; neither pain nor sadness is there, because He will dry every tear and, no longer will there be death, nor mourning, because everything wrong and imperfect that now exists will disappear...

An absolute silence reigned on that hill for a few moments... then followed and explosion of a joy. A deafening sound of applause and shouts of joy were heard; sounds of drums, musical horns, whistles, flutes and many other instruments. Children and adults danced gladly on the slopes of the hill to the rhythm of the music interpreted by the improvised orchestra.

It was a great celebration without antecedents. The shouts of joy, the applause and the music extended well into the night, but Chepe and Juan really did not know how long since they left half way through the afternoon, in the middle of the festive atmosphere of celebration with great enthusiasm and optimism among the people. The two cousins came to the man of the house to ask him to help them with directions to find the way that would take them to their next destination in the north.

They started getting ready to depart and when they were ready to leave, the man of the house took off his hat and bowed briefly with a grateful smile. The beautiful Sinú also smiled sweetly and with her brother raised their hands waving goodbye and wishing them well.

The two cousins started on their way on a trail that descended zigzagging on the slopes of the hill towards the northwest. They descended the last section quickly, stopping to watch for one last time the multitude that continued celebrating on top of the hill; then they continued on their trail...

Suddenly they found themselves next to a centennial *ceiba* tree, planted at the front of a church. The sky was darkening as the sun moved down slowly on the horizon. It was a beautiful sunset. Still surprised they examined their surroundings and then they looked at each other.

"We are in Barichara!" exclaimed Juan, excitedly. "We are in a town filled with history and beauty. Barichara means productive and land of abundance. This historical center was declared a national monument for the lovers of the beautiful and authentic towns. This one is a true display of beauty" continued Juan.

The first thing they noticed in this place was a beautiful sculpture of a couple of oxen, a tribute to those great and tame animals that help the farmers in their daily tasks in the field. Once downtown, they went to the church of Santa Barbara, a beautiful colonial temple sitting in a splendid manner in this distinguished city. Slowly they walked through the building admiring much of its beauty and tranquility, a very good environment to withdraw to for meditation and the transformation of the inner spirit.

The city offered calm and peaceful atmosphere with its street carefully paved with stones and the main town square surrounded by large colonial houses and old buildings preserved with great care by its inhabitants.

If something distinguishes Barichara, it is the beautiful shades of colonial colors between reddish and dark yellow stones with which the streets and the walls of the houses are constructed and even the arts and crafts. The sun, the dust and the air contribute to the warm and cozy atmosphere of this place.

"This is a charming town" said Chepe, "but we must move on to our destiny ahead. We cannot feel too much at home!"

They walked in silence through the stone streets in search of a vehicle that could take them to the town of Girón, their next stop in the north. But it was already too late and dark to allow them to continue on their trip. They did not have another alternative but to look for a place to spend the night.

CHAPTER 13

From very early in the morning the next day, they were ready to continue their trip up north to the town of Girón. Chepe looked in all directions enjoying the beauty of Barichara as if wanting to fix in his memory each detail of that cozy atmosphere. The morning was so clear that the hills in the distance could be appreciated plainly. The peaceful town woke up slowly to the tasks of the morning. Chepe tried to murmur in a low voice a cheerful song he had composed himself.

They went to the town center to find transportation and without wasting any time, they boarded the bus which was leaving at that very moment in route to the north of the country. From the beginning the highway started to climb up mountains while the sun was appearing among the hills as if wanting to greet the travelers.

Chepe and Juan, conscious that they were again on the way to unexpected adventures, sat down and looked at each other in silence. Both of them had great expectations of what was to come. They knew with certainty that nobody could foretell the events that were to happen during their trip. Soon they would come into lands and places that were totally unknown to them. The bus continued climbing until reaching the summit at the top.

"The view from here is fantastic!" commented Juan.

The air was cold and the sky seemed to be within reach. They had climbed a considerable distance into the mountains and little by little they seemed to drive into the clouds, which prevented them from seeing for long distances. There was no doubt; they were now at very impressive heights. Down, on the other side extended an unknown long valley, covered by a slight mist.

The bus began to go down slowly through a winding road; the mountain was very steep, with little or no vegetation, a semi-desert. It continued this way until arriving at the great canyon of the Chicamocha River, an immense and spectacular monument carved by nature, of reddish color, in the middle of a majestic mountain range. To all of this was added a chilling geography of steep abyss and imposing rocky depressions.

From the high viewpoints Chepe and Juan could appreciate the landscape, resembling enormous linen cloths, covering the high altitudes. Although unproductive, the mountains offered an extraordinary panorama, as well as the magic and the magnitude of their vast vegetation of cactus, thistles, and thorn bushes abounded in this place turning it into a delicate and hostile environment at the same time. The descent through this difficult road was laborious and horrifying. Witnesses of these dangers are a large number of crosses and small chapels with flower pots set along the road to remember those unfortunate victims of this beautiful and menacing place.

Both cousins observed with fear and distrust the bottom of the canyon through the windows of the bus that quietly descended on the highway towards the river at the base of the mountain. They were anxious to arrive at the town of Girón. This was a small village founded many years ago by the Spaniards at the borders of the so-called golden river.

There, one still feels the colonial past. It is considered as a monument of the period of the Spanish conquest. Its charming streets, narrow and paved with stones are filled with history, and offer the visitor the opportunity of time traveling to the past and feeling like in a true town of Andaluz, Spain. The traditional and religious atmosphere of the time is reflected in its beautiful architecture: the bridges, the small town square, the chapels and large houses evoke that spirit of the past which preserve itself intact. In addition it is possible enjoy the delicious treats and delicate crafts of different areas of the nearby regions.

Due to gold mining, this town acquired great importance in the region until the exhaustion of its mines. Girón at the present time is a peaceful village that preserves its past jealously. The Cathedral of the Lord of Miracles is one of its main attractions and the object of pilgrimage for many people. In the days of the Colony this region was the center of tobacco production along with cotton which the Spaniards exported to Europe. In order to remember this event, every year the famous town fair is celebrated. During this event the inhabitants of the region come down to Girón, to enjoy with their relatives and friends the activities of the fair.

The Power Of The Relic

The farmers take the best leaves from the different varieties of tobacco and extend them on the streets forming long curtains. They produce a very particular scent, something between bitter sweet and sour which visitors enjoy while they take a stroll along the streets. This is also the time to sell and to buy all kinds of domestic animals: horses, cows, sheep and goats, in addition to crafts of the different regions. These celebrations were propitious for the consumption of great amounts of drinks like beer and *chicha* prepared for this occasion by the inhabitants of the village.

The night of the arrival for Juan and Chepe was precisely in the middle of these celebrations. The streets were crowded with all kinds of people, men, women, children, and merchants. Music and dances in every place in addition to the entertaining chatting on the streets contributed to the festive atmosphere of the town. The *tiple*, the guitar and the maracas were part of the different instruments played by several musical groups. Many people in the streets drank and offered liquor to their friends; some of them already showed signs of being somewhat drunk.

With much grace and artistic expression the music was presented by the municipal band that offered large repertoire of folkloric rhythms and dances. Chepe and Juan spent the first part of the night, enjoying the music, the dance and the pleasures that this beautiful town had to offer. This brought them memories of the celebrations of their own town of La Mesa in the other side of the mountain where they also participated in the joyful celebrations.

Suddenly, already late into the night, a group of horse riders approached the town square through the highway that comes from the West. Clear and strong shouts sounded in the streets of Girón. The noise came from the shouts and the sparks produced from the horseshoes in the pavement of the streets. The head of the group came near followed by his companions, passing by the park along Main Street. The horses were swift, strong and of large stature, of Spanish breed; their reddish skins shone under the light of the streets; their black manes covered part of their proud and arrogant necks.

The riders were of medium stature, with faces serious and strong; with black hair the same as their moustaches, well cut. They dressed in white pants, black shirts and great straw hats. All of them had a machete on their waists and cowboy ropes in their hands. They rode in pairs sharing jokes resulting in loud outbursts of laughter. From time to time they rose in the stirrups to look around as if they were looking for something or somebody in particular. Nevertheless, they did not seem to have noticed the presence of the strange new visitors who were sitting in silence on a bench observing them carefully. The group already had passed by, when Chepe, suddenly stood up and asked in a loud voice:

"Who are you and who are you looking for?"

Very quickly and with an amazing ability, the men

stopped their horses, turned around and came back to the park. Both cousins were standing up, in silence and without any sign of fear, as they were surrounded by the riders who moved in a circle, grasping the cowboy ropes as they swung nosily to the ground. The rest of people remained immovable, sitting, or standing up maintaining a prudent distance, with great expectation as to what could happen in the next few moments.

Two shining machetes rose up in the air, then come down threatening in the direction of the two cousins while the other riders struck their cowboys ropes against the stone floor of the street. One of them, the shortest and fattest, with a moustache similar to that of Pancho Villa, the famous Mexican leader, apparently the head of the group, came near Chepe and then advanced towards him until he touched his neck with the end of his machete. Chepe remained calm in his place.

"Who are you and what are you doing in this town?" said Chepe finally, speaking with a santandereano accent which he had learned during its childhood to the South West of Girón.

"My name is Marcos" said the rider, "I come from the countryside and I am looking for a young fortune hunter who travels in company of his cousin."

Immediately he got off the horse, still with the machete in his hand. Chepe, kept his eyes on his face, watching him carefully and without any fear.

"And why are you so interested in finding him?" asked Chepe with a firm voice without moving his eyes from Marcos, who in turn kept his shining brown eyes fixed on Chepe's face.

"A strange man with a black hat has promised us an attractive sum of money for his capture. By the way you dress and speak, you must be a *cachaco.*" said Marcos. "The reason does not really concern me, but he offers a good payment if we turn you in."

"But I see that you are originally from this part of the country from the tone of your voice. What businesses brings you and your companion to this land, and who do you work for?" he asked.

"We come from the highlands and the favor and the protection of the king is with us," said Chepe.

The rider watched with great astonishment and confusion, because he never had heard similar words, with such authority and conviction.

"We will be here a couple of days, and then we will head north. That is our destination," added Chepe.

Marcos understood by the tone of his voice and the determination in it, the spirit of the mission for the young kids. Then he approached Juan and looking at him he asked coldly:

"And you… why are you so quiet?"

Juan remained still on the sidewalk by the street, with his feet separated to maintain a good balance and with a hand grasping something his pocket. With his green eyes, fixed on those of Marcos, he responded:

"If you persecute the innocent and the stranger without a reason, you do not deserve my words nor my answer."

The eyes of another rider flashed with rage and murmuring angrily, with the machete on his hand he approached Juan gasping:

"I would cut your head off Mr. impertinent," said the rider, while Chepe pulled out his sword.

"Mr. impertinent is not by himself..." intervened Chepe as he raised his sword on his right hand.

"You will die before you can touch my cousin..."

Things could have ended up in a disaster, if Marcos had not taken part, jumping in the middle of them with his bare hand extended up as a sign of peace.

"Excuse us Señor Chepe!" he said. "We do not want anything bad for you or for anyone standing here."

"We only served the King and our mission is to rescue a valuable relic that in the wrong hands, it could have dangerous consequences," said Chepe firmly and then adding:

"We have knowledge of difficulties in territories of the south and threats of destruction if we do not act soon. Our desire is to be free and to live peacefully, as we have done until now, preserving what is ours without serving any strangers. We are not at the service of any man, but we pursue those who try to enslave their neighbors or their fellow countrymen."

"For this mission I am not disarmed" continued Chepe as he moved his hand to his waist.

The sheath of the sword shone and the sword sparked with flashing colors like a flame with red, yellow and blue. Both riders were astonished as they had never seen something similar. Chepe's face showed revived determination and intrepidity, and it seemed to contain briefly the power and the majesty of the King.

For a moment, Marcos thought to have seen on his

forehead a mysterious mark; and taking a step back, with an expression of fear and respect on his face, he said to him:

"Tell me, gentleman what is the meaning of these words, and what is your intention?"

"The opportunity to choose is yours," responded Chepe, "for our part, a delicate mission awaits us. A war, although not official, was initiated thousands of years ago. Nobody will be able to live in the future as they used to live in the past and very few will be able to enjoy what they have now. But of these important subjects you will be able to learn if you are interested. Our assignment is to rescue the relic of the power from perverse hands."

The other rider, without paying attention to Chepe, interrupted saying:

"We have to hurry now, we have to go back home and it is already late... Let us leave these people to take care of their own fantasies."

He went away quickly while Marcos took a careful and cautious look around to make sure that the rest of his friends were still with him, and making a gesture of goodbye to the cousins, he said:

"Pardon me gentlemen... best of luck to you." Then he added: "I am interested in learning more on those subjects, so I hope that our ways will cross again."

After saying this, he and his group of riders went towards the outskirts of the town.

Juan and Chepe, on the other hand, followed the main street in search of Padre Nicanor who they found in the parsonage, next to the cathedral. He received them with a friendly spirit and he asked his assistant, a boy who must have been about twelve years old, to take care of their visitors. He for his part offered his services and took them to their rooms where they could leave their suitcases and provisions. When they returned, Father Nicanor led them to the living room for some refreshments before supper. After a lively and enthusiastic conversation, they moved to the dining room, where they were served an appetizing supper with the flavor of the santandereano taste: fresh fruits, roasted beef, rice and potatoes with cheese.

Before going to sleep Chepe asked about the information that they needed for their mission.
"In effect, as you know," said the Padre, "part of the information is in the chapel and is secret. Although I am the only person with the key to it, I do not know its meaning nor do I desire to know it, for my own safety. The code, is divided in two parts, it is of great importance and has remained secret until today. The other, is in a city in the Caribbean Sea. That person does not know of the existence of the first part or its meaning. All of this has the purpose of preserving the security of those who will have the privilege to find, El Dorado, which contains not only valuable wealth, but great secrets of science and technology." He who discovers these secrets will be able easily to dominate the world. For that reason it is truly important that they do not fall in unscrupulous hands.

CHAPTER 14

The town was still asleep when Father Nicanor took Chepe and Juan down to the inner chapel of the cathedral early in the morning the next day. The door was well secured with iron doors and a double set of locks. From the outside of the chapel some precious relics of gold and emeralds could be appreciated.

"The value of all these relics must be incalculable" thought Chepe when he saw them.

The Padre opened both locks with great skill and he invited them to follow him, securing them immediately once they were inside. Alongside the altar was a small table which contained some gold relics. Father Nicanor pressed the head of a small figure and instantly a hidden door was opened that gave access to a narrow and dark tunnel. He guided them to the entrance and invited them to go in while he illuminated the entrance with a lamp. The tunnel ended in a small room that contained only a table with a large open book in the center.

"The information that you need is found in this book" said the Padre.

As he approached with the lamp to illuminate the great book that was written in Latin, he exclaimed:

"Look here! Look here! Everything happened after the flood in the days of Noah. Look what it says here...!"

He bent over the book and paged through it, as if searching for something concrete.

"Let me see…! Let me see…" he said as he continued paging through.

After a few moments he exclaimed again with great joy, pointing with his finger to a place about the middle of the page:

"Yes… Yes… it is here; it says here…!"

"God blessed Noah and his children with these words: Be fruitful and multiply and fill the Earth. All the animals of the earth will fear you and have respect for you: the wild birds, the beasts, the animals that crawl on the ground, and the fish of the sea. Everything will be under your dominion. Everything that lives and moves and all the plants will serve as food for you. I give them all to you. If anyone spills the blood of a human being, another human being will spill his, because men have been created to the image of God."

Father Nicanor paused and then continued reading the book:

"God spoke again to Noah and his children, and he said to them: I make this agreement with you, your descendants, and all the living things that are with you this day, and with all the living things that came out of the ark; the domestic and wild animals. This is my covenant with you: I will never destroy the earth with a flood; then He added: This is the sign of the covenant which I establish for ever with you and with all the living things who are with you: I have placed a rainbow in the clouds which will serve as a sign of my covenant. Whenever the rainbow appears, I will remember the covenant that I established for ever with all the living things of the land."

Then the Padre continued reading from the book:

"In that time, the anointed one of the men made a raft of gold to commemorate the ark that had saved the life of humanity. This raft was consecrated and sworn in by that powerful priest and was kept as a sacred relic from those times. But later on, when the human race was scattered throughout the whole earth, the relic was brought to the new world, thousands of years ago."

Look...! Look...! It says here:

"At that time everybody spoke the same language. When they left the Eastern region, they found a plain in the region of Sinar. Sinar is the name of a vast plain between the rivers Euphrates and Tigris, designated with the name of Mesopotamia in the Middle East. They remained there and one day they said to one another: Let's make bricks and cook them in the fire. Thus, they used bricks united by a mixture created by them, instead of stones and used natural asphalt in those times."

"Later they said: Come, let's build a city and a tower that ascends to heaven. In this way we will become famous and we will not have to disperse over all Earth. But the Lord descended to see the city and the tower that men were building and thought: They are one people and speak one language; for that reason they have made this work, and now nothing in the world will stop them from doing it. It is better if we come down and confuse their language, so that they will not understand each other. This way the Lord dispersed them throughout all the earth and they did not finish the city."

The Power Of The Relic

Father Nicanor continued:

"From these events, two great cultures of the Middle East came to the New World bringing with them a civilization of advanced knowledge. One of these groups was the descendant of Arfaxad that settled down in the Caribbean. Those of the other group were descending of Nimrod and they settled down in the high mountains of the Andes. They brought with them the sacred golden relic or the raft. Examples of the influence of these advanced civilizations are the inexplicable and colossal monuments of Central and South America.

"Those of the first group founded an admirable city under waters of the Caribbean Sea which by the way will be your first destination. But before that, you will have to go by the Sierra Nevada of Santa Marta. This will be a small detour on your trip to the north. The second group went to the high mountains of the Andes, where they built their metropolis. There is found the famous city of El Dorado, about which many European conquistadores heard but none of them had the opportunity to find it. Your main purpose is to recover or destroy the sacred relic from the Middle East. In perverse hands, it is a threat and a danger to the welfare of humanity due to its great and mysterious powers."

"In effect" continued the Padre, "this page contains the first secret that you need. Here is a sketch of the sacred relic, the original raft. The *balsilla de oro* which was found by the Spaniards in the New World, was only one copy made by the natives intrigued by the power of the sacred relic".

Chepe, as if already prepared for this task, removed

a paper from its pocket, sprinkled it with clear liquid and then waited a few seconds for the liquid to dry. With great care and skill he placed it on the page of the mysterious book where the image of the sacred relic was. Next he pulled out his sword and pointing towards the paper he pressed the grip; a blue light, almost invisible, drew up on the paper a faithful copy of the sacred relic. Chepe returned his sword to the sheath and taking the paper that now contained the copy of the sacred relic; he placed it with extreme care in a small book that apparently was his diary. "That is all, Father" said Chepe, leaving the place immediately the same way as they had come in.

The following morning Chepe and Juan woke up with first rays of the sunrise. The fields and the valleys of the region looked full of life and vivid colors that demarcated the horizon. During breakfast they had a lively conversation with Father Nicanor. Juan was quite fascinated with the vast knowledge the padre had about the history of humanity. He would have loved to remain a few more days to learn more details about the great cultures of ancient civilizations and fabulous engineering works of mankind; about the disappearance of so many civilizations. He had an endless number of questions but there was not enough time. Father Nicanor promised him that next time they could speak at more length regarding these interesting topics.

After breakfast he took them to a room where they received the last instructions for their trip and a liturgical farewell blessing. Finally he warned them:

"On the way to the north there are many honest

farmers, noble and hard working, but also there are groups of violent men who are ferocious, strong and without scruples, that commit evil acts against the people and against nature. What they like most is to destroy; they kill for pleasure, without any apparent reason, they are avaricious and they store treasures and fortunes that they take from their innocent victims. They are greatly feared in those lands.

According to the Padre's instructions their next destination was Teyuna, the Lost City, located in the Sierra Nevada of Santa Marta. The two cousins boarded the bus about mid morning. The route from here to the north was very colorful, with beautiful fields, small farms and large open grassy fields for cattle, proper of the tropical climate. Now the mountains were left behind and the charming valleys and plains of this zone were ahead of them.

Half way between San Gil and Santa Marta an unexpected and unprecedented incident took place: next to the highway there was a massacre of ten farmers. The driver of the bus refused to stop for fear of his own life and that of his passengers, but at the persistent requests from Chepe, he finally agreed to it, only with the condition that if some threat arose they could go immediately. Chepe and Juan got of the bus as soon as it came to a stop and ran to examine the gravity of the situation.

The bodies of the dead farmers who apparently were killed with machetes lay on the grassy meadows next to the highway, covered with blood. The spectacle was macabre.

Suddenly they noticed that somebody was hiding behind the shrubs. Thinking that it could be the enemy, the two cousins threw themselves to the ground and waited for something to happen. After a few minutes everything remained in silence. Juan tried to slide swiftly towards the shrub where they had observed the movement. He approached cautiously, exploring the front and then the sides but he did not find anybody. He rose up slowly trying not to be seen. At this moment he noticed that somebody was running in the opposite direction into the trees. Very instinctively and even without thinking, he started running after the stranger. Juan was much quicker and in a matter of seconds he reached him and throwing him to the ground; he lay on top of him. Chepe was at his side in a matter of seconds, curious and ready to help.

"It is a boy!" exclaimed Chepe in surprise.

Juan rolled over to discover the nature of his enemy. Disappointed and a bit ashamed, he knelt down next to the youngster who was about twelve years old. He offered excuses trying to console him. The youngster rose up without saying word, with tears rolling down his cheeks. He remained this way for a few moments with his glance fixed on the ground. Juan through his arms around him, but when he let him free the young boy ran in opposite direction. Chepe and Juan thought that he was trying to get away again, but instead he went to the place of the massacre; he stopped next to one of the bodies and kneeling down he threw his arms around him and began to cry bitterly, calling him Father and asking him not to leave him.

At this moment the other passengers had approached with curiosity, making commentaries in low voice, and the women sobbed at such a tragic picture. Chepe kept in his anger while tears rolled down his face, looking at the sad scenario… an absurd and bizarre spectacle…, but he did not dare to interrupt the tender hug of that son to the lifeless body of his father. After a long while, the young kid, still on his knees, raising his face to the heavens he cried out:

"Papa, please do not leave me alone!"

Everyone present there cried bitterly as well, but the young boy did not realize what was happening around him or who was by his side.

Chepe stood there for a long time; immovable, angry, frustrated; finally he approached the boy and placed his right arm on his shoulders; he remained in silence, waiting a few moments for him to calm down, then he finally asked him:

"Who you are and what is your name?"

"My name is Jairo and now I am by myself… without a family. They killed my papa for no reason and now I am alone… Last year they killed my mom on the farm. But now I am going to kill them… when I grow up I am going to kill them…" he said among tears, with a mixture of sadness, anger, desperation, and a deep desire for revenge.

Immediately he returned to embrace the lifeless body of his Father, covered with blood; and to ask with the innocent and tender heart of a child not leave him alone.

Chepe approached the lifeless body the boy was embracing to study his conditions. To his astonishment he found that the body was still warm and while placing his ear to his chest he found a languid heart beat. He was unconscious but he still had signs of life. Without wasting time, Chepe took its sword and raising his eyes to heaven he poured a few drops of the water from the fountain on his right hand and then he put it on his forehead, his lips and finally over the incapacitated body.

Immediately the man opened his eyes as if waking up from a deep sleep. He looked around trying to find out where he was. When seeing his son at his side on his knees with his face covered with tears, he asked him:

"What's the matter son? Why do you cry?"

It was evident that he did not remember any details of the violent encounter with the criminals that roamed around this region.

"Come here son" he said with his open arms and a great smile on his face, still lying down on the ground.

Jairo threw himself on his father's open arms with great joy. They embraced each other, remaining there for a long time while the group of bus passengers watched them astonished and incredulous.

"Please do not cry my son, we are now together, you and me; for ever... for ever" repeated the father, assuring his son that everything was well.

Satisfied, Chepe contemplated in silence the emotional and moving encounter between father and son. He then looked at Juan and the two of them smiled with an expression of triumph on their faces. Jairo, now realizing the miracle that had happened, ran to Chepe to give him a hug of thanks.

"Thank you! Thank you very much! Now I will not have to be alone... now I am not alone..., I have my papa and he has me... thank you sir!

After saying this, Jairo ran back to his father who was now standing up, healthy and quite happy, but not yet understanding what had happened... the important thing was that he was again with his son. He knelt down to Chepe to thank him for the surprising miracle. Chepe took him by the hand and asked him to get up. "The honor and the glory belong to the King and Lord. It is He who has entrusted me the power this day."

Later Chepe requested them not to mention anything of this to anybody and embracing Jairo, he said to him:

"Remember son: He who is slow to anger is better than a mighty man and he who controls his temper is better that he who takes a great city. Revenge belongs to the Lord..."

Chepe rose and looking over the dead victims asked the bus driver to inform the proper authorities immediately so that these could investigate and carry out justice. And then looking at the yet incredulous passengers, he said:

"The government is not set up for fear of those who do well, but for fear of those who do evil. It is set up for the service of the King, to do good for you. He who does evil must fear, because the authority does not bear its sword in vain; it is for the service of the Lord, to do justice and to punish the evil doer.

"In the same way" added Juan, "the Lord gives this

warning: Do not mistreat or oppress your neighbor, nor to the widows or the orphans, because if you do and they come to me, I will come in their aid with great wrath and take your life. Then who will remain widow and orphan will be your women and your children."

Finally, Chepe suggested to Jairo's Father that he should do what was good and to take care of his son without looking for revenge and to always help his fellow men.

"Then he continued; he who has pity on the poor, the Lord compensates him for his good work. You do not rob the poor man, nor oppress the afflicted one, because the King will defend his cause and will take the life of those who disregard his precepts."

Minutes later Jairo and his Father were ready to return to their farm in the country side. Chepe and Juan observed them as they went their way. They were together again, as Jairo had cried out to the heavens in the middle of his desperation. Chepe and Juan stood there in silence looking at the Father and son in the distance as they turn around one last time to wave a goodbye with their hands.

CHAPTER 15

Chepe and Juan arrived in Santa Marta during the morning of a new day. This coastal city in the Caribbean was settled at the beginning of the 16th century and it is one of the oldest colonial cities in Colombia. It was strategically located near the Sierra Nevada to serve as a base for the commerce of the fabulous treasures coming from the Tayronas Indians. Thanks to their adventurous spirit, Juan and Chepe were well equipped for their expedition to these legendary mountains. They got comfortable shoes for the long hikes ahead of them and light cotton clothing. They were ready and anxious to start their new adventure in search of the Lost City up in the Sierra Nevada.

After a few hours of intense search, they managed to locate an expert guide who could lead them to the mysterious city. From Santa Marta, they went by truck in a long six hour trip through a difficult and open gravel road. Thanks to their guide, they had a chance to learn many details about this place on their way up:
"The Sierra Nevada is a beautiful and magnificent mountain that stands out majestically near the Caribbean," he began saying as they entered the long trail; "it is classified as the highest tropical mountain by

the ocean in the world. It is part of an extensive National Park that constitutes an important hydrographic reserve, formed by several rivers that supply waters to the large banana growing region and the important tourist area of this region. It has always been considered a marvelous place but at the same time a horrifying place; the conquistadors did not have much of an opportunity to get to know its history and its secrets, since it was jealously guarded by its brave and courageous inhabitants, the Tayrona Indians."

"Today," continued the guide, "this park protects the fauna and the flora of the humid forests of warm and temperate climates, and the forests of cold climates, and the deserts. This is an ecological reserve of incalculable proportions, which has an innumerable variety of plants and animals and is the home to an indigenous population composed of Arhuacos, Kogis and Malayos, who keep the customs of their ancestors.

"The Arhuacos Indians are skilful weavers; they elaborate by hand the famous *mochilas* or *tutus*. This tradition is of great importance for their community. The *Tutu* is the symbol of the mother earth, of the woman and the Arhuaca mother who carries her son on her back. The women learn to weave from their early age by watching and helping their mothers. The first tutu they make is given to the priest for the rituals of the life cycle. The others, before their marriage, are for themselves, their Father or their brothers; when they are ready to get married, they keep the prettiest one for the man they will marry.

At the end of the 16th century, the Spanish expeditions started off from Santa Marta with the

The Power Of The Relic

purpose of conquering the Tayronas. The native warriors fought against the invaders in a heroic way, but time and time again the conquistadores made them give away part of their territory forcing them to change their place of residence and therefore their way of life.

In spite of the superiority and persistence of the conquistadores, the intrepid natives managed to protect great parts of their civilization. This has been demonstrated in a surprising way in recent years, thanks to archaeological investigation in the Sierra Nevada. Out of this work has emerged the Lost City, one of greatest and most famous discoveries in the American continent of the pre-Hispanic times.

The Lost City is at the top of the valley of the Buritaca River, surrounded by a lush and productive vegetation of palms, cedars and ferns that hide a surprising variety fauna: wild birds, insects, snakes, monkeys and other animals. Close to this archaeological site live the Kogui Indians, descendants of Tayronas. This entire region, of one hundred thousand hectares, has become a forest and an archaeological national reserve. Recent investigations in this region have resulted in amazing discoveries of engineering feats made by the Tayronas: the system of terraces, stairs, avenues and channels are witness of their excellent knowledge of urban organization.

The Natural Reserve Maringa, whose name also comes from the Tayrona culture, is only twelve kilometers from the city of Santa Marta and two hundred forty meters above the sea level. In its entire expanse there are important archaeological remainders of the old highway system that linked the different villages with the ocean. Today, we can still appreciate the reproductions of ceremonial terraces and indigenous houses constructed by their direct descendants, the Koguis. These trails go into in a gallery of forests where the beauty of our nature can be enjoyed."

Six hours later, the travelers came near the foot of the Mountain. Pointing towards the Sierra Nevada the guide continued:

"In these mysterious mountains the fog is frequent, the forest is humid and the temperatures are highly variable. The gigantic trees go up to thirty five meters of height and maintain their foliage always green. The tropical vegetation, moss and orchids are abundant in this area. On the western slope, the forest becomes rather dry with thorny scrubs accustomed to the warm climate. The east is a permanent source of water streams.

The Tayrona Indians occupied the valleys of the Don River, Buritaca and Guacharaca in the North Slope of the Sierra Nevada. Within these rivers are the gigantic ruins of one old indigenous city that has had between three and five thousand inhabitants. The beauty of its coves, cliffs and mountains, its historical past and its natural and wild atmosphere, attracts many visitors."

"Teyuna is one of the most mysterious places in Colombia" said Juan to Chepe. "Its walls, terraces, paths and steps extend deep into the forest and up to high altitudes in the northwest of the mountain. Towards the north, the waves of the Caribbean Sea bathe the beaches covered with palms trees in the

The Power Of The Relic

Tayrona Park. At its back side stands out, imposing the highest mountain peak in the country, the *Pico Colon*."

"The trail to the Lost City is surrounded by thick and diverse tropical vegetation, which gives a sense of mystery. I have a feeling that a great adventure awaits us there" concluded Juan.

After six exhausting hours they reached the end of the dirt road. From here they took a trail up the mountain. The guide loaded two mules with the food and their belongings in order to make this a lighter and pleasant trip, thus starting the long ascent to Teyuna, the Lost City. The first section of the trail was through an area that the colonos had deforested in order to grow banana, yucca, vegetables and unfortunately, some illicit drugs like cocaine, marijuana and poppy seeds.

After climbing up to about six hundred meters above sea level the expedition had to continue through a trail shaded by tropical forests for more than two hours until they arrived at the colono house. They decided to spend the night there. After taking a light supper they arranged to sleep in their individual hammocks covered with mosquito nettings, while the guide made the necessary preparations for the next day.

After breakfast they undertook the long walk up the mountain through beautiful forests. Half way up, they found the Kogui Indian reservation. There they went through a village where they had the opportunity to see some natives. Although these were generally timid, Chepe and Juan, with their gentle, happy and friendly temperament, managed to establish a simple conversation with them, although they were a little distrustful.

In one of the rustic indigenous villages that were used frequently for special meetings, the guide made arrangements for overnight lodging. Before supper, the travelers could enjoy a magnificent bath in the cold waters of the Buritaca River. As during the previous night they slept in hammocks hanging in a safe place covered by tropical vegetation.

"Did you hear that?" Juan asked suddenly.

"It seems to be Indian drums" answered Chepe.

The music could be heard softly in the distance, above in the mountains, as if it was announcing some special ceremony. After a few minutes everything was completely silent again, interrupted from time to time by the sad singing of some nocturnal birds.

After breakfast, they took the trail that crosses the Buritaca River in several occasions; some times they went across swimming, others simply walking through its cold waters which descended from the high part of the mountains. From here they went through some areas half way destroyed by explorers. In the last part of the trail they had to climb a set of stone stairs of more than two thousand steps, built by the Tayrona Indians, until they reached the legendary Lost City of Teyuna. They set a campground next to the stone patio of the city ruins, and then they took a comforting bath followed by a light supper. The simple and primitive atmosphere of this place seemed to mysteriously transfer them to other times when the culture of these natives bloomed in these imposing mountains.

The explorers dedicated the following day to explore the ruins of this spectacular city.

Teyuna, seated on the banks of the Buritaca River

has been until now the most important nucleus of the Tayrona culture; it was possibly the capital of the region. The axis of the city was a path of stairs that began at the border of the river and climbed up to the crest of the mountain, unfolding to the left and to the right, forming secondary trails that went to several terraces as well, most of which also served as support for their huts.

The mission for Chepe and Juan was to find the Indian chief and priest who should be able to provide additional information about El Dorado, but they heard that the Indian chief had gone to look for medicinal plants, so they would have to wait for his return.

The walls, terraces, paths, steps and seats of the city were covered by the fog, which did not permit them to see a fair distance, giving this place an even more mysterious atmosphere. The way towards the top of the Sierra Nevada extended through the forest disappearing in the mist that seemed to embrace it. Chepe went to the hut of one of the natives with whom he had established a friendship the previous day. In a friendly manner he tried to initiate a conversation, trying to discover more details about this people.

"This must be one of oldest cities of the region" said Chepe, as he started the conversation.

"It is the greatest of several old cities our ancestors built," answered the native with certain nostalgia."

"Where were your ancestors before they came to these lands?" Asked Chepe, a bit intrigued, trying to find out the origin of this fascinating culture.

"The way they worked gold, the precious stones

and the ceramics, are very similar to some Indian cultures of central America. For that reason it is very probable that they have come from that part of the continent" pointed out Juan.

"The older people say that the ancestors had to flee from territories of fire where the gods punished them with volcanoes and earthquakes" added the native, "but with time also they punished us again by sending the conquistadores to us…"

"But it has been even worse recently" he continued in a somber manner. "The Sierra Nevada has been our home for many years. It has been inhabited mainly by natives, but lately armed groups have arrived; insurgents from the outside world who commit all kinds of violent acts, murders, mutilations, kidnappings, tortures, threats, spreading terror throughout, recruiting young kids and forcing our families to move. These groups operate in this region where the natives undergo the rigors of the conflict and live in extreme poverty. We feel left out and forgotten, and indeed we are, left out by the law and by the State."

"The conditions in which the indigenous communities live are precarious and difficult, especially in economic, social and cultural matters and regarding the protection of human rights. This continues without an effective strategy that could mend once and for all, this critical situation for our families" concluded the native bitterly.

They spent all the morning talking while they shared some hot drinks of herbs, which helped them stay warm in those cold mountains. Chepe and Juan learned much about the history of those people; now, with more knowledge about their past, they felt a greater respect for their culture. They could understand better, how with the course of the time the Tayronas had become one of the indigenous cultures most besieged by the Spaniards in the Colombian territory. When arriving to this region, they discovered with much surprise cities well established by the natives.

Among the most surprising things for the Spaniards was the high level of development of beekeeping, the cultivation of fruit trees and protection of the water sources. The Hispanics were also amazed at the knowledge the natives had of astronomy and meteorology, and their ability to exploit marine salt. Additionally they had developed an intense commerce by means of the exchange with tribes of Central America, Venezuela and many others from the center of Colombia.

The skill of the Tayronas in the art of gold working was extraordinary. The society was organized in hierarchic layers. In the upper level was the high priest, who at the same time was the healer, the chief and the judge. Their main deities were the sun, the moon, the frog and the jaguar. They lived in relatively large villages, governed by chiefs, who were at the same time the commanders during the battles of those times. The relative rank of the inhabitants was indicated by the location of their houses.

Chepe and Juan were very impressed by the ingenious way these people defended their ground from the forces of the erosion when building their cities on the steep mountains. With a special technique they placed great stones to carry strong water torrents by channels to water their crops without destroying their buildings.

The second night was interrupted again by the indigenous drums; this time they sounded faster and closer, as if they were celebrating something cheerful and festive, full of energy. Minutes later the rate became slow and gloomy.
"It seems like a funeral with a very sad music" said Juan trying to decipher some type of a message in the percussion, which continued well into the night.

The following day, Chepe and Juan came back to explore more in the vicinities of the Lost City. There they could observe the famous roads, the bridges and steps, the channels of irrigation and drainage, as well as different implement for domestic usage. They found the primitive works of engineering quite fascinating. The natives had developed a technique that allowed them to manage their resources and surroundings in an extraordinary way. For the following two days they continued examining every detail about the Lost City of Teyuna.

Since they had waited for more than four long days for the return of the Chief, Chepe and Juan began to suspect that something was wrong, but they did not know how to find it out. Their native friends assured them, that the Indian chief would return soon; but the fifth day came and still there was no news of his return.

Then Chepe called one of his friends to speak alone and to try to convince him that they could help him in case the chief was in any type of difficulties.

"I only need to see him" he said. "If he is in poor condition, I am perhaps the only one who can help him."

With certain fear, the native, agreed to tell him about the nature of the situation.

"It is true that our chief is in the mountains looking for medicinal plants; somebody is with him because he is blind. As a result he does not wish to receive any visitors. He feels ashamed if somebody would see him in that state. How can a blind chief and priest, guide and heal his people? This would be an insult and a misfortune for our old chief!" he said finally.

Chepe put his hand to his cheek while he thought about the next step.

"I can help him but I need you to take me there!" insisted Chepe.

"Impossible!" answered his friend, "when the chief does not wish to see anyone, it is necessary to fulfill his desires. All of us fear him and respect him!

"It's OK, it's OK ..." said Chepe, trying not to force him into doing something he did not want to do. Then he made a second attempt, trying to make his argument more clear.

"Do you wish that your chief be in good health and able to see again?"

"But off course!" was his immediate answer.

"If it is true, then we will have to find a way to see him. You must help me!" insisted again Chepe.

"I will try to see if this is possible, but I will have

to go alone to the mountain to convince his assistant; perhaps this way we can obtain something..." said the native.

And it was done that way: the native went to the place where the chief was and tried to persuade his assistant of the importance of this visit. After several hours of deliberation the old man finally agreed to see Chepe, but only if he went up alone; he was not willing for anyone else to see him. Chepe accepted the conditions for the interview without any problem.

CHAPTER 16

Both of them went up the mountain in search of the old Indian Chief. They found him lying down on a mat and his assistant seated at his side under a rudimentary hut made with branches of trees and palm branches to protect him from the sun and the rain. His young aid was there to help him feel as comfortable as possible under the present circumstances. On the floor, there was also an Indian drum.

"Perhaps this is the drum we heard during the last few nights" thought Chepe.

"We use this for a ceremony of the magical spirits" said the guide. "We have been performing that for several nights but the spirits are angered and they do not want to come when we call. It is for this reason that we have not yet returned to the city."

The assistant announced the presence of Chepe to the Chief. He raised his fragile hand as a welcoming sign. Chepe, in turn bowed to him respectfully. After this formality, Chepe approached the old man slowly; he bent at his side and remained there a few seconds observing him with admiration and compassion. He appeared to be about seventy years of age. The weakness and lethargy of his body indicated difficult times in his life. Chepe looked around his surroundings and then fixed his glance on the chief and his young assistant. Looking up to the sky he murmured some words and taking his sword he sprinkled a few drops of water from the fountain on his hand; immediately he passed it over the forehead, over his eyes and over his body. The old man opened his eyes and looked at Chepe and then he look around his surroundings without saying word. As if waking up from a long dream, ha had a big smile on his face; he knelt down next to Chepe in an act of gratitude. Chepe took him from his hand and asked him to get up because he was not worthy of such a thing.

"The glory and honor belong to the King and Lord" said Chepe, "because it is He who has granted me this power."
The Chief was now in perfect condition, with no sign of blindness or any other disease; his body was filled with supernatural energy, which he had never experienced before. The joy and a big smile now had returned to his face; after so many years, once again he could enjoy the matchless beauty of these mountains which he had walk during his youth. There he stood for a long time; delighting himself with the beauty of nature.
Finally, placing both hands on his chest in attitude of reverence and after a brief bow, with great curiosity he asked:
"Who is this king of whom you speak to us? The only kings of whom I have heard previously have brought us only mistreatment and destruction."
Chepe approached him with a friendly smile and fixing his glance on his eyes he answered:
"The king I speak about is quite different and for some, perhaps incomprehensible and of unexpected

actions. Our Lord and King is good and generous; He is compassionate and merciful, slow to anger and abundant in mercy and truth. He alone can pardon the transgressions of men and their sin. He will not consider innocent the guilty one; he punishes the iniquity the men. The Lord and King is exalted to the highest; his name is over every name; every knee shall bow at the calling of his name and every tongue will confesses that He is the King of kings and Lord of lords."

After saying this, Chepe realized that the chief did not seemed to understand what he was talking about, so standing by his side he related his own story to him; explaining to him at great lengths the character of the King that he had known in the eastern mountains, close to the small town of La Mesa. The old chief stayed there for many hours... still enjoying his renewed body and trying to understand what he had heard from his new friend Chepe.

Chepe approached the old man once more. He now seemed to enjoy a new life.

"What is your name and what is your history?" Chepe asked with great curiosity, without moving his glance from its face.

"My name is Tairo," answered the old man. "I have been hiding in the mountains as a survival strategy."

"I was born in these mountains many years ago and as a descendant of warrior leaders I was given the opportunity to choose between the incognito life or the life of the invaders. So I decided to be transferred, along with the last survivors, to the high and mysterious mountains of Sierra Nevada; in this hiding place we have lived in relative peace."

"But this is not everything" continued Tairo. "The legend says that many years before the arrival of the invaders, strange beings had come to this part of the world. They brought with them great technologies and science of great power. They have their sinister empire in a secret place up on the Andean mountain range, where they hide a magical relic. Thanks to the relic they enjoy great power, even today.

"They have much gold, much more than the invaders took from the inhabitants of this Sierra Nevada. They are surrounded by a great mystery and only in rare occasions they have come out to attack our people; also there is a legend that they keep a large number of natives from the mountains as slaves." Chepe listened with much attention, and then he asked:

"And what do you know about the sacred relic, the *balsilla* of the power? And where is its hiding place today?"

"I do not know, nor do I desire to know it. Everybody has a great fear and horror of those strange beings and the power of the relic. Everyone shakes in terror when it is even mentioned," responded Tairo. Then he added "They are indestructible and horrible beings. But this is not all; something very interesting happened at the arrival of the Spanish conquistadores who were looking for gold and wealth, things that those beings had in abundance. But it did not go well with them. The search for gold became a terrible history of intrigues and mystery. Those that have tried to acquire their wealth or their power have lost their lives or have returned totally ruined… it is a curse…"

"El Dorado is a wonderful city, ruled by a powerful monarch, who instead of using a suit when he bathes in the lake, something that was against the divine dignity, he bathes every day with gold dust that adheres to his body; at dusk he would come off as he submerged in the waters of the lake which is on top of the mountain. In this manner great amounts of the precious metal went to bottom of its waters. The sovereign was not concerned about this wastefulness."

Tairo tried again and again to discourage and to dissuade Chepe from his search. He tried to convince him that the search for *El Dorado* could be a disaster for him and for his companions.

"The Indians of the Andes also tried to help the conquistadores," he continued. "They answered all the questions and satisfied all their curiosities giving them precise details about the extraordinary sovereign, who was superior in wealth even to the powerful Inca emperor. This motivated Francisco Pizarro to prepare an expedition with the objective of finding the coveted kingdom of *El Dorado*. In his preparation he used good part of the large booty he obtained in the conquest of Peru.

His army which left Quito with the purpose of trying carry out this fabulous conquest was made up of two hundred Spaniards, four thousand natives and two hundred horses, which represented an impressive wealth in those times. A good number of *llamas* used to carry their cargo, flocks of pigs and provisions of all nature. In addition to the ammunition and arms, tools for the manufacture of new equipment, they also took seeds and all the necessary provisions for the conquest of *El Dorado* and for the establishment of his own new empire."

"No dominion in the old world would have been able to support t such and expensive expedition; only the arrogant conquistadores could allow such luxuries. What they acquired in one conquest, they would spend in the preparation of the next one. Francisco de Orellana joined Pizarro in this venture. He had participated previously, like Pizarro in the conquest of Peru. Orellana left his government post in Guayaquil to participate in this adventure."

"In spite of the great preparation of the expedition, all of it was insufficient for the great difficulties of the hostile nature and the unhealthy climate," continued Tairo. "The calamities began when they crossed the mountain range, where a good part of the Indians died. They were accustomed to the mild climate of the mountain plateaus; but when they arrived at the valleys of the Amazon, the situation was even more complicated.

"The physical and climatic adversities of the virgin forests, which had prevented the success of previous expeditions towards the interior of the continent such as: the humidity, the fog, the mosquitoes, the tropical rains, began to be felt with greater intensity among the expedition, especially among the Indians that still remained; those that had survived the passage through the mountains. Soon Gonzalo Pizarro found himself with no Indians and no *llamas*. The *llamas* either died or were sacrificed, like the horses and the pigs. Thus they found themselves with no means of transportation and with no provisions."

"Due to the humidity of the tropical forest, their clothing, the food, the seeds, and the weapons began to deteriorate. Even the gun powder became of no used for anything. To these also added the continuous annoyances caused by the clusters of insects, taking them to state of nervousness, exasperation and violence among their own people in the expedition. The situation was made even worse by the continuous attacks of the Indians hiding in the forest, which attacked them frequently with poisoned arrows."

"As far as getting new supplies from Peru, every attempt to go in search of provisions failed. Every group that attempted to separate from the main expedition fell into the hands of the enemy. Suddenly hunger became their most faithful companion. They finally arrived at the borders of the Coca River, the Napo River and then the Amazon. In order to continue their journey they needed other means of transportation."

"They began the construction of a small boat, good enough to resist the attacks of the Indian enemies. The wood was abundant and the nails were made with the horseshoes of the dead horses. Along the Coca River and later the Napo River, they sailed for the first time in this strange boat. Due to the hardships of the diseases and in the lack of food, Gonzalo Pizarro decided to camp at the border and explore the new place. Orellana continued the expedition down the river taking on board the fragile ship fifty seven men."

"Orellana promised to return in twelve days but he did not come back. Pizarro spent days and months waiting and finally decided to return to Ecuador. The return trip was more difficult than the outgoing one. Sixteen months after they have left Quito commanding a formidable army, they re-entered the city with eight men who seemed more like ghosts, dresses in rags. The spectacular expedition was reduced to that; a sad end for those who dared to go in search of *El Dorado*. Pizarro returned ruined, a true state of calamity... it was a curse..." concluded the Indian Chief.

"And what happened with the other companions of Pizarro, who had left in search of provisions?" asked Chepe quite intrigued.

Tairo kept silence for a while before answering:

"Francisco de Orellana decided to undertake his great adventure in charged of the fifty seven men who accompanied him. Instead of going in search of food and provisions, he decided to go himself in search of *El Dorado* but since the boat he had was not enough for this great mission he undertook the construction of a bigger ship.

"In just thirty five days, he and his people made a new boat in which they continued their trip. This was the first boat manned by Europeans crossing the greatest river of the world. This was called first Trinidad, later Orellana and finally the Amazon River. This last name was given by Orellana himself, who believed to have seen women warriors in one of his landings. The legend says that indeed during a fight he sustained with those women warriors, Orellana lost an eye."

"The immense river did not offer wealth, it did not offer gold. The natives lived from fishing and mandioca crops. The wonderful landscape replaced the necessity of wealth. The river and the virgin forest provided food for them; the materials for their houses and as far as their dresses, the Indians used different materials and the skins from the animals they hunted. What else would the Spaniards hope to find in that green place of grief and despair?"

"Nevertheless, Orellana never gave up on the search of his dream, but this took him to his own destruction" continued Tairo. "Always sailing in search of *El Dorado*, that fantastic place, he arrived at the Atlantic sea. He had crossed the greatest river of South America, having traveled across the whole continent. The first point they touched in the Caribbean was the island of Cubagua, in the Venezuelan coast, where they met Spanish fishermen who welcomed him and his companions. Now they could at least boast of being the first explorers of the Amazon."

"Shortly after, Orellana traveled to Spain where this history captivated the attention of his superior. He was named governor of the lands he had explored. Two years later he tried again to cross the Amazon, but in this occasion in the opposite direction… He still insisted in continuing the search for the wonderful *El Dorado*. But this time he failed again…

Not many days after entering the river, he was attacked by serious fevers and diseases, which finally took his life there… at the borders of the greatest river of South America, without ever reaching his dream, of finding and conquering the famous *El Dorado*. Everything ended up in ruin, in disaster… in calamity… it was a curse." concluded Tairo, the Indian Chief and priest of the Lost City in the Sierra Nevada.

CHAPTER 17

After fulfilling their mission in the Lost City of Sierra Nevada, Chepe and Juan went to *Cartagena de Indias*, the Heroic City, founded in 1533 by the Spaniard Pedro de Heredia. With an excellent geographic position it did not take much time for this city to become the strategically most important point for the world of gold treasure hunters and a point to begin with innumerable marine trips to the old world. While its fame expanded, its beauty increased and its interesting booty grew even greater. Continuous attacks happened one after another. Hundreds of pirates and adventurers, in search of wealth attacked the unprotected city without truce. Because of this the Spanish crown ordered the immediate construction of castles and fortified walls to provide protection for it.

Chepe and Juan went to the old part of the city. They wanted to visit the Castle of *San Felipe de Barajas*, located on the hill of San Lazaro, to the east of the historical center of the city. In front of the fort, both cousins marveled at the talent and advanced engineering that allowed them to build such a magnificent construction.

Juan explained to Chepe: "This castle is considered the most outstanding work of the Spanish military engineering in America. This fortification, which consists of a series of walls with very broad bases that narrow towards their embankments, constitutes a formidable military bunker. The batteries and parapets do not aim towards the fortress, but rather they protect each other; this way it was practically impossible to take the city. It is said that the enormous stone blocks for the fort were extracted from the coralline reefs of the bordering coasts, and taken by the slaves all the way up the hill."

"To the colonial Cartagena came large convoys of Spanish *galleones*, carrying royal mandates, weapons, slaves and merchandise. From here they left for Havana, Cuba, where they would meet other fleets that controlled the commerce and the market of the New World. The galleones carried the tributes, the silver of Peru, the gold of New Granada, the tithes collected by the clergy, fine woods, the emeralds and the wealth of the Spaniards who returned to the mother land. The returning ports were Havana and Cartagena. For the navigators this last one was the safest for the maintenance and repair of the boats, before crossing the Caribbean which was plagued with pirates."

"Many galleones which did not have the luck to arrive at their destination lie at the heart of the Caribbean Sea, within this bay outside of the city," continued Juan. "But what is still more interesting: The Castle of San Felipe, that rises imposing watching towards the Caribbean Sea, was constructed with the price of blood. The natives were not quite strong enough for this type of work. Thus the Spaniards brought black Africans as slaves. Defenseless and at the mercy of their masters, they worked day and night, supporting the inclimency's of the weather and the cruelty of the Spaniards. Thousands of slaves died in their construction.

"It is said that the blood was cruelly used to prepare the mixtures to set up the stones on the defending walls. It took two hundred and eight years to build this fort. Many other constructions were built at the cost of this superhuman effort, like for example the convent of *La Popa*, built at the beginning of the 17th century. From there you can see the whole city of Cartagena.

The builders equipped the castle with a diverse defensive system, thus assuring its impenetrability. The walls were not raised in a perpendicular way from the ground, but inclined towards their interior, in order that the bullets from the enemy canons bounced without causing much damage to its structure."

"On the other hand the canons of the fort were placed strategically, in front of the bay, so that any suspicious boat that came to attack would be perfect target for the cannons. The pits were also added, in which any intruder would fall who tried to penetrate the city by climbing its walls. Part of the defensive system was also the surprising declivities, the inclines, the tunnels and strategic artillery. The interior was also a fundamental part of its defense, the tunnels that connected the different sectors of the fort permitted them to move without being detected by the enemy. The underground quarters had sufficient capacity for more than three hundred and fifty men; and the deposits of weapons and food supplied were sufficient to resist several months of outer siege."

After enjoying a very memorable self guided tour of the castle, the fort, and the city walls the two cousins made arrangements to search for the contact that padre Nicanor had mentioned to them before their departure from Giron: Hernan Casas. The task was not difficult; his house was located in the area of the city called Bocagrande but there was no need to go all the way there. Chepe got in touch with him by telephone. After arranging an appointment to have supper in the city center, they walked to an establishment where they could hear a sound of the happy and cheerful music proper of the Caribbean Coast.

There you could hear a mixture of voices and the pleasant music of the accordion. The place was clean and with an excellent view of the ocean waters. Many people of distinguished background frequented this place. Chepe and Juan sat down and asked for two cold fruit juices to calm the thirst produced by the hot and humid temperatures. At the very moment they were getting ready to leave a man of dark skin approached them with a warm smile on his face.
"Welcome to Cartagena, please have a seat and have another drink... I will buy," said the man, as he offered two chairs at his table.
Chepe vacillated for a moment, but then he thought that this would be a good opportunity to make a new friendship and to learn more about the city of Cartagena.
"Very well, but I will buy" said Chepe with a great smile as he extended his hand to greet his host.
"My name is Camilo Rendón," said the man with a

Caribbean accent.

"I am Chepe, and this is my cousin Juan," replied Chepe as he shook his hand.

"You guys are *cachacos,*" affirmed Camilo as he signaled the waiter to come over to his table to take his order. "Please bring these gentlemen whatever they would like to drink; as for me, please bring me a cold beer," he ordered in a courteous way. The cousins on the other hand requested two glasses of mango juice, very cold.

They spent several hours, chatting and laughing at the jokes and the good humor of the Caribbean coast. Camilo had studied Law at the National University, in the capital city of Bogotá. Wanting to be near his family he had returned to Cartagena two years ago, where he was now teaching at the University of Cartagena. Ha had a great sense of humor and an endless number of stories about the Heroic city, which fascinated the two cousins.

"The *cartageneros* are proud of our history and of our past" said Camilo as a way to introduce one of his stories. The Heroic City does not carry this name in vain. Did you know that Cartagena is one of the few cities in the world that valiantly and victoriously defended itself against the attack of the British? This happened a few centuries ago but our old folks have never forgotten about it."

"The defeat of the British Navy in Cartagena is an event unknown for most people" Camilo began saying, as he played with the half empty bottle of beer on the table.

"In October of 1739 England declared war to Spain, planning to take this city. The city where the wealth of the Spanish colonies was concentrated and the commerce of the Caribbean were controlled.

Although the origin of the war was the commercial rivalry between the two great powers, the real cause of the conflict was an incident near the coast of Florida, which happened when the captain of a Spanish coastguard vessel, Juan Leon Fandiño, intercepted the Rebbeca ship under the control of Robert Jenkins. He cut his ear and after releasing him he was sent with this insolent message: "Go and tell your king that I will do the same if he dares". This event irritated the British in such a way that the Prime minister declared war on Spain, pressed by the commanders who wished to seize the new markets.

In March of 1741 the British arrived at *Punta Canoa*, putting on alarm the city of Cartagena. This was the largest military fleet ever to travel the waters of the Caribbean Sea: two thousand canons ready to use and one hundred eighty six boats, between military ships, frigates, and transport ships. The fleet was far superior to the so-called Invincible of Felipe II of Spain, which only had one hundred and twenty-six ships.

The British forces, directed by Admiral Sir Edward Vernon, had twenty-three thousand six hundred combatants between sailors, soldiers and black slaves from Jamaica. In this expedition also came four thousand recruits from Virginia under the orders of Lawrence Washington, half brother of the future liberator of the United States, George Washington.

"The defenses of Cartagena was not over three thousand men including regular troops, six hundred Indians armed with bow and arrows brought from the interior of the country, plus the ship's crew and soldiers of disembarkation of the only six military ships which the city had: the Galicia that was the flagship, San Felipe, San Carlos, Africa, the Dragoon and the Conqueror. This small contingent was directed by men ready to fight until death: the Virrey Sebastián de Eslava, general lieutenant of the Royal Armies with a long military experience, and under his direction the famous general of the Navy, Don Blas de Lezo, man of the sea that had already participated in many battles and naval expeditions, losing a leg and his left eye.

In spite of some discrepancies regarding dissensions about strategic matters between Blas de Lezo and the Virrey, they decided to unify their actions under the direction of the former; in this manner they could resist with great firmness and heroism the attacks of the British forces."

Camilo, who had finished his beer, asked for another one while he made a pause; when the drink arrived, he continued:

"Vernon entered the bay triumphant with his ship Admiral, with the unfolded flags and the standard of general and chief, escorted by two frigates and a packet boat. Assured he had won the battle, he dispatched immediately a mail to Jamaica and England with this part. After he ordered the disembarkation of its artillery and then he commanded to cannon the Castle of San Felipe from sea and from land with the purpose of softening the resistance."

"The defense was carried out only by six hundred men under the command of Blas de Lezo and Des Naux. This one had already resisted in the island of Bocachica and was determined to fight against the British attack; the defense was ferocious. Vernon resolved that his infantry could take the fort easily, which had suffered considerable damages. The night between the 19 and the 20 of April the decisive acts occurred:

The attackers advanced between the shadows in three columns of grenadiers and various companies of soldiers, in addition to the slaves brought from Jamaica who went in the vanguard. Their march was slow due to the heavy military equipment that they transported and the enemy fire they received from the trenches and the top of the fort. The advance stopped just before the walls by lack of foresight. The ladders destined to cross the pits were too short; the aggressors were perplexed; not having the necessary resources to facilitate their arrival to the castle. The defenders, on the other hand, redoubled the fire from the top of the walls, which resulted in a frightful slaughter of the British troops."

"At dawn, the macabre spectacle of the dead, and the large number of mutilated and injured soldiers moved like souls in pain, around the castle of San Felipe were the evidence of the catastrophe undergone by the British Navy. The Spanish soldiers with their bayonets caused immediately the disorderly retreat of the attackers who had lost hundreds of men along with all their armaments.

The British continued bombing the city from the sea during the following thirty days, without obtaining anything. The diseases like the cholera and scurvy ended up decimating the troops; hundreds of corpses floated in the bay. All this caused a desperate and amazing situation. Vernon, arrogant and a man of bad temper reproached the slow and careful General Wentworth, supreme head of the disembarkation troops, for the humiliating defeat."

"The discords came to an absurd and critical point. At the end the British High Command ordered the retreat, which was made in a slow manner in the middle of incessant cannon shots until there was nothing left. The last sailboats left the 20 of May, but the English set fire to five of them for the lack of crew. On their return to Jamaica they had to sink another boat. The situation was dramatic; each boat looked like a hospital."

"With the arrogance and the pride proper of the empires, the British took the victory for granted; they did not know the unfortunate and disastrous end. They went ahead and made commemorative medals showing the Spaniard De Lezo kneeling before Vernon, giving to him the sword with the inscription "the Spanish pride humiliated by Vernon". In those medals De Lezo appears with his two legs, his two eyes and his two arms to cover the fact that he was a mutilated man. In the reverse there were six ships and a port, and around the inscription: "Who took Portobelo just by six ships, November of 1739".

"Of these medals, still some are preserved that confirm the truth of the facts but that they were reason for ridicule for a long time on the part of the enemies of England, being greater the shame of its authors, to the point of which king George II prohibited all publication on that assault, with the idea of leaving this painful episode forever buried in history. Since these events, the British never again seriously threatened the Spanish empire that subsisted for one more century."

Camilo took one last drink from the bottle and placing it on the table he continued:

"In the same way as people do not know much about this heroic fact, there is also a mystery about the aid received from strange beings in that unequal battle."

This last statement captured the attention of Chepe and Juan in an extraordinary way.

"What type of mysterious beings?" Juan asked immediately with great curiosity.

"There are rumors that indeed during the most critical moments of the battle, when it seemed that the city of Cartagena was almost in the hands of the British, some unknown beings, of medium stature, brown skin, black hair and with white clothes arrived at the city to help the tired soldiers commanded by the Spaniards. Their presence, firm and powerful was sufficient to strengthen and encourage the soldiers and to give the final and decisive victory over the British forces."

"There are those who affirm that these beings fought shoulder to shoulder with the defenders of

The Power Of The Relic

Cartagena providing strategy and additional reinforcement. According to these rumors, they disappeared as mysteriously as they arrived, but they left behind a metallic document that possibly contained something like a map, perhaps the indication of their origin. It is very probable that they are inhabitants of a submarine city located some place in the Caribbean" concluded Camilo.

"And that map, where is it?" Chepe asked greatly intrigued.

"Nobody knows, but everything seems to indicate that it is very possible that it is still in the castle of San Felipe, perhaps in some secret place..."

Late at night, Chepe and Juan went to the city center to the street of the Tower of the Clock, where they had the dinner appointment with Hernán Casas. They stopped at the entrance of the walled city where a group of apparently native young people of this city, played some happy tunes proper of the Caribbean coast, accompanied by guacharaca, maracas, tamboras and accordions.

This was a group of six boys between twelve and eighteen years of age. Mauricio, one of the acordeoneros apparently was the one who directed them. The repertoire was cheerful, between tunes of porros, cumbias and vallenatos.

"The folklore of the Caribbean is always happy and full of life. The rhythm of the accordion and the tambora run through the blood of the people from the coast." said Camilo, without losing the opportunity to dance skillfully to the rhythm of the happy music.

One of the typical dances of the north of the country is the mapalé, which is danced in Cartagena and almost all the towns of the Caribbean coast. This like most of the coastal dances is performed in pairs and it requires much ability and a good physical condition. Juan, the more daring of the two cousins had the opportunity to experiment with this dance; meanwhile Chepe observed him entertained. Juan enjoyed dancing a couple of dances with a beautiful young lady from the group; he was so entertained that Chepe had to remind him of their appointment for dinner.

CHAPTER 18

Hernán was a man quite knowledgeable in the subjects related to the Spanish conquest and more specifically of the history of the Spanish galleons used to transport the royal treasures from Cartagena to Spain. Both cousins arrived early for the dinner appointment and took advantage of it to choose a table in a corner of the restaurant where they could speak with some privacy.

Although Hernán arrived a few minutes behind schedule Chepe and Juan were not impatient. The restaurant's menu included typical local dishes so all three of them ordered seafood. During dinner, Chepe could obtain important data about the treasures taken from Colombia and their possible whereabouts.

"It is true that most of the gold that went to Spain left through the port of Cartagena because this was a safe place for the Spanish ships. But a large part of it never arrived at its destination but ended up at heart of the sea" Hernán began relating.

"The golden age of the pirates began with the trips of Columbus to the New World and the same could be said of the shipwrecks; the ships loaded with great treasures aroused the greed of the buccaneers and were also exposed to other dangers during their trips, like the currents, the storms, the rocks and reefs. In this sense, no place could compare with the Caribbean and the waters of the Atlantic under the dominion of the Spaniards."

"They were thirty caravels, the first ships of the Spanish fleet that were shipwrecked in these waters. These were in charge of taking their country's precious metals and merchandise of great value. Among the sunken ships was the main ship called El Dorado, which left The Espanola Island on July of 1502, although Christopher Columbus himself had warned them about the imminence of a hurricane and disastrous storms in the waters ahead."

"Columbus, who had just returned from Spain, could not prevent the departure of the loaded ships. Three days later, in the Straits of Mona, located between the Dominicana Republic and Puerto Rico, a hurricane destroyed the ship *El Dorado* and twenty-five other ships. There have been found remains of some of them in the reefs and beaches of the Straits, but still remain to be discovered the remains from seventeen boats, among them El Dorado with its fabulous shipment."

"In 1553, a furious storm whipped a Spanish fleet next to Padre Island, close to the state of Texas. Of twenty ships only three were saved and the sailors who did not drown died at the hands of the hostile Indians who waited for them on land and whose presence prevented the rescue at the time. That catastrophe, in terms of losses of ships and shipments, is one of the three most important shipwrecks suffered by the Spanish fleet," said Hernán.

"The other two great shipwrecks took place in 1715 and 1733, both by the Florida Keys. The rescue of the sunken ships of the Spanish fleet in 1715 constitutes one of the most important examples as far as the recovery of treasures. Until now the search for the others has yielded nothing, probably because they sunk in very deep waters."

"The American treasure hunter Mel Fisher tried to find these ships; this task took him sixteen years. His tenacity was compensated in 1985, when divers found the Atocha and he was told that in its interior, there were many objects, coins and ingots of gold and silver valued at about four hundred fifty million dollars; this was the most important treasure found until now from a shipwreck of that time. Using a sonar and suction pipes to clean the sediments and the sand, Fisher's team rescued an enormous amount of ingots of silver, coffers full gold and extraordinary jewels. Part was sold to collectors and the rest ended up in some museums."

The Caribbean waters can be an authentic paradise for all those who are interested in looking for sunken treasures" Hernán finally said. Chepe and Juan listened to the stories with much attention and curiosity.

"Well, these treasures lie at the heart of the Caribbean, but the important question is: where can they be found and how can they be retrieved?" asked Chepe.

Hernán scratching his head thought for a few moments, and then he put his closed fist on his chin and answered:

"I hope you have some more free time tonight to meet another person, a friend of mine. We will find him at a bar, not too far from here. Perhaps he has some ideas or suggestions as to how to accomplishing this mission."

"Excellent!" exclaimed Chepe with excitement as he got up to pay the restaurant bill.

The three of them went out in search of the place Hernán had mentioned to them; it was a short distance within the walled city. They walked by the narrow colonial streets, arriving at the front door of the establishment. It was a bar of European style, built at the same time as the Heroic City. It seemed as if by magic the clients were transported back in time to the 17th century, the time of the colony. The tables and chairs were outside, on a brick patio. The stars shone on a blue sky, the salty air of the sea blew, refreshing the atmosphere; and the cheerful music of the accordion and the maracas contributed a special atmosphere in that historical place.

Just as Hernán had said, his friend was there seating next to a table, under a beach awning. He was of short stature, dressed in a white shirt that ran over his beach shorts. On the floor, next to his chair was his straw hat. By his appearance and especially from his accent, you could tell that he was from Antioquia, a province located at the center of the Colombia. Hernán had mentioned that this friend had lived in the coast for more than ten years and was an expert in the history of the Caribbean Sea.

Hernán introduced Chepe and Juan to his friend and then asked for drinks for the four of them. The subject of the conversation turned immediately to the

Caribbean Sea: its mysteries, the sunken boats filled with valuable treasures, and the dangers of navigation in these waters due not only to the pirates but also to the natural fury of its waters. One of the subjects that captivated their attention was the strange disappearance of ships in this enigmatic sea. Hernán's friend began his story as the cousins listened with great attention:

"Many places of this sea have been catalogued as mysterious; some of their secrets have been understood, in other cases the phenomena are inexplicable, as is the case of the so called *Bermuda Triangle*. As its name indicates it, it is a space in triangular form that covers a large area located between the Bermuda islands, Puerto Rico and Melbourne. It is also called triangle of the Devil. This place was and is witness of incredible phenomena that has intrigued the entire world.

The disappearance of boats and airplanes in those places is attributed to many causes," he continued: "some scientists maintain that in that place there are great fields of energy coming from the Earth and are the reason why communications are lost; other fanatics of science fiction think that the triangle is related mainly to extraterrestrial creatures and UFO's.

There are also those who think that this place is the vestibule that unites this dimension with another yet unknown; if this theory is certain" continued the man, "the people who disappear there are not kidnapped, but are rather transported to another dimension. One more theory is that this place is the old Atlantis, a city that supposedly existed thousands of years ago, with very high scientific developments, which then disappeared without a trace."

At the end of this conversation Hernan took Chepe and Juan to a more isolated place next to the patio to speak in private. From there they could observe the sea under the beautiful and calm night, only interrupted by the sound of the waves; the moonlight reflected on waters of the Caribbean gave it a charming aspect.

From there, the Caribbean Sea seemed subtle, delicate and innocent, incapable of causing the great tragedies that were attributed to it. They remained there for a long time in silence, fascinated by the waves of the sea. Hernán finally interrupted the silence:

"According to padre Nicanor there is another theory that explains these events. They say that long ago, years after the universal flood and as a result of a great human dispersion from the Middle East, some highly advanced people sailed by the Mediterranean and then towards the New World. Years later they built a city under the Caribbean waters, very similar to the Atlantis but with more advanced technology. No one knows for certain to this day," continued Hernán. "But nobody can deny that these strange phenomena happen. For several years there have been many boats and airplanes lost. Some of them have become very famous, as the case of the disappearance of flight 19 in 1945" concluded Hernán. "You must find this place to decipher this enigma."

"Much has been written and spoken about the Bermuda Triangle, but until now, nobody has been able to decipher this enigma. This responsibility and privilege have been kept secret until now like an exotic adventure for us" said Chepe to Juan in a prophetic tone, and then he continued, "according to Hernan, the first clues to locate that place are located somewhere within the castle."

The two cousins entered several of the tunnels of the castle in search of the map that would indicate to them the location of the sunken Spanish Galleon. This would take them to the location of the supposed submarine city. The search was long and useless; the tunnels crossed each other making it look more and more like an endless labyrinth. They did not know for sure what they were looking for, and this troubled them. Maybe if they could find an inscription that perhaps would provide a clue as to location of the map, or if they could find the map itself hidden in some corner of that labyrinth; that would tranquilize them. After several hours of searching, Juan noticed something strange in one of the tunnels. One of bricks on the floor produced a hollow sound when stepping on it. Surprised, Chepe struck the brick, time and time again perceiving a sound, like an echo, in the wall in front of them.

"Extraordinary!" exclaimed Chepe. The sound of the brick must indicate the key for a secret entrance in this wall. Making sure that nobody was observing them, he moved carefully to the place where he had noticed a type of switch in the wall; when pressing it, a small door in the opposite side was opened giving entrance to a secret tunnel. They entered the tunnel noticing with astonishment and certain preoccupation that the door closed behind them. The tunnel was low and narrow and quite dark. The way in front of them descended leading them to a room at sea level.

An old wood table surrounded by four chairs of colonial style was the only furniture in the room. Two low doors in the form of arches connected this place with other adjacent rooms, which were also slightly illuminated but apparently vacated.

"Look there!" exclaimed Juan. "At the other side of that room is the sea and something that looks like a submarine!"

Both of them walked in that direction, looking around carefully in search of anyone who could be there. When arriving at the last room, they located the place that Hernan's friend had indicated. They proceeded to try one of the keys he had given them, but nothing happened; then they tried the others without success, none of them worked.

"It is possible that we have the wrong door," thought Juan disappointed. "I am sure that we are at the place they indicated to us."

They went over to some ruins nearby without any results, then they decided to return to the same room once more. After meticulously looking around they found a rare instrument in a corner; from the form of it, it appeared that it was used to draw up maps. This was the only object they found there, so they took it with the hope that it could be of some use later on. Further down in another room, they found a strange diagram with drawings representing the figure of three men in triangular form. The three angles converged with lines in a place marked with an X.

The Power Of The Relic

"It is possible that this is a type of clue indicating the place where the city is located," said Juan.

The cousins began to imagine what all of this could mean.

"The triangle.... extraordinary!" indicated Chepe.

They continued the search for more clues among the ruins:

Astonished they observed that in the center of the patio a diagram was drawn, similar to the one found in the previous room. Now they had to find the points where the vertices of the triangle begin and then had to draw up the lines from each one of them. For this, they would have to use some precision instrument, just like the one they had found.

Once this was solved, they would have to locate the second clue to be able to enter the tunnels or passages that would perhaps take them to the submarine port. The man from Antioquia who they had met at the bar had given them a clue to help them find the entrance; they thought it would be possible to get access without much difficulty. Chepe introduced the key in the lock of the second door, which opened with a smooth sound, allowing them entrance to another underground tunnel that disappeared under the waters of the Caribbean.

Crossing the labyrinth, the two cousins entered a new passage. Their presence there activated a type of elevator that lowered them to another level where they found another narrow passage. In a corner near the elevator they found a human skeleton, apparently from the colonial time.

"It is probably from somebody who used to work in this port, whose life ended up in a tragic manner," said

Chepe.

A handful of keys and a wood cane were found next to the skeleton. The wood cane had an unknown inscription; Juan pick it up with the thought that such object must be there for a special purpose. They found a written note with a possibly decipherable message; after examining the note at great length, they recognized that it was writing with characters from the Middle East. It indicated that it was not possible to find the hidden door without a special power. Chepe stopped to process the new message, repeating for himself: "The power! The power!"

"I hope that with much luck and some cleverness we can decipher this enigma before we find the next door" said Chepe.

After the strange surprise they had just found they began to look for the next entrance.

The tunnel ended at a heavy iron door that prevented them from going any further. It appeared that it could be opened only from the interior. The other possible way was a small hole on top of the door, but neither one could fit through it, so they decided to return to the place where they found the skeleton to search the strange place looking for additional clues.

The only part they had left to search was behind the door with a mechanism similar to the one they found first. The one giving entrance to the labyrinth of the castle. Chepe placed the key in the bolt in many different ways but everything seemed to be useless; they were trapped. The return door was closed leaving them isolated in the tunnel. The solution had to be there with them, and that was his weapon of great power. Chepe introduced the end of the sword in the bolt and as by magic the door opened allowing them access to a new room. The room consisted of two levels. From the upper level they could see in front of them a beautiful golden box, which they could not reach from where they were. In the lower level they found a large idol; it was apparently an indigenous god, carved in rustic stone. Juan suggested using the wood cane they had found in the first tunnel. Chepe placed it in the mouth of idol, and a mechanism was opened immediately which gave them access to the second level allowing them access to the gold box which contained two thin leaves of a precious metal, very fine, whose properties they still did not know.

There was no exit from this level, so the only way to leave this place was through the lower level. Chepe stood next to the idol with his hand placed on this forehead trying to find a solution to open the door from the inside; suddenly he recognized that the answer was indeed there, in the head. Not in his, but in the head of the idol. He touched the head of the idol with his sword and the mechanism was driven immediately that opened the door allowing them to leave the hall into another tunnel.

Once in it, they crossed the last part of the labyrinth without finding any exit. In the middle of this situation, Juan remembered the note they found in Middle Eastern writing next to the skeleton. On the last hidden door they understood that the moment had arrived for interpreting and for using the message contained in it.

Chepe turned off a light switch leaving that place totally in the dark.

After a few seconds he removed from his pocket a small lantern of ultraviolet light projecting it on the wall. They could now see an old door through which they could enter. Behind that door they found a large room, white and totally empty. From here they went into another large room; in this one they found a table with a beautiful scale model of a city with three concentric circles surrounding it.

"This could be the map left by those strange beings of which Camilo spoke to us about," exclaimed Juan in a low voice but full of excitement.

"Yes, it could be" said Chepe as he considered it an excellent possibility.

In center of the scale model there was a mechanism where Chepe placed a small steel piece that Camilo had been given to him and following its instructions they opened one of the many doors around the room. Without thinking much about it, Chepe went through it. The next room contained an intricate network of stairs and doors that communicated with each other in a complicated design. It seemed to be a place made to confuse any intruder. In the wall of the maze of stairs they saw a diagram that seemed familiar to them, as if they had seen it before.

The next challenge was to find the precise door that would take them to the submarine port. Chepe thought for a moment: there could be a relation between the first map they found and the diagram they saw in the previous room. After analyzing them in his mind, he reached a conclusion: the door must be located where the three imaginary lines of the triangle converge in the design. Finally they could find the exit to the waters.

A complex submarine construction appeared before their eyes; it constituted the axis of a great marine wonders. Astonished, the two cousins entered the building and walked through it until they arrived at a room that seemed to be the control center.

CHAPTER 19

Two men of oriental appearance and elegantly dressed in white came out to meet them as if they were waiting for them. To the surprise of Chepe and Juan they gave them a friendly greeting of welcome. After a brief bow of welcome the two men guided Chepe and Juan through a narrow hallway at the end of which a small submarine was waiting for them. Again, with friendly bow the two men invited them to enter the strange vessel. Once inside, the two men proceeded to operate the controls in silence. It seemed as if they communicated by mental telepathy. Without exchanging a word, their activities were perfectly coordinated.

The small control cabin was well illuminated and equipped with all types of navigation instruments and communication equipment to keep them well informed as to the state of the vehicle. Minutes after boarding the small ship it started off for a long trip northwards in a wonderful and fascinating silence. During the trip, which lasted several hours, both cousins seemed to be in a trance ... enjoying a fantastic dream.

Later on they approached a spectacular submarine city; little by little it appeared more majestic as they approached it. Soft lights illuminated the tall and massive walls that surrounded it. As they observed the design and geometry of the city walls, it reminded them the design of the walls of Cartagena. The ship entered the port quietly. Chepe and Juan waited inside until they were invited to disembark. Their eyes searched around this wonderful and stranger world trying to capture it all in their minds. Their companions opened the doors of the vehicle, inviting them to follow them through a short wharf at the end of which another man was waiting for them. He was of medium stature, brown complexion, black hair and a black moustache, well taken care of.

He was well dressed in white; on the collar of his shirt shone a beautiful gold badge possibly indicating his rank or hierarchy in the organization. Next to him were two men of lower stature and of indigenous appearance, also dressed in white.

The man of the gold badge approached them as he gave them a formal welcome. "My name is Aram, descendant of Hazar–Mavet, son of Boast, son of Heber, son of Arfaxad, from the territories of Chaldean of the mountainous region of the east.

Chepe and Juan greeted him with astonishment, not understanding the meaning of this strange greeting. Turning around, Aram invited them to follow him through a corridor in the direction of a large room. The two men of native aspect followed him in silence, one on each side.

"Welcome to the city of Mizpah–Harim," said Aram, as he invited them to follow once more towards a reception room.

The transparent walls of the corridor and the main room were of a fine crystal, surrounded by marine choral of bright colors; the place was wonderfully constructed and decorated with exquisite architectural details. All the furniture in it was also made of a material similar to crystal.

A soft music seemed to come out from all directions. From time to time the music was interrupted with brief announcements on details of the state of different locations in the city.

"It is an incredible place... a fantastic place!" said Juan. Without interrupting, Aram observed at a short distance, understanding their state of astonishment. Finally he approached them:

"I do not believe you have ever seen a place like this one before; I imagine you have many questions about it. But there will be enough time to satisfy your curiosity and to answer your questions. Now you must enjoy our hospitality."

Having said this, he invited them to seat on a comfortable sofa next to one of the crystal walls where the marine beauty could be enjoyed.

The lamps had been placed strategically to illuminate the choral and the plants outside the wall. Fish great and small came by, near the wall looking inside with great curiosity or simply attracted by the light inside the wall. A soft music contributed to help you become accustomed to this wonderful place; a true paradise; a vast virgin territory populated by exotic marine creatures, enchanting landscapes and gorgeous colors; a world of silence and mystery, filled with life, in the middle of clear, blue waters.

Through the wall, sand caverns and slopes could be

observed, rock walls that descended vertically to the bed of the ocean; coralline formations whose textures and varied colors decorated the environment. This world was inhabited by a spectacular diversity of marine plants and fish, sponges and reefs, barracudas, sharks and octopus; truly a world of fantasy!

After a few minutes, two young men brought refreshments to them. The drinks were served in silver goblets, accompanied by treats and cakes served in crystal plates and small silver forks. The young men that served them indicated with their hands that could proceed to enjoy the refreshments. After a bow of respect they turned around and walked away disappearing down the hallway.

Still filled with admiration and astonishment about this place, they took the drink goblets and with great curiosity they tasted them. A small swallow at first and then they drunk the whole content. It had an exquisite flavor, neither one could say for sure what exactly the flavor could be compared to. The cakes and treats on the other hand had a consistency similar to those made with wheat flour but they tasted sweet, like a natural fruit.

After finishing the refreshments Aram and his companions met again with Chepe and Juan who now felt re-energized. They had not noticed it before, but right after the refreshments they were full of energies as if the day had just begun.

Minutes later the two men of oriental appearance who had brought them from Cartagena in the strange submarine also joined them. Aram began the conversation.

"As you now are starting to realize, this is a city with highly advanced technology and mostly superior to that of the outside world. It is what has been called technology of the future; it is clean, pure and perfect, if it is used in an appropriate way. Unfortunately it can be dangerous and could cause great damage to humanity if it falls in unscrupulous hands; in the hands of people without principles and without respect for life or the environment."

"Unfortunately, some aspects of our technology have been made known to the outer world, with disastrous results; their inhabitants were not prepared for such a privilege. That we have been able to verify with the use of the fantastic atomic energy" concluded Aram, as a deeply disappointed father with his children.

"This is the reason why the presence of the City of Mizpah–Harim continues to be a mystery to the eyes of the external world. None of the enormous advances of this city will be within reach of the outside civilization. Only when they grow in wisdom, at the same rate they grow in knowledge can they inherit such powerful technology."

Then he continued with this warning:

"The City of *El Dorado* contains great powers and deep secrets of ancient technology which must be rescued to prevent its wrongful use. That coveted booty of great power must be recovered or be destroyed."

"This area of the Caribbean Sea, denominated the Bermuda Triangle, is a location of excellent conditions for the creation of the city of Mizpah–Harim... the natural energy is more aggressive than in other places of the sea. The current of the gulf creates a phenomena of great speeds, the polarity of the currents, the gigantic vortices and the strong cross-winds make this location an excellent source of natural energy; a privileged center to take advantage of the forces of the sea. Many days of the year there are violent storms that cause an enormous load of energy. It is channeled, taking advantage of it to support and maintain life in the city of Mizpah–Harim," explained Aram.

"The inhabitants of this city, have put in practice the inherited knowledge of the natives of the American continent; they had the special gift of understanding and knowing how to use the natural resources. The presence of the natives has been of great importance in the use of our natural resources."

"The foundation of the city and the development of our technology have their bases in the ancient secrets and powers brought to the New World by our ancestors. Much of this knowledge also came to the new world with the men who now live in the city of *El Dorado.*"

"How can this be possible?" Asked Juan a little confused "*El Dorado* was discovered by the Spaniards many centuries ago and all their treasures were taken to Europe."

"My dear friend" answered Aram: "*El Dorado* was never discovered by the Spaniards. They never understood its meaning or the content of it and this was the major reason for the disastrous failure in the search for that fantastic place. That magnificent place not only contains great wealth, but more importantly, it contains the deep secrets of a very advanced technology; very similar to the one used in the city of Mizpah–Harim."

"Do you mean to say that the city of *El Dorado* still exists?" Asked Juan quite intrigued.

"Indeed, it still exists in the high mountains of the Andes where the Spaniards never imagined that it could be found," answered Aram. "But lets go now," he said, inviting them to take a walk around the city to show them what he was speaking about.

He took them to the residential area. The quality of the houses was different and far beyond what Chepe and Juan had seen in the outer world. It was a project with a very advanced design, constructed under the concepts of an exclusive model for the city. It demonstrated the development and application of modern technology, oriented to give an end product of admirable perfection, with excellent results; solid and hermetically sealed by the waters, and most of all quite useful for the entire community.

There were also other areas dedicated for the relaxation and the recreation of the inhabitants. Parks interconnected with trails surrounded by gardens, green areas and plazas that complemented wonderful sport fields taking maximum advantage of the space as well as the marine resources. The education and the culture were also fundamental elements in this plan, assuring therefore the success of future generations and the continuous expansion of the great city.

One of the most spectacular designs in this place was the sports arena, constructed in a complex and large field dedicated for the practice of physical development and physical recreation.

"Sports are fundamental to stimulate good habits and discipline in the community; it is well known that from a healthy body gives rise to a healthy mind. This way we prevent laziness and vices that only lead to destruction" said Aram, in a wise and philosophical manner.

"The ideas that are presented to the community encourage the participants in these projects to debate them, to modify them, or to enrich them, in order that between them all, a complex mosaic may be built, a dynamic model for the future of Mizpah- Harim, a city with broad leadership from the community. This is an innovating idea for the evolution of future developments and the perfect operation of the system. The easy mobility of our people is associate with this type of urbanism; nonpolluting vehicles, operating on fuel cells or electric motors and designs that allow them to move in a fast and quiet fashion without contaminating the environment.

"These are intelligent transport systems, with a high ranking of unattended navigation. This method, totally computerized, avoids any type of incident, with orders of synthesized voice and automatic communication."

"Transportation for the city inhabitants has been designed as a complement to the technical advances of communications. Every person carries a two way micro radio that allows him, with the use of privet frequencies, to communicate with anyone of his colleagues or members of the family in an automatic, fast and efficient manner. The use of a small receiver and emitter of video images is used with high performance avoiding unnecessary relocation. The technology in telecommunications allows us to maintain a continuous and permanent flow of information at a professional and communitarian level."

"The concept of a city and civilization has a new definition here. It is a notion different from the traditional city of the outside world. The urban concentration has made possible the great social, technological and community advances that have influenced in a decisive way this unique civilization."

"As far as the human factor" continued Aram, "the accelerated growth of the population has created the necessity to carry out studies on community housing with respect to centers of work, study and recreation. As a result of the shortage of available space it is possible to build greater constructions, and even more attractive environmental surroundings, resulting in a more efficient society than those of the external world."

"The optimal use of the space in this city, leads in a natural way to a setting that favors the combination of houses and areas of work. But this does not produce in any way isolation, nor segmentation of the inhabitants; the nuclear family stays united, in contact through the cycle of life, without isolating parents and children, old and young, as is the case in the so called advanced civilizations of the outside world which has resulted in a social disaster of division, isolation and poverty."

"The purpose of keeping the families within the same area," Aram continued to explain, "is that each nucleus comprises a residential level with a suitable density along with the appropriate services, equipment and employment, in order to maintain self-sufficient and functional units within the community."

Chepe and Juan were surprised and impressed by the coexistence of the different social groups in this highly developed city. The community sites like the gardens and sport complexes were truly authentic places for a social encounter of adults, young people, children and the elderly.
"A social and family wonder!" exclaimed Juan.
There they coexist, and they live, work and entertain together; people with different racial, social, and religious characteristics, of different ages and different sex.
"It is fantastic!" said Chepe, "as he observed people there from all parts of the earth; from Asia, Africa, the Middle East, as well as native Americans living and working in harmony."
"Now let's go to the most special place of this city which is located bordering the waters," said Aram.

CHAPTER 20

They walked through several hallways to the other side of the city, not very far from the park. In front of them was now a majestic and colossal temple. From this place they could observed through the transparent walls the beautiful caverns and chorals of various colors; rock walls that descended to the bottom of the ocean, coralline formations that surrounded and decorated the place. A spectacular diversity of marine plants and tropical fish adorned this sacred place giving it a truly supernatural aspect.

"This is the place of adoration" said Aram with certain pride.

The interior decorations gave it an aspect of a celestial palace. The temple was quite large, designed to accommodate great multitudes of people, but at the same time it provided an environment for spiritual meditation.

At the far end, there was a small chapel and in its interior was a magnificently decorated sanctuary. The ceiling and the back wall were totally covered with gold, as well as the frames of the large windows. In the heights, hanging from of the ceiling as if floating in the air, two cherubim were carved and equally covered with gold, with their wings extended and their face looking towards the center of the building.

In the center, almost underneath the cherubim there

was a pulpit with a great opened book of golden covers and white pages that shone under the light. Distributed in pairs at each side of the entrance were four magnificent candelabra. Every ornament of the chapel was of silver or of pure gold and the doors were made of fine crystal that shone as pure diamonds.

"This is the community's sacred place. Here everyone approaches the King and Lord with their liturgies and adorations or just to meditate."

Filled with astonishment, Chepe and Juan looked around with admiration and respect. In different places of the temple there were people on their knees in attitude of adoration or sitting in attitude of meditation; some by themselves, others in family groups, with parents, grandparents and children. Chepe and Juan were there in silence for a very long time, astonished by the beauty of that place and absorbed in the sacred atmosphere.

Suddenly they noticed something amazing at the far end: a magnificent cross of about twenty meters high and about ten meters wide hanging ,which seemed to emanate light in all directions filling the surroundings with solemnity.

When noticing this Juan exclaimed:

"Look Chepe! It is similar to the one we saw in the other palace and the sign above it also reads: "King of kings and Lord of lords."

Under the cross there was a great ivory throne with six steps, a round back, two lions standing up next to the arms and another twelve on the steps, one at each end of the steps. In front of the throne was a large table, apparently made of crystal and on it there were table settings for twelve. All the glasses and dishes were of pure gold. The beauty and majesty of this place was absolutely impressive, full of splendor.

Crossing several corridors they went to the station of external communication, used for marine or space navigation. In an immense hangar they found a large number of navigation crafts and vessels of different types and designs, ready to take off and contiguous to this, a wharf for takeoff and arrival of these vehicles, which kept in constant movement with people leaving and entering the city.

"As you can observe" said Aram "we have perfected a new technology of submarines that move at high speed, propelled by technology and movements based on those of some marine animals; it is the result of taking advantage of the natural energy in the propulsion of the submarine."

"Fantastic!" Was the only observation of Juan, who was excited to find out new things about this city.

The external design of the ships gave the impression of being a perfect mixture between a fish and a sea turtle; the fuselage, extended and articulated, facilitated the agile and fast movements; the surface was covered with small silver-plated scales seemed to be in continuous movement due to the reflection of light.

Alongside the wharf there were the ships of space exploration. Aram then explained:

"These ships are amphibious, which gives them the opportunity of moving under water, going into space or moving on land surface without any difficulty.

Although relatively small, they have sufficient energy, which allows them to be outside our city for many days before returning to re-charge at the base."

"In effect, this technology combines the characteristics of the submarine and the spaceship. Its design resembles a gigantic jellyfish that thanks to its design allow it to slide with facility in the water. But when it is outside, it can move at great speeds on land or through the air and outer space. It has in addition the possibility of staying static, floating in the air. Its design is truly surprising."

Very intrigued when observing all this, Juan asked:

"Do you mean to say that your people sail in the sea, on the earth atmosphere and the outer space?"

"Indeed, that is the case" responded Aram.

"If that is the case, how is it possible that you never have been detected by the Earth inhabitants?" asked Juan once again.

Trying to find an adequate answer for his curios visitor, after a deep sigh he responded:

"We have devices of high technology that make our vessels invisible if it becomes necessary or when they are in imminent danger. With the passage of time we have considered that it makes more sense to avoid the enemy through invisibility than to have to face it. Often, the best way to solve a confrontation is to avoid it. This is the reason why our city has chosen to focus our efforts and resources in the development and improvement of the technology of invisibility. Thanks to this technology, our ships travel in any direction without any danger."

Chepe who had been trying to assimilate and to

process all its information, asked:

"What about the accidents and disappearances of ships in this area of the Caribbean Sea? They cannot be all strange coincidences or the result of the acts of nature, are they?"

"I was afraid that this question would eventually come up. You are certainly a pair of very intelligent and inquisitive young fellows. I already knew that," said Aram. "Many of these disappearances of which you speak, have been the result of the natural fury of this region; others, the product of interventions that we have believed necessary. But this never has brought fatal consequences; they have been only interventions of warning."

"For example" continued Aram, "a few years ago, a DC–8 of the North American company Braniff Airlines, during a trip from New York to Panama, underwent a minor inconvenience due to a slight confusion and a small error, but nothing major happened. The sky was clear and the plane maintained an altitude of three thousand meters. In the control cabin the ambient was calm and relaxed when they saw the Bahamas; but something unexpected happened suddenly: the airplane began to vibrate, every minute stronger and with greater intensity then followed by a descend that seemed impossible to control. The DC–8 did not respond to the controls of the pilot who tried to avoid a rapid descent into the waters of the Caribbean Sea."

"The airplane was going to crash inevitably but only two hundred meters above the waters, the large machine straightened the nose and the mortal descend stopped as mysteriously as it had begun. In Miami, the pilot was able to land minutes later to unload some of the passengers who were slightly wounded, but mostly scared. There was nothing mechanically wrong with the airplane. The mistake was ours; that plane was confused with another airplane heading for Chile with a large cargo of weapons which we were trying to intercept."

"In December of 1945, four months after the end of the Second World War, five bombing torpedo carriers took off of from the Naval Station of Fort Lauderdale, in Florida; supposedly for a simple patrolling mission and a shooting exercise with a boat that served as a target to the south of the Bimini Island, the most western of the Bahamas. On board of the Avengers, the powerful flying machines were five pilots, with six years of experience in the Navy and nine crew members."

"The weather was excellent, it was clear and sunny with only a few clouds pushed by a breeze of the northeast appearing in the sky. "The flight conditions are ideal", declared one of the crew from flight 19, the name given to the mission. The return was planned to take place at 16:00 hours. But at 15:45, the radio of the squadron leader called the control tower:

"Urgent Call to the tower! We are not sure about our course; we are no longer able to see land!

"Which is your position?"

"We are not sure of it, we are lost!"

"Set course to the west."

"We do not know where is west... everything is abnormal... strange... even the sea looks unusual."

After half hour, the controller was frightened as he received a new message:

"We do not know our position exactly. Perhaps we are two hundred twenty-five miles from the base. It seems that…"

"There was some interference, then some incomprehensible words, followed by total silence."

The control tower concluded that the group was lost. Immediately, a large hydroplane took off; a true flying giant machine, outfitted with all the necessary equipment for a rescue and with thirteen men on board. Half an hour later, the rescue airplane communicated that it was near the last probable position of the Avengers. This would be its final message as well. In the evening the control tower had to accept the hard evidence: The hydroplane would not return either. It had disappeared in the middle of the same mystery as the Avengers, whose survivors it was trying to rescue.

"The next day, early in the morning, a battle group made up of two hundred and forty two airplanes, eighteen boats and an aircraft carrier with its thirty five airplanes, participated in the most intense sea and air search in history. The search was carried out over an extensive area, over the Gulf of Mexico and hundreds of kilometers of coasts of Florida and the Bahamas. But nothing was found; not even the smallest indication of the six airplanes and the twenty-seven crew members."

"As a result of these events, many hypotheses were created, all mysteries and impossibilities:"

"A collision in flight? In that case the remains of the Avengers would have been found."

"A failure in some of the systems? It could not have been simultaneous in all five airplanes. In addition, these airplanes were constructed in such a way that they would have floated the time sufficient to allow the crew to escape in life saving boats."

"An abrupt change in the wind direction, that would have pushed the ships for hundreds of kilometers off route to the south? In this case they would have flown over the Antilles, an easy point of reference. If they had crashed they would have located the cabins near the Bahamas. There were other thoughts as well: the possibility of the magnetic phenomena caused by the UFO's and the possibility of the white storms; sweeping winds in which rain is intimately mixed with the mist of the sea, a supernatural force sufficient to disintegrate an airplane. But then how could the hydroplane also disappeared?"

"After several months of investigations, the members of a commission from the Navy reached the conclusion that no hypothesis was able to explain the disaster."

"The disappearance of flight 19 attracted the attention of the entire world upon this region" continued Aram.

"Nobody dared to pronounce the name of the Bermuda Triangle with its sinister history. Twenty years later, an article of a North American magazine, related for the first time the tragedy of the Avengers to other inexplicable disappearances that had happened in this area."

"What is true about this incident," continued Aram, "is that the technology of the new atomic bomb, was only a new born baby, but a baby with great power that threatened to extent to other nations with fragile and unstable policies. Therefore, our intervention was necessary" emphasized Aram "again, with the purpose of preventing a future tragedy with incalculable consequences for humanity."

"But there was no catastrophe at all in this case. All the pilots and the crew members were returned safe and sound to the corresponding agencies with the specific message that the new technology of the atomic bomb had to be dealt with high security to avoid futures disasters. As you have been able to realize, such warnings were not taken seriously" said Aram.

"A very similar account happened to two English airplanes" continued Aram. "Again there was no human disaster. The reasons can not yet be revealed but we can assure you that all the people of these ships were left unharmed."

First was the Star Tiger, a Tudor IV of the company British American Airways, which had made the stop at Lisbon and Azores. It was January of 1948; the airplane had to arrive at the airport of Kindley Field, in the Bermuda, before reaching its final destination in the city of Kingston, in Jamaica. On board there were thirty one people. At 22:30 hours, Kindley Field received a message from Captain McMillan, the pilot of the Star Tiger:

"Our approximate position is six hundred forty kilometers to the north of you; we hope to land on schedule. The meteorological and mechanical conditions are excellent."

"The arrival at Bermudas was planned to take place soon after midnight. But the airplane would not give any signs of life after the message from Captain McMillan. Thirty airplanes, ten boats and nearly thousand men started off in their search, but they never found any sign of its occupants, either dead or alive. Or at least those were the reports…" said Aram, assuring them then,

"The passengers and crew members were returned unharmed."

"Almost a year later, in the morning of January of 1949, another Tudor IV of the same company, the Star Ariel, took off from the Bermudas with a crew of seven people and thirteen passengers towards Jamaica. The weather was splendid; the pilot transmitted his last optimistic message:

"We are flying at a cruising altitude, the temperature is pleasant and we are planning on arriving at Kingston, our destination, right on schedule."

"The North American Navy was performing maneuvers and exercises to the south of Bermuda: a battleship, an aircraft carrier, cruises and destroyers, interrupted their exercises to explore the area between these islands and Jamaica. After the warning of the possible disappearance of this airplane about two to three hundred kilometers from Bermuda, two destroyers moved immediately towards that point without finding anything more than a sea in perfect calm."

"But how can you manage nature in such a well coordinated and organized manner?" asked Chepe.

"It is indeed possible to control the forces of nature, just like the ocean currents and the winds. To a great extent the existence of our city is due to it. Allow me to demonstrate:"

Saying this, Aram pressed a small button on a small remote control that he took from the pocket of his shirt, illuminating a map located in the wall, where the different localities from the city stood out, including two concentric circles that apparently indicated the external perimeter and the outer walls."

"In effect," they continued, "this wall is for protection. The marine forces that can easily destroy the city are used for our own benefit; in order to support and to provide life. Through these mechanisms the marine energy is channeled for the support of the city and all its technology. It also allows us to control the atmosphere of the sea and the winds that blow upon it. We have learned all this technology with the advanced knowledge we brought from the Middle East and we have achieved all of this with the help, the talent and the cleverness of the natives who live with us."

"Innumerable legends of the region" continued Aram, "speak of boats found empty, with still hot food on the tables, and airplanes that disappear without having at least sent a distress signal or request for help. The absence of any remains is often used as an additional proof of the mystery and power of the Bermuda Triangle. Some of these stories are true but others are not more than legends. One of the incidents of most importance is the sinking of the Spanish boat

El Dorado which had taken valuable treasures from the Indian Natives. Some of these treasures now are in our possession, you will be able to admire them when you wish to do so" concluded Aram.

"Please, tell us about El Dorado, its secrets and how it could be found," requested Chepe.

"The value of El Dorado is more than its treasures and jewels. The fundamental thing is the knowledge that it contains. It can actually represent a great danger for humanity, if it falls into the hands of unscrupulous people with no respect for life. It is for this reason that the City of Mizpah–Harim tries to protect its advanced secrets even at the cost of unpleasant means. The European conqueristadores did not understand the meaning nor the great value contained in the legendary kingdom of *El Dorado*."

"It is a question of balance between benefit and danger to humanity. It is at this point where the difficult decisions require wisdom and determination. Quite often there is no alternative nor is there a way to wash your hands in an innocent manner ..." said Aram in a philosophical and melancholic way, as if making a long introduction to the following story.

CHAPTER 21

With a display of his wisdom and knowledge, Aram had gained total attention from Chepe and Juan who listened carefully trying not to miss a single detail of whatever this masterful scholar said. Anxious to know other important events, almost in unison they asked:

"Please continue; please tell us more about this place." Aram accepted happily and began saying:

"In the year 1940 humanity was crossing one of the most difficult moments in history. The crisis was the War. The situation was an evil leader trying to dominate the world and to exterminate the Hebrew race. His name was Adolph Hitler. Of all the conflicts that isolated the civilization of the 20th century, the main one is without a doubt the Second World War. The great economic crisis, the ascent to power of dictators in several European countries and their border problems ended up triggering an armed confrontation, in which almost all the nations of the world got involved."

"After several years of territorial disputes and the western democracies not able to avoid it, Germany initiated the invasion of Poland in September of 1939. France and England went in to help and declared war to Germany. This was then the first stage of a war conflict; Germany was able to take its immense power and its weapons from the Polish plains to skies of England, and even was able to sustain fights in the Sahara deserts and in the cold fields of the Russian tundra."

"In 1941 the German armies were wining victory after victory. The world observed with terror and astonishment the surprising war machine that Germany had made in such a short time. Hitler, the absolute holder of the country from

1933, reconstructed an industry in crisis and raised the fighting spirit of his people now asphyxiated by international treaties. The moment of revenge seemed to be within his reach. The democracies and the free world held their breath when the German troops attacked the Soviet Union. However, this adventure would be known as the greatest strategic error Hitler made during the war. The German forces, tired and whipped by the rigorous Russian winter, ended up defeated and forced to retreat. The war with the speed of light with which Hitler put in danger the freedom of the world was stopped forever by another dictator, a hard and implacable Russian dictator much like Hitler."

"This was Joseph Stalin, who obtained in just a short time what the western democracies were not able to do initially: to defeat the Germans. At the end of 1941, when the German divisions were on the verge of suffering the hardest defeat in front of Moscow, the Japanese attacked the United States of America turning the conflict, until that time European, into a world-wide conflict."

"During 1942 the coalition of nations that had decided to put an end to the empire Hitler wanted to impose on Europe, began to strike with firmness and efficiency at the German armies. Japan, an ally of Germany in the east, decided to take the opportunity to create a great Asian empire for themselves."

"The situation was desperate. The technical advances in military matters obtained by the German industry, threatened the possible discovery of the atomic energy for use in war, an event that would be totally disastrous for humanity. It was at this crucial moment that our people decided that they would not have a choice but to share the secret of the powerful atomic energy to the allied forces, headed by the United States for the defense of the world and the liberation of the Hebrew race."

"Preventing the extermination of the Jews that was planned by Hitler at this moment required the crucial intervention of the City of Mizpah–Harim with its technology which we never thought, would later end up in the hands of the enemy" Aram made a brief pause and with much disappointment in his voice he continued:

"This plan was initiated by the brilliant physicist and scientific leader, Robert Oppenheimer. He was a key man in the intervention of our people with the purpose of assuring that this powerful technology was developed by benevolent hands. Oppenheimer was absolutely indispensable in the invention and materialization of the first atomic bomb. He was born in New York; from a well to do family of German-Jewish origin. He grew up in a family who loved art and music; thanks to his intellectual restlessness and curiosity, he became a true scientist."

"He studied at Harvard University, where he obtained with honors a higher degree in chemistry. In the following years, the precocious young man traveled to Europe and had the opportunity to work with some of the most brilliant physicists at the forefront of technology of that time, pioneers in the investigation of the atomic phenomena."

"The Nazi threat was imminent. The United States knew that the Hitler of Germany was prepared for total war, for world domination and that possibly they were on the way to discover nuclear fission. Oppenheimer and other experts supposed that the German scientists would try to produce a controlled chain reaction that would make possible the development of a bomb with a destructive power much superior to any other conventional explosive."

"The scientists alerted President Roosevelt, after obtaining the support of the famous scientific genius, Albert

Einstein, who was in exiled from the Nazi regime. In the middle of a great secret for everybody, the President authorized to finance a project destined to develop new weapons; specifically, the atomic bomb. Ironically, many renowned scientists, forced to flee from their homes in Germany, Italy and Hungary, joined the researchers of the United States. Some groups studied the possibility of building a nuclear reactor, while others worked on the separation of uranium isotopes needed for a chain reaction. At the beginning of 1942 Oppenheimer was asked to take charge of coordinating all these efforts."

"The project of the army of the United States to develop a nuclear weapon received maximum priority. It was at this critical moment, when the city of Mizpah–Harim made the difficult decision of releasing the wild tiger, in this case, to share the technical secret of the atomic power, which would allow the total and decisive triumph over the wicked forces that tried to control the world and to exterminate the Jews off the face of the earth."

"The project was given the code name "The Manhattan Project", directed by the Colonel Leslie Groves, who had initially referred to the scientists investigating the atomic energy as "an expensive collection of lunatic scientists", and then recognized that Oppenheimer had the skill and potential necessary to direct these divided colleagues under situations of great pressures. The physicist suggested that all the project investigators move to a single laboratory to work together in the small town of Los Alamos, in New Mexico, a region he knew very well, because he was owner of a ranch nearby.

"In March of 1943, a boarding school for men was transformed into a well guarded and highly secure and secret facility. Oppenheimer was named scientific director;

insisting that all information be freely exchanged among the scientists. Their travel to foreign countries was severely restricted. Oppenheimer stimulated an atmosphere of confidence and respect which produced enormous progress."

"With great efficiency, Oppenheimer stayed at the front of the complex project. The highly awaited test of the first atomic weapon of the world took place on July 6 of 1945, about ninety kilometers from the air base of Alamogordo, New Mexico."

"The device being tested was named "The Fat Man" due to its bulbous form and was set up in the desert on a steel tower. At 5:30 A.M, by means of a remote control the first atomic bomb was detonated. With a rumbling roar a fireball of green-orange color rose over an area of a kilometer and a half in diameter. The chain reaction shook the earth and the steel tower disappeared."

"A smoke column rose towards the skies; high and mighty to form a mushroom eleven kilometers high. The first nuclear blast performed by mankind left the military observers who were present at the event, overwhelmed and satisfied. Some congratulated the director, but Oppenheimer saw this event with skepticism; his satisfaction with this great scientific achievement was moderated by a deep sense of responsibility for its future consequences."

"The first atomic bomb used in war would be used against a single enemy: Japan. At 8:14, local time, the bomber Enola Gay unloaded its only cargo: "the Little Boy" then it moved away quickly. Minutes later the atomic bomb exploded, producing an intense brightness that ignited the sky and caused strong winds. From a fire ball of four hundred meters of diameter, which produced an intense heat of approximately three thousand degrees Celsius and with unimaginable destructive power, produced a mushroom cloud that rose twenty kilometers into the skies."

"Three days after Little Boy fell on Hiroshima, a replicate of the Fat Man was dropped on Nagasaki. Japan surrendered unconditionally on the 15th of August, completely disheartened, after the attack with this new weapon. It was a clear victory at a very high price. This extraordinary and cruel event changed the history of humanity forever."

"The invention of the atomic bomb was viewed as the climax of the victory of the United States over its enemies of the II World War; saving the life of a million soldiers who could have died during the invasion of Japan. But the skeptics expressed their own point of view and Oppenheimer himself, two months after Hiroshima, predicted: "Humanity will curse the names of Los Alamos and Hiroshima."

"Nevertheless, the following year he accepted the position of president of the scientific advisory of the Commission of Atomic Energy, thus becoming, the most influential adviser of the government and the army about the subjects of nuclear energy."

"Meanwhile Stalin's Russia was involved in a political isolation from The United States called the Cold War and initiating a new armament race. The 29 of August of 1949, before it was anticipated, Russia detonated its first nuclear bomb. The secret of how to take advantage of the tremendous atomic energy could not be stopped now in spite of our severe warnings and advice. So the secret was shared with Russia even against our will. This was not the original intention of our people."

"Although many participant scientists in the "Manhattan Project" did not support the creation of new weapons; the former collaborators of Oppenheimer, believe that the national security of the United States required the fast development of a lethal and still more destructive weapon: the hydrogen bomb. As we had originally requested, Oppenheimer was against it. It was our position that now the two world nuclear powers faced each other like two scorpions in a bottle, each one able to kill the other, at the cost of its own life. To proliferate the new weapons, the wars no longer would have winners or losers, but only victims."

Aram stopped awhile before concluding his history. Putting his hand on his chin, he took a few steps around the room and finally said:
"And thus concluded this chapter, or better yet, I should say, the beginning of one new one..."
"Hitler ended his life by committing suicide and Japan suffered a great defeat with the loss of thousands of innocent lives... His greatest mistake was to try to exterminate the Hebrew race off the face of the earth. There is a great promise that was given to them by the King and Lord thousands of years ago:
"I will bless those who bless to you, and to those that curse you, I will curse.
And in you all the nations of the earth will be blessed."
"One way or another justice is served on earth; as the King and Lord says:

"Because I will reduce to silence
all the evildoers of the earth;
I will eliminate all the wicked
from the earth.
The nations will fear the King;
all the earth sovereigns
will recognize His Majesty.

The Power Of The Relic

*The King shows himself in his splendor.
He hears the request of the poor,
and He does not despise it.
The King watches from His sanctuary;
And from His throne He contemplates the earth,
He listens to the outcry of the captives
and He releases the imprisoned;
 those who trust in Him. .
The storm goes by and the evildoer vanishes,
but the righteous remains for ever..."*

CHAPTER 22

After Aram finished telling them about the promise that the King and Lord had given to the Jewish race they sat down to rest for a while. There, they were joined by other people from the city in friendly conversation. Towards the evening, as Aram had promised earlier, the two cousins were led to the room where the wealth and treasures of the city was kept; there they would have a chance to see the valuable and wonderful jewels and treasures, never seen by an outsider before.

They walked in direction of the temple through the delightful gardens; when crossing to the right, they ran into a large passage that took them to the entrance of an extraordinary building next to the temple.

Chepe looked around with much curiosity as they entered a massive open room, decorated with ornaments and instruments apparently from their ancestors; a perplexing sensation was perceived there. The room was beautifully built with four rows of columns. From the foundations to the cornices, and from the outer part to the great vestibule to the back, it was done with polished marble blocks, adorned with gold and precious stones. The amount of gold that was there was incalculable: shields of different sizes, various utensils and weapons of the same metal decorated every space. The wealth and the artistic value of the place and its content were incomparable. Its splendor exceeded the imagination of the young cousins.

Finally, Chepe and Juan were before the legendary gold relic. It was all by itself, over a small table, very similar to the one they had seen for the first time in the Gold Museum of Bogota. Chepe examined it carefully at great length, with great curiosity. Aram observed them at a short distance, then approached them saying:

"This is a beautiful relic, very similar to the relic of the power."

"Do you mean that this is not the authentic one?" asked Chepe with great interest.

"The raft of the power was consecrated thousands of years ago in the lands of Babylon, after the universal flood. That relic was brought to the New World by men of the Middle East. Its power became evident in the new world. Intrigued by the legend, the natives constructed a copy of the raft for their ceremonies" explained Aram.

"This is absolutely fantastic!" exclaimed Chepe.

"But please allow me to relate the history from the beginning" continued Aram:

"Shortly after the universal flood a great human dispersion took place. Mankind grew with much power and knowledge, setting up a powerful kingdom on earth. Those men, possessors of great wisdom, constructed the Tower of Babel and the city of Babel. It was the beginning of a great kingdom in the land of Sinar. From there they went to Assyria, where they built Nineveh. They also founded Babylon and some of the other great nations of the old Middle East.

After the flood, the Creator had asked men to populate the earth. He did not want for them to group themselves in one place. But the opposite happened when they found land in the fertile valley of Sinar, where they settled down serving strange gods. Their intention was to be united, to consolidate a great empire in that place that would dominate the entire world.

But their plan failed when the Creator confused their

languages, which forced them to disperse themselves everywhere; the dispersion was total. Of these men, two large groups traveled towards the west through the Mediterranean Sea and then towards the so called New World. Our people settled down in the Caribbean. The other group preferred the mountains of the Andes, where they have remained from those times.

Just like us, those men came from the Middle East bringing with them highly advanced knowledge," continued Aram. "They developed and built extraordinary air ships for transportation, which they flew around and over the Nazca desert of south Peru. In that place strange drawings have been discovered on the ground, testimonies of the landing images used by those strange navigators."

"In the desert they drew animal representations, spiral and straight lines. Apparently these were landing runways for their ships, similar to those of the modern airports. These signals and drawings were the guides for their vehicles; therefore, such designs can only be appreciated from the air. These men had the technology to fly in sophisticated ships."

Chepe found this last story quite fascinating. Later he took Juan to a separate place and commented:

"These are not extraterrestrial beings as the natives of South America have thought in the past. They are the survivors of the flood and they come from the old Babylon, a highly developed culture!"

"Old Babylon?" asked Juan. "How do you come up with the theory of the old Babylon?"

With a gesture of preoccupation, Chepe fixed his glance on his cousin.

"Have you not read in Biblical history about the Tower of Babel and its admirable scientific development? The archaeological findings, as those of Nazca, are not more than the relics of these old visitors who arrived here with a technology much superior to the one already existing here. Then, the natives considered them like gods."

"Incredible! This is incredible!" exclaimed, Juan.

"But there is more" continued Chepe. "These beings also established contact with other indigenous cultures, like the Mayan and the Aztecs. As a result of this contact there exist the pyramids and the famous Mayan calendar with a surprising and inexplicable exactitude; these were created several thousands of years ago with an extraordinary complexity that astonishes our archeologists and astronomers.

The Mayans determined the correct way that the sun, the moon and the planet Venus are in the same alignment only every one hundred and four years. Of the old cultures, they were the ones who came closest to the calculation of the solar year. The present one is of 365.2422 days, whereas they, using their own instruments and from the height of their pyramids, got the number of 365.2420 with a difference of only a thousandth of a day. Remembers that this was thousands of years ago…"

"How is it possible that the old Mayans could make such a precise astronomical observations long before the invention of the telescope?" inquired Juan.

"This has been the result of the communications of these cultures with those visitors who arrived from the old Babylon; survivors of the tower of Babel. The calendar and the pyramids were the result of a highly advanced technical and scientific knowledge," concluded Chepe.

Juan remained in silence, reflecting about what his cousin had said, about the origin and the nature of the people who were waiting for them in the mountains of South America. Juan was also an eager reader, based on his studies of old history, he tried to understand how the stories of the first books of the Bible, so often considered as legend, could be true.

"This is a true puzzle," thought Juan. "Would it be possible that those men were related to the legend of other native Indians in South America? And that the earth experienced catastrophes of planetary impacts like the extraordinary story of the universal flood and other phenomena as they register in the Bible? That the Sun stood still in the skies, that the Red Sea was separated and then came together again, that manna fell from the sky and fed the Israelites, that great plagues flogged Egypt?"

"And if these legends could be really true," Juan continued asking very anxiously, "would it be possible that events of our Solar System had been able to originate catastrophes, tides and enormous earthquakes on earth as it says in the history of the flood? The total disappearance of humans over the face of the earth had been documented in almost all the old archives, and the mass extinction of the animals was demonstrated in the vestiges found in the caverns and the archaeological excavations everywhere around the world?"

Although Juan had studied history, where old legends and written documents were evidence that corroborated these theories, it seemed fantastic and difficult for him to believe it: The existence of a culture of the Middle East in South America!

Juan asked Chepe again:

"How can you be sure that all these legends are true and that they are related?"

Taking his hand to his forehead as if searching for a suitable answer, Chepe expressed his answer with a deep thought:

"You know that the British museum has thousands of small Babylonian clay tablets that have not yet been yet translated or published? These offer very interesting

information about the Solar system related to human historical events. This is evident for those who have knowledge of old languages and can read and decipher the texts and hieroglyphics of Assyria and Babylonia."

After this interesting dialog, they returned to the room, next to Aram, who then returned to his story:
"Those beings are known as the men of blue skin."
This immediately caught Chepe's attention in a profound way.
"The men of blue skin?" he asked, to make sure he had understood well.
"Indeed" responded Aram, "this constitutes something very strange in nature, but actually it has a biological explanation: the blue skin is due to genetic anomalies caused by decades of family intermarriage, as those people used to do for the purpose of preserving the purity of their race."
"Also this is attributed to the altitude of the land where they settled down. Their skin, started turning blue due to the noticeable diminution of oxygen at more than five thousand meters above the sea level, apparently due to the high production of hemoglobin. The excess of this sanguineous compound is pronounced through the skin, with the blue tone that it produces. This is the reason for which some natives call them, the men of the blue skin."

"For many years those men lived peacefully near the native Indians. But soon a sinister leader named Hifar arose who propagated strange ideologies within his people. He taught that at first there had been two races on this planet: the one of the men of blue skin and the one of the other men. The First was that of humans, possessors of the light of creativity and superiority; they had been a divine race, extremely intelligent, of great beauty and special creativity.

The other was an inferior race, without many attributes or knowledge. At some time during its evolution, they began to envy and to hate the men of blue skin, the superior race. For the purpose of destroying them, they came up with plan of mixing the two races. Hifar assured them that after several centuries of such intermarriage the two races disappeared as a result of a universal catastrophe caused by flood; only a few were saved from it.

Hifar spoke of the existence of a being that had created the two races and assured them that the inferior one had intermixed with the superior for revenge. Hifar needed to make of his people the superior race, to recover the power of the men of blue skin. Finally these men decided to support him in a fantastic project that would end-up with the foundation of the secret and mysterious city of *El Dorado*.

He maintained that the race of those of blue skin came from the Middle East; that they had come through a migration through Egypt, Persia, Greece and Rome and that they had been the creators of great cultures and had reformed the old civilizations that flourished in those areas. The collapse of these cultures, maintained Hifar, had been due to the degeneration caused by the mixing of the superior race with the inferior race. For him, all the moral and mental faculties were the product of racial origin, dominated by the men of blue skin.

According to this leader, the natives represented the inferior race in the New World; as a result they were put under a cruel slavery on the part of the men of the blue skin, who lived in the city of *El Dorado*. They lived there with the express mission of creating a great elite, with an extensive and well-consolidated power.

With this idea they justified the right to capture and enslave the aborigines who lived in the high mountains of

the Andes. This implied that the mission of the city of *El Dorado* was to create a structure and an empire that could impose a global system of perfection and harmony under the command of a superior race."

"Hifar was proclaimed as a charismatic leader. He made them believe that he was the possessor of supernatural qualities maneuvering with great ability the magical powers of the golden relic; being elevated as the emissary of the Creator, as a predestined guide.

He came to exert absolute power through a macabre plan of manipulation of his own people. He accomplished his decisions by means of terror, intrigue and intimidation. His rivals and contenders were silenced and eliminated. The decisions taken supposedly were made unanimously by his people, but this was not certain.

This way, Hifar was consolidated little by little as an infallible and invincible leader. His intention was to turn the city of El Dorado into a self-sufficient empire, a vital factor for the formation of a superior race and to subdue the people he had destined to serve; to maintain a high standard of living, while the inferior race was to perpetually remain as slaves and servants.

A global system governed by that privileged race would give as result the elimination of the fight among classes, something considered as non-desirable. The final intention was based on a peaceful, coherent and dynamic society, perfectly governed by superior men...

There it was; the macabre plan. The purpose was to establish a new empire; in spite of all the differences of languages and customs; with only an economic, political and religious system at a world-wide level, which is being developed at the moment in the city of *El Dorado*. But they would obtain it only with the power of the golden relic.

Hifar did not manage to complete his plan in those

times. But in the past few years a new leader has been trying to carry out those sinister plans of world-wide dominion dreamed by Hifar…"

Aram remained in silence for a while as he looked around the room as if giving time to Chepe and to Juan to process this new information. They in the meantime, were overwhelmed, looking to the outside through the transparent walls. Finally Aram approached them to say:

"The purpose of your mission is to rescue or to destroy, if necessary, the powerful relic and in this way to prevent a great human catastrophe."

"But how can this be possible?" asked Chepe with incredulity. "That is a strong and powerful empire. In addition, it is hidden in an unknown place!"

"It is true that the empire is strong and powerful," said Aram "But you have the infallible power of the sword! The power that no one else has ever had on this earth! You must not be afraid nor be troubled in your way, because this power is greater than the one of that empire," continued Aram trying to encourage them with a spirit of optimism.

"The city of El Dorado is located high in the Andes, to the south of the ruins of the Indian Kuelap Empire. These ruins are in almost inaccessible places of those mountains. We have a map with its location.

There is no doubt that this is a difficult trip… an arduous and dangerous task, but remember that you are not alone in this mission," he assured them again, reminding them of the King and Lord, of Father Carlos, Bachu and Tachia who had been with them, training them, and preparing them for such a delicate assignment.

Saying this, he handed them a map, which contained more details of the location of *El Dorado*.

"Write down your plan and your purpose in your dairy and set it on your memory that it may not be forgotten. Fix it clearly in your mind and your heart so that it will come to pass. The mission will have to be carried out as it has been indicated to you; if you march towards its fulfillment, your objective will be fulfilled completely just as planned and at the opportune time," Aram ended saying in a prophetic tone.

After this conversation he invited them to have supper with him, in company of his closest advisers. He sat at the head of the table; to his right was the man of Indian features and to his left, another man of medium stature of Eastern features.

The table was elegantly set for five people; covered with a white tablecloth and set with utensils of gold and silver. Aram rose, and after giving thanks for the food he invited them to participate in the meal. The atmosphere was welcoming, hospitable, ceremonious, and solemn, with soft music, special for such occasion; the special atmosphere allowed Chepe and Juan to meditate more about the nature of the events that awaited them.

Once they finished the delicious dinner, they were taken to their comfortable guess rooms. There they spent the night before their return to Cartagena.

CHAPTER 23

The next destination was the city of Leticia, located in the heart of the Amazonian forest. The trip from Cartagena was by air, in an airplane that made this route daily to carry the mail and special merchandise between the two cities. The first part of the journey was over the magnificent and breathtaking landscapes of the plains of northern Colombia and then over the open fields east of the Andes. From the windows of the airplane they could observe the extensive cultivations of the productive lands, as well as open savannahs of grass populated with cattle and horses.

After several hours of flight, the cousins discovered in the distance the overwhelming and wonderful rain forest. The first impression for Chepe was that of flying over an immense green ocean, formed by the dense tree tops and tall palms trees that demanded the coveted sun light, in the permanent and insatiable competition for their existence. From the air they could also see the winding mighty waters of the rivers that wandered through the Colombian rain forest on their way towards the Atlantic Ocean.

"This is a true paradise," said Juan as they descended from the airplane.

"Yes, you are right, a green paradise but full of great secrets and dangers," answered Chepe, as they now walked to luggage claim.

Ramon was waiting for them as they were coming out of the airport. He was a good friend of Father Nicanor and had agreed to provide accommodations for Chepe and Juan for a few nights while they organized their expedition towards the jungle, on their way to the Andes Mountains of Peru. His house was located a short distance from the airport, within the city of Leticia. Leticia is the capital of the Amazon province and an important commercial center in the South end of Colombia. Transportation was mainly through waterways, which offered an excellent opportunity to see closely the famous and feared piranhas, and the black caymans, as well as endless species of animals and tropical plants. The hot and humid climate generally is accompanied of intense rains that flood great areas, turning this place into a true sea.

From the very first moment they arrived, Chepe and Juan fell in love with the imposing and delightful spectacle offered by the Amazonian rain forest. Unfortunately this place is being subjugated and civilized by the predator hand of man. While the missionaries may have been attracted by human souls, the colonists on the majority were attracted by the wealth of the region. They brought with them a new culture and a new way of life, founding a few cities on the borders of the rivers. Today, those cities are a point of reference for the tourists who come to enjoy the beauty that this region offers. Most of the population of this region is aborigine of various communities, like the Huitotos, Yaguas and the Tucanos.

They talked awhile with Ramon before starting their way home. On the way he talked with much pride about the value of the rain forest.

"The Amazonian region is the greatest ecological reserve of this planet and biggest lung; its area is distinguished by the channel of the impressive and magnificent Amazon River and it is covered, almost in its totality, by an impenetrable vegetation that has taken thousands of years to become what it is today. A large part of this rain forest belongs to Colombia. Much of it extends over a waved topography, whose altitude varies between one hundred and five hundred meters above the sea level.

The rest of it is shared between Brazil and Peru."

As an expert tour guide Ramon continued:

"The Amazon river, with its great volume, has a length of more than six thousand kilometers, through which they are more than six thousand islands. It begins in the mountains of Peru and it ends at the Atlantic coast of Brazil. Large rivers of Colombia, like the Putumayo and the Caquetá are tributaries of the Amazon. An intense commerce has developed between the different villages of this extensive region. Francisco de Orellana, the Spanish conquistador gave this name to the river. He and his men were the first Europeans to travel its waters in 1541. According to De Orellana, during his expedition, he and his men sustained a battle with women of war –the Amazons– which is how he lost an eye. This old mythical story inspired the name of this fascinating river.

"To venture into this territory, besides being a spectacular ecological field trip, is an opportunity to learn about its history that speaks of great adventures and colonial expeditions which have claimed a high number of human lives. And in more recent years, the cruel exploitation of the natives on the part of the companies that with impunity have been destroying and annihilating great extensions of this forest, a forest preserve that will never be able to recover."

"Today, in Leticia," continued Ramón, there is a greater conscience about our environment; about the native population and the importance of safeguarding the fauna and flora as a preserve for everybody to enjoy. The Amazon region invites us to appreciate a creation filled with an exceptional enchantment and beauty. To be here is to coexist directly with nature; is to have the opportunity to know this massive river that sometimes becomes a sea. We have the opportunity to venture into the tributary rivers and to listen to the sound of the forest, to observe the gigantic trees, and to admire the famous pink dolphins that come along the boats. If they do not astonish you by their color, they do it by their intelligence; they are part of the enchantment that characterizes the Colombian rain forest. In short, all of this is a journey that will transport you to a fantastic and prodigious world that without actually seeing it is very difficult to imagine," ended Ramon.

The following days, Chepe and Juan enjoyed Ramon's hospitality as they learned many details about the wonderful and yet frightful and terrible rain forest. During this time they were also preparing for the long journey ahead of them. Two days latter everything was ready. Ramon chose two skilled Indian guides, experienced and well knowledgeable of the rain forest, the river and its dangers, as well as many of the native dialects. They started their journey in company of their guides leaving behind several friends.
    In the city of Leticia they embarked on a small canoe in a long journey towards the Andean mountains. This contrasted with the elaborate expeditions of the Spanish conquistadores, who with thousands of soldiers and Indians, used large numbers of ships, as well as the old colonists that carried with them horses ready to be used in case they found any hostilities on their way.
    On the contrary, the two young cousins, had preferred to travel light, to be able to face any misfortunes or surprises they might find on their way without major difficulties.
    The first day they arrived at a small village where few natives lived. According to the guides, they were not very friendly. But much to their surprise the natives preferred to flee with their women and children after burning their huts, instead of having to face the strange visitors; their fear of

outsiders was evident.

They continued for several kilometers without finding anybody. Later they arrived at a village inhabited by people who had their huts hidden on the trees and half way submerged in the waters. They had abundant fish and food, in addition to many canoes, which indicated the good conditions of living. The women covered themselves with beautiful fabrics woven by hand. These people were shy and little sociable; they ran away at their presence, just like the previous ones.

Three hours later, already deep into the forest, they arrived at a town where they discovered a small group of friendly natives. The men had round discs of wood hanging from their ears; their women were of brown skin color and very beautiful, wearing a shining crystal in their lips. Their clothes were of lively colors, covering only from the waist to the middle of the legs. They lived on a simple way, centered around a nuclear family formed by the parents and their children.

Chepe and his companions remained with them for two days. Juan took advantage of this time to try to find some information about the city of *El Dorado*, but these people did not seem to know anything about that subject. In view of this Chepe asked to make arrangements to continue their trip. He appeared to be anxious to get moving again towards their destination as soon as possible. And so they did, but they had not advanced much when they decided to return back to the same village following the recommendations and warnings of the Indian guides who considered that the conditions ahead were not good and that the provisions were not sufficient.

The following day Chepe requested that one of the guides should go ahead along with Juan, with the purpose of exploring during a day, then to return back to the village. After several hours of traveling, both emissaries found a small group of natives who lived in small straw huts. Juan realized that they could obtain provisions there but decided not to make contact with the native Indians but to return back to his cousin to give account of the result of his exploration. With this information, Chepe decided to resume the trip, in search of the new town, but their plans were frustrated again because the region was flooded as a result of torrential rains falling in the high part of the forest.

On the way back, one of the guides who was standing up in the canoe, lost the balance and fell to the water. Chepe and Juan were alarmed, because this zone was infested with piranhas. These fish usually have an extraordinary appetite and devour their prey in a matter of minutes, leaving only clean bones. In spite of the cloudy Amazonian waters that prevent their visibility, their sensitivity and acute sense of smell helps them to detect their prey and to attack them at a slight movement or the slightest scent to blood. The guide tried desperately to swim towards the canoe but it was already at a considerable distance. In the middle of his anguish, he remembered the advice that he should remain calm and float on the water in order not to attract the attention of the voracious piranhas. He tried to contain his anxiety, waiting for the aid of his friends, but every second seemed like an eternity. Suddenly, from the bottom of the water, a gigantic turtle arose that served like a support and life-guard for him. Seconds later, their companions, rescued him unharmed. They were convinced that it was large piece of wood. Once the guide was out of danger, the enormous turtle went down and disappeared in the cloudy waters of the river.

Once safe and sound on the canoe, the guide, explained to his friends:

"The piranhas, as you look at them from the distance, in their own habitat, are very beautiful creatures of many colors; with red, green and black, round bodies and a great nose. They have gained great reputation for their teeth: pointed, triangular and as sharp as knives. Its lower jaw overlaps the upper one, facilitating this way its closure forming a deadly trap. When the piranha bites something, it easily breaks it in small pieces. The power of their teeth and the fact that they travel in colonies make of these creatures, terrible enemies of the animals who live in the Amazon and of those men who venture themselves into this waters; their prey disappears very quickly, in a matter of minutes" concluded saying the guide.

His companions, who had paid closed attention, exploded in a loud outbursts of laughter, observing the calmness and tranquility with which he had made such a meticulous description of the ferocious fish that minutes before could have had him for lunch. After overcoming this misfortune, they started their journey again in search of a town where they could obtain additional provisions.

They navigated for three days through the wide river, until they found a village of Indians who lived in an island. They had much food such as fruits, corn, sweet potatoes, mandioca, vegetables and abundant meat and fish. They remained there for a day in order to get supplies. The following day they left in company of two local Indians, who offered to go in another canoe ahead of them to show them the way to the mountains and to explain many other details about the rain forest and the mighty Amazon. During the trip, they fished twice a day and hunted wild animal for food. What was left over, they threw it in the waters so that it could serve as food to the fish in the water.

"This way nothing is wasted," explained one of the natives to the four visitors.

The dark of the night was almost total; suddenly they saw that a boat had stopped right in the center of the vast river. From nowhere a large canoe approached one of its flanks and three men with their luggage boarded it. It then moved away in silence, just like it had arrived, vanishing in the deep penumbra, taking a valuable shipment, perhaps of illicit merchandise.

The boat did not have any identification; it was propelled by a small electrical motor that allowed it to move with greater discretion. Apparently it was there to transfer passengers and merchandise from bigger boats coming from different places in the jungle. It would then transport them into a city hidden in the heart of the forest. With much curiosity, Chepe and his companions decided to approach the boat with great caution in spite of the difficulties, but they did not manage to make sense of anything happening there. The light was very tenuous and every once in a while they encountered trunks and branches in their path which at this time of intense rains abounded in the course of the river. To make matters worse, they also found on their way several canoes that suddenly crossed their path without any lights.

Under these circumstances they decided to continue their way. All of a sudden in the middle of the night, lights and the silhouettes of some buildings in front of them drew their attention. When coming closer, they realized that it was a city located in a lake formed by the overflow of the river. It appeared almost invisible for those who journey by this route. Chepe thought that the intention of its founders was to build a refuge camouflage in the borders of the Amazon, hidden away and protected from the noise of the outside world. In the morning blue sky some vultures flew over this part of the river; these appeared to be common birds in this part of the forest.

But the sensation of isolation of this city, protected permanently by the shadows of the dense jungle, was false. It was in fact an important a river port for this area. Its docks were always in constant movement with boats coming from neighboring cities located in the higher or lower part of the river. In the middle of this economic activity, the social deterioration also was made evident in this city, made up of a relatively large population. The children, apparently immune to the visible contamination of waters of this lake, bathed happily in its borders, without any apparent concerned of the risks to them or to their parents.

At noon the suffocating heat and the humidity typical of this part of the tropic, caused the inhabitants of this place to take refuge in their hammocks hanging from the trees or within their straw huts. In the evening they go back to resume the work in the market place or at the docks; waiting for the arrival of the night which is much, much busier than the day.

CHAPTER 24

Sailing a little more towards the west they arrived at another city. It was small, very clean and with a colonial architecture well preserved, prosperous and very famous for the quality and variety of its agricultural products. Every year the great celebration of the fruit fair took place there. Its growth was due to a great extent, to the exuberant nature and the tropical beauty of this remote place. Everything was happy, with an atmosphere of simplicity, almost primitive. During the day the children played in a terrific football field of green meadows; well maintained. At night a magnificent music band entertained and amused the town people and its visitors. People danced enthusiastically in the park. Chepe and its companions had the opportunity to enjoy the hospitality and the festive atmosphere of this community.

The following morning, they decided to remain a few more hours, while they gathered provisions for the days ahead and to have lunch before restarting their journey. At noon, a cool breeze calmed the unbearable heat of this place that together with the humidity, used to be intolerable.

The majority of the inhabitants were quite friendly, very proud of their annual town fair which took place next to the docks; during this day you could see all the exotic natural treasures of the Amazon exhibited on the streets: gigantic pineapples, papayas, guaraná, guanábanas and many other fruits of strange and exquisite flavors. Juan, before this spectacle of tropical wonders, said jokingly to Chepe;

"With all this abundance and all these wonders and wealth of the Amazon, who needs *El Dorado?*"

They went to a nearby restaurant for lunch. The waitress

said to them as they came in:

"We live happy in this paradise!"

A group of musicians played a happy piece of music, whose lyrics was a delicious inspiration for the mind and the spirit. At the front, there was an old church surrounded by beautiful gardens with gorgeous tropical flowers and a well cared grassy meadow. At the other side the sun shined over the surface of the waters whose destination, like the one of all the water of the surrounding areas was the one to render its tribute to the Amazon river and finally to the Atlantic Ocean.

The first hours of the day, everything became a charming scene. The multicolor sunrise transformed the boats, the waters of the lakes and the surrounding vegetation into an enchanted and spectacular world never seen anywhere else; only in this rain forest. Although the region offered foods in abundance, the population in general was not satisfied; fishing and agriculture were the main activities, but no longer was there work for everybody there. In the bars people talked about the little opportunities that they had, especially the younger generation which was the most numerous. Some complained about the corruption of the local authorities, that made the local resources disappear, and others complained about the authorities in Bogota. All these commentaries indicated that there was much dissatisfaction among the inhabitants.

Juan, placing his hand over his forehead in attitude of preoccupation commented to Chepe.

"With so many blessings that this people have received in this wonderful garden, one would think that they would always to be glad and thankful with the Creator."

"For the afflicted one every day is a bad day, but for the one that is happy, every day is a day of celebration."

"That is true," affirmed Chepe, as he agreed with his cousin, then adding;

"The lazy man wishes but he does not obtain anything and he remains afflicted, but the one that works diligently prospers."

Their expedition continued toward the west arriving at a floating city inhabited by tall and strong natives dedicated to hunting and fishing. This way of life allowed them to provide meat and fish in abundance for their families. Their women were tall, beautiful and attractive but timid and afraid of any strangers. Chepe and its companions decided to stay a day in that place in order to get specific direction from the aborigines about the best way to take towards the Andean mountains. The natives accepted happily to help and offered to send guides to show them the way to the mountains.

After traveling for two days they arrived at an old city dedicated to exploitation of rubber. The old city is truly a sad story that only left signs of destruction and contamination of the environment and desolation to its native inhabitants. The history of that region was written in the many years of invasion; the time when colonists crossed the plains and mountains of South America with soldiers and servants looking for land and gold, while others came with the best intentions; to find a pleasant and safe place to establish their homes and to see their families grow and develop.

Chepe asked his companions to camp there for a few days in order to learn about this place and to evaluate the fragility of the forest under the powerful and imposing hand of the colonists. Many people had amassed great fortunes in this place, and then went to the large cities in the interior of the country or foreign lands leaving this place in utter misery, contaminated and poor.

Once they were settled in their camp, Chepe met with one of the native chiefs to investigate more about the impact the colonists activities had produced in the local environment and its inhabitants. The native's face showed evident signals of preoccupation. Chepe asked him directly about the origin of his apprehension and concern.

"The situation for our people and the forest has been a disaster without precedents with the arrival of the colonists that came over here to get rich at the cost of the blood of our people and the destruction of our forests. With their arrival, the natives had to face a predator more voracious than ever before had penetrated this jungle. In the beginning, the natives received them with kindness; they cooperated with many of the first immigrants. The natives taught them to fish and to hunt, and the best ways to cultivate the ground. Without their help, the colonist would not have survived."

"Nevertheless, due to the form in which the colonists have abused the land and since the agricultural resources are limited, great tensions have arisen between the invaders and the natives. Wild animals abounded in the forest before the arrival of the conquistadores; the rivers offered plenty of fish and the land offered lots of fruits and vegetables to satisfy all the necessities of its inhabitants. But these men took our land, devastated the forests with machines; the trees were converted to saw dust; their horses ate the meadows, their pigs and cattle ate and wasted our crops. Now we are the ones who suffer the consequences; many of our people die from starvation," concluded the Indian chief with a gesture of sadness and resignation, longing for the good old times.

For his part, Chepe was a quiet witness of the destruction that the new settlers brought to this fragile territory. The rivers were contaminated from the use of machineries and the waste resulting from the lack of responsibility of mining companies. Once the damage is done, those companies move on to other places to continue with their implacable and devastating business in search of quick fortunes, but behind are left the natives who do not have another alternative of life. The forests disappear, the wild animals are extinguished and the waters, now deleterious, are not suitable for the fish or other aquatic animals...

"So it is a sad landscape left for our people who in the past enjoyed an incomparable paradise... but so fragile and vulnerable," said the Indian chief, sadly.

"The forest cries, longing for the past when its beauty was fresh and radiating. The ashes and the ruins of the lands have turned into graveyard what used to be a spectacular garden. All its enchantment has been transformed into tears of pain, humiliation and infamy. It is now very much changed, hardened, more deteriorated, on the verge of becoming extinct... just like a dying mother who does not want to leave the children she has nourished for such a long time."

The native could not hide his deep pain before the horrible cruelty perpetrated against Mother Nature. Chepe looked at him with admiration and sorrow as the native searched for a tree trunk to sit on. His appearance was that of an old and decrepit man as he shared the progressive deterioration of that place. He was great and splendid in years past, but now he was languid, sad and old. He remained in silence there a long time, without moving or pronouncing another word.

Suddenly a voice came out of him which seemed to come from the heart of the jungle. Chepe listened stupefied. The native was no longer speaking about the forest, but about himself and his people. As Chepe observed him, he noticed that the chief was now speaking in his own native language and that he did not want to look at him. Immediately afterwards, he exclaimed aloud:

"The forest is dying!"

"And what can we do now?" asked Chepe in a sympathetic tone.

But there was no answer. The Indian chief had left in the direction of the trees that still grew at the distance; and he never heard again about those people, of the native inhabitants of that territory...

Chepe turned his glance one last time in the direction where his friend, the Indian chief had disappeared. A little while later, Juan approached him interrupting his thoughts.

"We have to hurry! We must leave right now; we must continue towards our destination in the high mountains," Juan said with firmness and authority. "There is no time to waste; everything is ready; we must leave as soon as possible!"

"No, no! Let's wait," said Chepe as if waking up from a deep dream. "The way is long and it is better that we rest now and leave tomorrow, first thing in the morning. As soon as everything is in order, we will start off."

To following day, Chepe and his companions gave one last look at the sad village, reduced to a miserable and desolated small number of houses before leaving in the direction of the high mountains. Two hours later one of the guides ran into something sinister in the way. Some small animals appeared squashed in the trail by someone who left clear tracks on the ground of giant feet with claws. The experienced guides studied the marks carefully and warned the group that this was a giant being and asked them to be alert of any imminent danger. Luckily, in spite of this they did not have any misfortune during the rest of the day.

At dusk they set up camp and hung their hammocks for an evening of rest. When it got dark, the strange creature made his appearance near the place where they were, trying to hide among the trees, under the pale rays of the moon which filtered through the thick foliage. It was large and hairy, with the appearance of a human being, with beard, moustache and radiant and brilliant eyes. But soon he disappeared in the dark at night as mysteriously as he had arrived. The third night of the trip both Indian guides were sitting, guarding the camp and armed with loaded guns, ready to fire at any intruder. When that creature appeared again between the shadows, the natives shot at him several times as it began to growl and left running towards the forests.

The guards were very sure that they had hit their target, but they could not find the smallest sign of blood. They continued advancing for several days, always looking for any possible indication of the presence of that strange giant, but they never saw it again. Nevertheless, later they heard from some natives who affirmed that they had seen an extraordinarily large creature, similar to the one they had seen with their own eyes before, and told them that they had seen it hiding behind the trees, apparently with a wounded leg.

Chepe and his companions continued advancing in the thick forest, towards the distant mountains of the Andes. After several days of leaving the bed of the Amazon River they found a small Indian village where their inhabitants built their houses in the trees. The men were of medium stature, brown complexion and brown hair. The women, whose appearance was similar to those of the men, were very timid and very rarely left their homes. Their faces showed an expression of tranquility and happiness.

These people were very experienced in handling the blowpipe and skilful hunters, but afraid of the strangers who, according to their legend, live in summits of the Andean mountain range. They had bare feet. Their large and peculiar feet help them to climb the trees with an extraordinary ability. The green colors of their clothes allow them to conceal easily in the foliage of the forest to hide and to protect them. In addition they found abundant food there. They were skilful with their weapons but very distrustful, although peaceful and hospitable.

They were also experts in the arts of navigation, fishing and swimming, but they preferred to live in the trees where they felt more secure. These were without a doubt the most agile and developed native group Chepe and Juan had found in the Amazon. Chepe and his friends decided to remain a few days there to enjoy their friendship, their generosity and company.

As a gesture of special hospitality they offered a great celebration in honor of the new visitors. During this event something rather surprising happened: the natives spoke to them about the existence of very tall men dressed in black that lived in mountains in a secret place and had control of the legendary and mythical city of *El Dorado*. These natives also said that these mysterious people had enslaved a great number of natives, never allowing them to leave the city.

Chepe was rather surprised to hear this news and tried to obtain more details about the location of that mysterious city, but the inhabitants did not have more information, because they always were afraid of exploring those places. During the following days he continued his investigating to confirm his suspicions. He reached the conclusion that this was really related to the existence of a mysterious people, with immense power... not more nor less, than the men of blue skin.

Noting the great interest of Chepe of knowing more details about this subject, the natives told them about a legend:

"The legend says that long ago, thousand of years ago, strange beings, perhaps extraterrestrial beings, came to these places and that their knowledge and exploits were truly amazing. So great was their influence that they became legendary beings, a symbol of divinity and fear for our ancestors… These beings were equipped with special powers."

"In fact, very little is known about those beings," continued the chief. "They were friendly and benevolent to the natives; they taught them new arts and different techniques of building large structures and how to cultivate the ground. Thanks to their powers they helped the natives built great cities, help consolidate cultures and create powerful empires. Remarkable cultures of the antiquity were born here; our ancestors treated them like gods, offering them sacrifices and giving them valuable offerings of gold and jewels" concluded the chief.

A few nights later, when all were together sharing familiar stories, Chepe and Juan discovered an object in the sky that went towards the north from a mountain in the south of Peru. The object disappeared in the horizon, leaving a luminous sign in the firmament. Minutes later the sky was illuminated for several hours with mysterious lights that descended randomly forming circles and drawings of various colors. It was something inexplicable that had never been seen before in those places.

CHAPTER 25

Leaving behind their native friends in their beautiful surroundings, they followed their path through the forest following the course of the river towards the mountains. In spite of the enormous volume of the Amazon River, in this part of its route, its surface gave the impression of not moving. It seemed like a vast lake. It was a vast open field of waters in which they moved up the river in a slow and exhausting trip, but without major misfortunes. After three days, Chepe and his friends arrived at a village located on the river borders. While resting there, something unexpected happened: Chepe separated from the group in order to be by himself to think about all that had happened in the last few days and to process the information they had obtained from their native friends. He was deep in his meditations when his cousin Juan surprised him as he came searching for him in the forest. Both of them spoke at great length about the nature and the purpose of their mission and the great risks and dangers that surely were ahead of them in the future.

Meanwhile, both guides began to get impatient about the long delay of the two cousins, who they now considered their leaders. After two hours of delay they decided to go searching for them. It was then that they were attacked by a group of Indian warriors from the south, experts in the use of spears and arrows which they used with the terrible and feared poison called curare. As consequences of this encounter Juan and Chepe were separated momentarily from their companions. But Chepe, aware of the danger at hand, immediately went in pursuit of the Indian soldiers.

When they noticed the presence of Chepe and Juan they undertook the flight, leaving the guides, luckily unharmed.

After this incident, they resumed the advance up the river until dusk. The night was terribly dark; and the fog and the dense humidity covered the trees and everything in the surroundings. For the first time the noise of the nocturnal animals sounded strange to them. Minutes later the fog vanished and in the clear firmament appeared the stars and the radiant moon. The shadows of the enormous trees projected on the waters giving them a mysterious beauty. Chepe and Juan remained in the shadows for a long while meditating in silence, perhaps with similar thoughts but not daring to say a word in order not to interrupt the peaceful night. They decided to spend the night in this place, looking forward to a time of refreshing before continuing the journey.

Meanwhile, the strong rains that lashed the mountain formed mighty water currents causing floods in the low parts of the jungle. The waters were not very deep, but they made the journey more difficult, forcing them to move very slowly. The group marched all day through the marshy lands until they arrived at a small patch, dry and clear; a very appropriate place to rest awhile. They decided that it was a perfect place to spend the night. The moon, as in the previous night, shone on the horizon surrounded by titillating stars that from time to time seemed to hide timidly behind fleeting clouds.

The evening had already grown dark when they noticed strange animals that flew in silence under the trees moving like birds. They approached the new visitors with certain curiosity and then they moved away quickly. Chepe giving a voice of alert said:

"These are vampire bats, one of the many varieties of this species that live in these forests of the Amazon!" Then he continued, "they are the only true vampire bats in the world, and just as the mythical creatures with which these are associated, they feed on blood. So be very careful tonight. These animals have the capacity to move in complete silence. This is a key to their survival since it allows them to approach their prey without being detected. Once they find their victim, they use their sharp teeth to open a small wound in the skin, sufficient to cause bleeding; because the vampire bats do not suck the blood but rather drink it or lick it, once it bleeds out of the body."

After such a warning, his companions were quite scared; so much that they did not want to camp out in this place. Chepe tried to assure them that they were not under any danger; he explained to them that these animals would not attack the group, but noticing that his message did not produce any positive effect on his friends, he decided to use another strategy, this time, visible and impressive. Taking his sword, he drew up a circle around the small camp and then he drove it in the ground.

"This place is now protected against any danger or threats from the enemy" said Chepe in a firm and convincing tone. The sword was standing on the ground next to his hammock, radiating a tenuous light. Now they felt assured and protected, able to rest peacefully.

The young friends woke up with the first rays of the morning sun that filtered through the green trees; they looked around with a certain anxiety to make sure that they had not been attacked by the ferocious bats and to verify that all were safe and sound, as Chepe had assured them. At his side, the sword still remained standing, driven into the ground.

The noise of his companions woke up Chepe, who felt for a moment that he was in a different place. The preoccupation about the previous night had disappeared but now he had the feeling that a new danger was imminent.

When studying the ground with the new sun light he noticed strange tracks that disappeared in the water that flooded part of the ground where they had set up camp. He called Juan to share with him his preoccupation. In addition to this, he had also overheard the previous day the guides talking about the presence of warrior women in these surroundings, but they did not have precise details about their location.

"These can be the legendary Amazon women of whom the natives and the conquistadores like Francisco de Orellana spoke," said Juan.

Chepe did not answer but he continued studying the tracks with more thoroughness and curiosity. After a few minutes he asked the most expert of the guides to follow the tracks he had found. This he did with an extraordinary skill following an old trail that led them to the ruins of an old city hidden in the middle of immense trees. Finally, after discovering these ruins, they had to accept that the legend of the Amazon women could be a reality.

Nearby they also found several tombs quite old, hidden among rocks and trunks of fallen trees. After examining them at great length, Chepe concluded that they had to belong to warrior women because next to the feminine remains there were swords, lances and daggers. Farther ahead, in the same path, they found another tomb, the one of a woman buried along with her weapons. Other similar remains were found in the forest, hidden behind dense shrubs, offering a natural protection against any intruders. After careful study of the different details of these ruins, Chepe went to his companions:

"This finding demonstrates that indeed warrior women exist in these surroundings. It is very possible that they are the famous Amazon women. From now on we must move more cautiously, very carefully."

Juan proceeded then to relate to them what he knew about these legendary women:

"According to the legend, after defeating the forces of Francisco de Orellana many years ago, the Amazon women who had attacked the famous Spanish conqueror took some of his men as prisoners. During the return trip, they killed the crew of one of the ships and after some combats, they finally defeated Orellana. They joined the men still remaining; but without losing their dominion, they managed to maintain a society run by the women. Their descendants still live in these forests."

"Previously, these women killed their husbands, once they had daughters to assure this way the feminine descendants and the continuity of their community. They decided to let the men from the conquistador live but they never allow them to go to war or to work in the fields. They must remain at home taking care of their fortunes and their children. The women are in charge of looking for food and provisions.

"According to the legend they are also in charge of the boats when they go to war," continued Juan.

"Originally they lived at the borders of the Amazon river, near the place where the city of Leticia is today. They controlled great amounts of land, including that of the North Rivers, and founded many cities; they fought against the Huitoto Indians, another indigenous people who used to control this area. Famous for their valor, they attacked the neighboring towns and marched against the Indians, putting them into servitude, taking their wealth and their jewels, but they never mixed with the Indians."

"The legend also affirms that these are beautiful and gorgeous women, charming and seductive. No men take part in their system of government and they are led by a queen. The presence of the men is allowed solely to carry out certain specific jobs that they assigned to them, according to the occasion."

To finish his history, Juan explained:

"To assure the survival of their race they join with men, but the women keep the girls. They have the peculiar tradition of cutting one breast, with the purpose of facilitating the use of the bow and arrow and the handling of the lance. The men take care of the boys in addition to guarding the treasures."

After this story and the discovery of the tombs and the old city, Chepe was quite sure that they would find on their way these frightful and charming Amazon women; it was just a matter of time. After many hours of traveling they arrived at a small city of straw huts; the natives who lived there were quite friendly. The guides suggested spending the night there to rest, to get new provisions for the days ahead and to take advantage of the opportunity and hospitality offered by the natives. This they agreed to do.

Early the next morning, Chepe woke up his companions in order to resume the trip, after obtaining the food and supplies they needed. The morning was fresh and the dew evaporated, turning into a dense fog that covered the grounds and the forest giving it a mysterious appearance. In spite of these circumstances, Chepe and his friends continued advancing towards the mountains. The climate conditions were turning more and more difficult. Juan had gone ahead a little way since Chepe was now moving slowly, examining the ground, trying to look for new indications or tracks of the Amazon women. Suddenly, one of the guides gave a shout alerting the others to come immediately.

"Look there! We have found what we were looking for!" he said, "Look!" he repeated, pointing towards the trees where they discovered the shadows of several women who fled in the opposite direction.

All of them started a quick race after them, trying not to loose them, but the women disappeared quickly into the thick forest.

As they arrived at the place where they had seen them for the last time, Chepe wanted to warn his companions of the imminent danger, but they had already disappeared into the forest. Seconds later he heard a scream of distress. His three friends had been caught in a trap. The surprise was so great that at the first moment he did not know that to do. It was obvious that his friends needed help, but he would have to think quickly about an effective plan to rescue them.

"Could it be that they were hunting here? Or could this be a plan to catch the intruders?" Chepe asked himself.

"I believe that they do not even know who we are. Perhaps they are only looking to defend their territory from unwanted visitors," Chepe continued thinking, as a thought of self consolation.

"That is a possibility and it would not be uncommon for these legendary women. I hope that my companions are still alive when I come up with a plan to rescue them".

Immediately afterwards, he proceeded to examine the ground and the surroundings where he saw his friends for the last time, but he did not find any sign of struggle on the part of his friends. Then, he went in the direction in which he had heard their voices when they were taken away. The area began to grow dark and the stars and the moon came out slowly announcing that soon it would be night. Chepe arrived at a small brook that went in the same direction of an old trail. At its borders grew some wild shrubs, grass and flowers, that seemed to lead to a garden.

"Finally! Here are the tracks I am I looking for," though Chepe, as he discovered the tracks that continued up the river.

"This is the path that the Amazon women followed, after capturing my friends," Chepe said to himself with hope and optimism.

But apparently the enemy moved quickly, because after three hours of walking and running through the dark jungle barely illuminated by the light of the moon, he had not been able to locate any sign that would indicate the proximity of his friends. So he decided to rest that night to recover his energies and to be able to continue the search of his friends the following day.

The fresh breeze of the dawn that blew on his face woke him up with renewed energies. After some time in the new trail, he saw in the distance through the trees, languid lights that could be a sign of an inhabited place. Minutes later those signs disappeared under the new sun light. Before him was a quiet scenery, a world full of mystery. As he observed the shadows of the jungle before him, he noticed that the forest was awaking up with new and magnificent colors: the green gushed forth in different shades on the high trees and the prairies; a white fog formed a thin layer over the water of the brook. In the distance, under a blue and purple sky, the snow crowned peaks of the Andean mountains could be seen shining for the first time. Chepe stopped a little while to contemplate the extraordinary spectacle offered by these mountains, conscious that that would be the final destination of his adventure. Looking away in the opposite direction, he tried to find in the forest a path that would lead him to the place where his cousin and the two guides had been taken.

"At the right time I will have a chance to go there, to the western mountains, in search of the mysterious kingdom of *El Dorado*. For the moment, I must concentrate all my efforts into rescuing my companions, safe and sound," Chepe said to himself.

He followed a trail into the thick forest, which descended smoothly following the brook. At a short distance before him appeared a green plain that extended towards the south, until it disappeared again into the jungle.

In the blue firmament, for the first time before his eyes was the condor of the Andes. It flew very high, and quickly one moved away to return to mountains, becoming a small undetermined point in the infinite sky.

Chepe, looking over the green plain discovered something moving in the distance. Seconds later, when paying more closed attention, he could distinguish what seemed to be a group of people traveling on foot. But they were too far away, at least a kilometer, although it was very difficult to say with certainty due to the rolling hills and the great number of trees on the way. He tried to find a shortcut to reach the group of people more quickly because he hoped that they could give him some clues as to the whereabouts of his missing friends.

"I believe that the fastest way will be through the plain," though Chepe, accelerating his pace under the exhausting noon sun.

But he could not reach them. It was as if the strangers had disappeared under the shadow of the forest. The tracks guided him towards the south, ending in a depression formed by the many years of passage of a small stream that then descended towards the forest on the other side of the plain.

CHAPTER 26

By the gorge, in the middle of the meadow, a footpath descended among aquatic plants towards the other side of the woods; Chepe could hear how little by little the water moved away murmuring through the tunnels covered by the vegetation. It seemed as if it had left the fresh air in the plains. Here, in the forest, the air was sweeter, humid, slightly scented by the flowers, as if the spring had awakened to greet the new visitor. Chepe stopped; he took a deep breath, as if trying to read a message in the air of the mysterious forest.

"Ah... the scent of spring! It is better than many hours of rest to get new energies" he said aloud, filling his lungs time and time again with that enchanting and refreshing air. When noticing fresh tracks on the meadow, he left running along the footpath that went towards the south. Suddenly he stopped excited; he went towards the right, moving away from the first trail to examine closely the new trail which went in a different direction. There were tracks of boots similar to the ones wore by his cousin. He was very sure that they were those of Juan; he was perhaps trying to escape. However, just ahead those tracks mixed again with the tracks of his captors. The tracks vanished again in the grass.

"The tracks I saw are very clear. Yes, I have no doubt that they are those of my friends," said Chepe, to himself.

In the meadow he also found a piece of wrinkled paper apparently left by Juan.

"This was not left here by chance. It must be a clue,"

Chepe thought. "I believe that Juan managed to leave his enemies momentarily for this purpose. Good, now at least I know that they are alive. These are very good indications; it means that my search has not been in vain. I must go forward".

Small clouds, under a blue sky, pushed by the breeze of the afternoon provided a fleeting shade to the forest. It was two or the three in the afternoon when he began to descend slowly along the trail. The sun disappeared hours later; the dark of the night soon prevailed bringing with it all of its mystery.

The captives must have been far ahead, on the way to the south. There were no more signs of them in the extensive forest. Chepe stopped very exhausted since he had not rested all day and still there was a long journey waiting ahead of him.

He had before him a difficult dilemma: to rest tonight and to risk that the distance became greater or to follow ahead as his energy allowed him. Unless the enemies also had decided to rest, otherwise he would be left way behind, although he supposed that even the Amazon women would need to rest.

"If I stop to sleep" he thought, "I will be left far behind, but if I follow them at night, I will not be able to find their tracks in the dark to follow them. Perhaps I can follow the tracks in the dark but if I loose them, when the daylight comes back again it will be difficult to find them again. Even more, only by daylight I will be able to see the tracks clearly, if the prisoners would try to escape".

"For now I must rest a little to be able to continue" Chepe said finally. "Yes, I need to rest and it is good to do it during the night, because I cannot run the risk of losing the tracks; that would be a very serious mistake… If the moon illuminates sufficiently, I could take advantage of it to follow the trail, but even if it did, I do not believe the moon light would reach the ground through these thick forest".

He prepared his hammock and lay down on it; he was so exhausted, he immediately fell into a deep sleep. The following day he awoke before the sun appeared in the sky. Once standing up, Chepe looked towards the south but still the dark surrounded the background. Trying to devise a rescue plan, he said aloud, as if somebody could hear him:

"I believe that they must be already very far. Something tells me that they have not rested during the night. Now only an eagle could reach them. An eagle!" he repeated, remembering the condor he had seen the day before. "If one of these creatures could help me... I must follow them anyway. I must start off immediately; the tracks are still fresh..."

Chepe laid down on the ground placing his ear closed to the ground. He remained in that position for a few moments trying to perceive any signs of movement, but it was useless. Thus the second day of the search began. During the long day of his journey through the dense jungle, he only made brief pauses to rest. The day was long and debilitating; sometimes he walked, other times he ran; he even had to climb over large tree trunks that lay across his path.

This way he crossed part of an extensive and solitary forested area with its gigantic trees and threatening dangers. Neither the burning noon sun, nor the humidity of these places, nor the difficulties of the way seemed to discourage him, because the single thought of the his friend's uncertain situation, made him recover all his energies, allowing him to continue, almost without rest, following the tracks that went towards the south, going deeper and deeper into the dense forest.

At the end of the day he arrived at a place with many fallen trees; enormous trunks covered the ground, consequently the sign of the Amazon women was made more blurred and difficult to follow. Chepe was astonished as he could not find any sign of people or animals; everything was calm. This silence was not normal in the forest that now was hiding behind a dense fog. The humidity made the air dense and difficult to breathe. Although the moon shone in the stormy and partially cloudy sky, its light did not to penetrate the ceiling formed by the foliage of the high trees. These circumstances, would allow him to rest a few hours, or at least take a break from his arduous trip.

"I feel very tired" thought Chepe, looking back at the way he had come in search of his companions, and immediately he decided to spend the night there.

There was something strange in this region; the roars of the wild jaguars were heard and the terrified whine of the nocturnal birds; the frogs in the marshes croaked in an off key concert. The stars shone weakly at the time that the moon hid behind clouds. Since he was so exhausted, he decided to ignore all these noises and in a moment he fell into a deep sleep.

At the dawn of the following day, the fresh and humid air woke him up. He turned over in his hammock and looking at the morning sun that shone in the horizon with red and yellow tones, he rose up with a jump and immediately he got on the way. He had decided that this was the day to find his friends; this very day. He was very sure that little by little he had approached the place to which they had been taken.

It was about an hour before noon, when he saw at the distance the shadows of a city almost hidden among the tall green trees. He stopped for a few moments to study the details of those structures but it was difficult to identify them and to define exactly what they were.

Now, in front of him, extended a long strip of land flooded by the rains, great and heavy vines hung around the trees in this marshy area. Chepe looked around examining the ground looking for some sign that would indicate the path to follow. He sat down to rest awhile while he thought about a plan to follow the rest of the day. Suddenly he saw recent tracks on the ground, very easy to distinguish. This seemed quite suspicious to him and seemed to indicate that the captors were not trying to hide their tracks, but were leaving this evidence on purpose so that he could follow them.

The only thing he could see was trees, marshes and fog. The sun light at noon could not penetrate sufficiently through the dense foliage of the trees; therefore the path was a little dark. Chepe had walked many hours without taking any rest, but his firm determination to find the whereabouts of Juan and his companions grew stronger as the day went by. He considered himself a young and strong fellow for the task at hand but now he was completely alone. This distressing search had started to take a toll on him; he had to march in silence, bending down from time to time in order not to lose the tracks on the ground. With time the way became more and more difficult; everything was gray and dark due to the dense fog that had begun to cover the surroundings. For the first time he felt the penetrating and bitter cold of the dense jungle, but he had to continue the trail with the hope of finding his friends as soon as possible.

Suddenly, as if a large curtain had been opened before his eyes, the city whose lights he had seen hours before in the horizon appeared before him. The evening sun shone on the city giving it a yellow tone, like that of gold. It was built of stone, the same as the wall built around it.

This fort was built in the center of a clear area in the middle of the forest in an excellent strategic position. It was an architectural wonder built by the Amazon women with surprising engineering talent. The main defense of this city was the stone wall that protected it all the way around. In the front it had an enormous iron door as the only exit and entrance for its inhabitants. In the center of the city there was a tower more than twenty meters high that served as a lookout position to protect themselves from possible intruders. It had been designed to resist all kinds of enemies; it was practically invulnerable. So powerful was its defense, that until now it had survived all kinds of invasions and had been able to remain invulnerable.

Chepe moved discretely towards the door trying to find how to enter without being discovered. Suddenly, he saw among the trees some shadows that moved with great agility. He quickly laid down on the ground and listened carefully, but nothing else happened. He thought that it would be prudent to wait a few minutes before proceeding. He knelt down and waited. An absolute silence ruled the surroundings; only the noise of the branches and the leaves of the trees that moved with the soft wind could be heard. Suddenly three women armed with spears and ready to use them, surrounded him.

"I cannot escape" Chepe thought, "I am tired and the search no longer makes sense, now they are the ones who have found me. At least now I will be able to see my companions," he kept thinking with certain resignation, trying to see the positive side of this situation. "Hopefully they are in good conditions".

The three women made signs to him to walk in the direction of the city entrance. Chepe obeyed and moved slowly in the direction they indicated. The slight breeze of the forest seemed to have calmed his nerves; in spite of being in such a difficult situation, he was relatively calm. The future was now uncertain for him and for his friends who presumably were captives within that fort.

The path that led to the entrance was made of stones, similar to those of the old colonial times. The doors and the walls similar to the medieval castles, revealing perhaps this way the time at which this city was built. Although the doors were very large and heavy, they opened quite easily.

The external walls were surrounded by a deep ditch full of water, with voracious piranhas that would devour any intruder who dared to approach the fort. Of this were the silent witness the human skeletons and the skeletons of some unfortunate wild animals that had accidentally fallen there.

The bridge that allowed access to the city was lowered to receive the new guest as the doors were opened. Opposite the door at the city center was the high tower from where several women watched over the fort for any uninvited visitors. Without introduction or any special reception, Chepe was taken with great haste to the royal palace, which was guarded by two warrior women equipped with their conventional weapons: the spear, the bow and the arrows.

At a sign of the three women who accompanied him, the guards opened the doors allowing them entrance. After crossing the first room they arrived at a hall with high walls, at the end of which there was a throne, and in it a beautiful woman, presumably the queen of the Amazons. In front of her, resting in the floor in a bed was a small girl, of about two or three years, apparently in a deep sleep. At each sides of the throne were standing two guards ready to defend their leader. On the right hand was another woman standing ready to serve the queen.

The queen addressing Chepe with a firm voice said:
"Welcome to this place. Your friends are well."

These rough and brief words, gave him the certainty of the well-being of his cousin and his guides, which was the only thing that concerned him at this moment. Then the queen continued:

"We are sorry about any inconvenience we may have caused to you... That was not our intention; I need your help and the easiest way to bring you here was through your friends. Recently, we have heard much about your powers and for this reason we have wanted to bring you to this place..."

Having said this, she asked the guards to leave the room, but there was certain hesitation, as if they did not understand her request.

"Everyone, get out now!" the queen again ordered her guards.

All left the room with certain displeasure leaving only the queen and the little girl sleeping next to the throne.

Then the queen turned to Chepe and said:

"I had lived in much tranquility, enjoying great prosperity in this place. But one night, as I lay down with my only and beloved daughter, an unexpected illness came upon her affecting her in such a way, that now she is like dead. I have looked all over for anyone who could heal her and give life back to her, but everything has been in vain. I issued an order to bring me all the magicians, the healers, wizards and fortune tellers from this area of the jungle, but none could do anything for her.

"My daughter dies!" she said with her eyes full of tears.

Kneeling down in front of the little girl who remained immovable in the bed, not being able to control herself, she cried bitterly over her daughter, caressing her face and asking her in vain to wake up. Tears kept rolling over the beautiful cheeks of the queen. The atmosphere was full of sadness, sorrow and pain.

"You are my life and the reason of my being!" said the queen to her little one with a broken heart and tears of great sorrow. After a few moments of quiet mourning, the distressed mother arose with the little girl in her arms and placed her on a blanket in front of Chepe. On her knees she pleaded with him to help her; to return life to her adored daughter. Chepe observed her with compassion for a brief moment, searching for the right words to say in such a delicate situation.

"There is no wizard, neither fortune teller, nor magician, nor astrologer, who can heal your daughter and give her life back as you wish" Chepe assured her. "But a mighty King exists, who has the power to give life and to take it away; His are the wisdom and the power. It is He who gives wisdom to the wise and intelligence to the intelligent ones."

After a short pause he continued:

"The greatness of the Amazon women has reached great reputation in this region and its dominion has extended over a large part of the jungle. But now it has been permitted that this illness fall upon your daughter, to give you the opportunity to know that the King and Lord has power over all mankind. He is the only one who has the power over all humanity, to give life and to take it way" repeated Chepe with firmness.

Immediately, he knelt down in front of the little girl and remained looking at her tenderly for a few moments.

"I know that you have the power to heal her" said the afflicted mother.

"The power belongs to the King" answered Chepe, placing his hand softly over the languid body that remained rigid, barely with any signs of life.

Not waiting any longer, he gave one last look of

compassion to the grieving mother and pulling out his sword and holding it on his left had, he placed a few drops of the water from the fountain of youth on his right hand; immediately he placed it on the forehead of the little one, then on her mouth to moisten her dry lips. Her eyes opened immediately as if she were awaking up from a deep sleep. Her eyes were green, just as those of her mother; they sparkled like beautiful emeralds. Her cheeks now had a reddish color; she was full of life once again.

She greeted Chepe with a broad and innocent smile; he raised her from the blanket where her mom had placed her moments before and placed her on her mother's arms with much joy. The queen picked her up with tears of joy and much happiness. Looking at her with incredulity she held her fast against her chest to feel her new life, to make sure that this was real, that she was not a dreaming...

"Mom!" said the little girl drying her mom's tears with the palms of her hands. "Mom, please do not cry, I am well" she said trying to convince her mom that everything was normal again. The two of them joined together in a long-drawn-out hug, crying for joy.

Chepe, not wanting to interrupt this touching and transcendental moment of happiness, moved towards the door to leave, but the queen still holding her daughter in her arms, stopped him and kneeling down before him, she said:

"Thank you...! Thank you very much! I would like to pay you! All my treasures are yours for what you have done!"

Chepe took her by the hand and asked her to get up as he bowed down to her as a sign of respect.

"The honor and power belong to the King..." Chepe reminded her.

He fixed his glance on the little girl with a smile of satisfaction for a brief moment. Looking now in perfect health, she looked back at him with a sweet smile. Once again Chepe bowed briefly to the queen as he left the room; he exited through the large door to the outside patio. Once there he lifted his eyes to the sky murmuring a few words of gratefulness.

It had been a long day, filled with many surprises. He knew that his friends were free from danger, but he did not know yet when he could get together with them again.

Now he felt the immeasurable and rewarding satisfaction of having had the opportunity to carry out a pious act in favor of his fellow human beings.

He looked around for a long time. For the first time he had a chance to survey and to get acquainted with that place.

CHAPTER 27

Most of the homes were inside the perimeter of the city. At the right hand side of the lookout tower was a large structure, similar to a castle. Great parts of the ground were covered with stones. A small area of it was designated to grow a variety of flowers and medicinal plants.

On each side of the main door of the castle there were two other doors. All of them were decorated with gold in the upper part. The large columns standing next to the doors, were round and crowned with designs of Greek style.

Chepe stopped half way to study in more detail this new place, astonished by its architectural features, so different from other places he had known during his journey through the jungle. The women who guarded him also stopped to give him time to become familiar with the surroundings.

Returning his glance towards the guards, who remained at his side, he noticed their distinctive physical features for the first time. They were really beautiful and charming. Their green and shining eyes, like emeralds, were the most attractive feature of their faces. The brown complexion and the long hair of brown color made perfect harmony with their slender bodies. Their upper body was covered with leather blouses that revealed their sensual, round and firm breasts. Around their waist hung a smooth leather skirt of brown color that covered their legs half way. Their appearance was hard, warrior like, but sensual. Their captivating and seductive eyes were fixed on him.

After a few minutes a large number of women had gathered around to take a look at the new visitor with much curiosity. As they were all together, Chepe discovered a

The Power Of The Relic

very interesting detail. They were all very similar in physical appearance. It was quite amazing; the only difference was in their stature. Quite opposite to the legend, they all had two round, prominent, firm breasts. In regard to their physical conditioning as women warriors, they were truly fearsome; of agile and flexible body and, trained with an iron discipline, just as they were famous for in the legends.

The dusk had begun to hide the forest and the sun disappeared on the horizon while the city was illuminated with tenuous lights of torches placed in strategic places in the city walls and on the outer walls of their houses. The light from the stars shining in the sky emphasized the beautiful and slender figures of the women guards who led him in the direction of a building located by the city wall.

Interrupting Chepe's thoughts, the leader of the guards said:

"Now we are going to have supper and then you can retire to rest; you have had a long day." The first room was designed and furnished to provide rest or to entertain visitors, which probably did not happened often in this place. The wood furniture was simple but it indicating their good taste in crafts and objects of decoration. In center was a large chair with gold ornaments indicating the importance of the person for whom it was designated.

"Looks like a throne" thought Chepe.

In front of it, forming a semicircle, there were ten chairs distributed around the hall, other furniture that was used for multiple purposes, with tables and armchairs to rest.

The following hall, to the left, was the formal dining room, with a long table, and high and comfortable chairs. The one located at the head of the table was also decorated with fine gold plated ornaments indicating to be the place for a high ranking leader. In the center of the table were a large vase and several cups of bronze.

"Let's get some refreshments and then you can take a good night's rest," the leader of the guards said, as she invited Chepe to sit down on the chair placed at opposite end of the table. The other two women took their seat on each side of the table. A few moments later they were served drinks. Taking their respective glasses they looked at each other, tasted their drink and then invited Chepe to do the same. Chepe took the glass to his lips, took a small swallow and savored it for a few moments trying to identify what it was but could not recognize its flavor. It was similar to the guanábana juice that he liked so much but, definitively was not the same. In any case, it seemed delicious, nutritious and refreshing; in a few seconds he finished the whole glass. He noticed immediately the wonderful effect this drink had produced on him. He felt renewed, with much energy and totally recovered from the long day.

"Good, now you can rest; we will see you tomorrow," said the leader in a friendly tone.

Immediately afterwards she led him to one of the rooms next to the city wall.

As soon as he was alone, he got into his bed which was smooth and comfortable mattress with soft covers. It had been a very long time since he had enjoyed this pleasure. The bed was clean, fresh and slightly scented with perfume with the gentle touch of feminine hands. The lights were extinguished and the city disappeared moments later in the darkness of the night, being left only a shade of light in the trees that vanished in the middle of the jungle.

The sky was clear the next day when Chepe woke up. Only a few clouds moved slowly across the sky, dragged by a smooth breeze that refreshed the atmosphere as the sun shone on the patio paved with stones; he could not see anyone in the surroundings. As he got himself ready for the new day, a woman arrived whose face was quite familiar; indeed, it was the same one who had welcomed him the previous day; she came to greet him:

"Good morning" she said in a dry and serious tone.

"Good morning" Chepe responded with a cheerful and friendly tone.

However, his attitude did not produce any effect on the woman, whose expression was a mixture of timidity and ferocity. They left the room and she indicated to him a sign to follow her. They went out, made a left and then crossed the patio paved with stones, walking across through it with long strides in the direction of the castle. At the end of the pavement, Chepe could see a great variety of fruit trees that were part of an extensive orchard and a garden of vegetables that were used for their food.

At the other side of the city wall there was a forest of shrubs and behind these, forming a natural wall were trees of extraordinarily height, as he had never seen before. Now he could understand how it could be possible that this city was never found before.

Suddenly the woman stopped in front of the castle and signaled to follow her through an alley that led to an extensive patio located in the back of the castle. At the opposite end of the patio was a large group of women getting ready for their routine morning exercise but there appeared to be no leader among them. They began with a few minutes of warm up exercises and then began to run on site as a military unit. At the same time they sang something in unison. All of them made the same movements simultaneously with an amazing precision, demonstrating the strict discipline with which they had been trained. Later they took the spears to use for target practice, which they did on a wood board with concentric circles, hanging from the stone wall. Immediately afterwards they came to practice with their bow and arrow using the same target. Their accuracy with both weapons was extraordinary. As in all the previous exercises, the rigor and the agility on execution was perfect, especially considering that no one in the group appeared to be a visible leader. It was as if enjoying a perfect symphony orchestra executing a musical composition without the presence of a director.

After having enjoyed this wonderful spectacle, Chepe and his guide turned towards the left, to continue through a wide alley which bordered the city wall; after a short walk they arrived at a narrow entrance that led to an underground large and square room. The interior was decorated with diverse samples of military weapons belonging to their past civilizations. The entrance to the following room was protected by a heavy metal door with several locks. The guide who had not said a word, with attitude of confidence and serenity proceeded to open it. It was total darkness inside; she proceeded to light up a pair of torches located on the wall. The room was illuminated revealing an incredible wealth that Chepe could not imagine could exist. Suddenly, he was surrounded by hundreds and hundreds of gold objects, brilliant emeralds, masks, pectorals, hangers, batons of command, nose pieces, a great number of shining pieces that with their brightness made it hard on his eyes. This was a place of wealth only known previously as a legend; the materialization of the dream of the Spanish conquistadores.

Finally Chepe could understand the reasoning of those ambitious travelers, as he had before his own eyes the fabulous treasures that the conquistadores searched for such a long time. The golden jewels and the relics offered a spectacle of such magnitude under the flickering light of the torches. It was impossible to describe it. It gave the sense of being in the presence of ancient ceremonies of their ancestors.

He continued looking around at every detail, not being able to hide his curiosity and with great astonishment he discovered that there they also kept human military trophies. Hanging on the walls he found several severed heads, perhaps those of the rulers of their enemies; these gave a macabre, gruesome and sinister aspect to the place.

Chepe stopped for a little while trying to understand the conflicting sense of that place of incalculable wealth, surrounded by death. He fixed his glance for a brief moment on the woman who had been his guide and companion for the day, without saying a word; then he went to the door as a clear sign that he wished to leave the room as soon as possible.

Luckily, after such experience, Chepe had the opportunity to finally meet again with his cousin Juan and his native guides. It was a joyous reunion; the encounter was exciting and refreshing for everyone but as soon as they had spent a few minutes together, they were led to the main castle where a delicious dinner was offered to them. It was specially prepared for them who now were considered guests of honor. Late into the night there was a special celebration as a tribute to such worthy guests. In spite of the rigid, warrior like and highly disciplined character, at the time of festivities the attitude of the Amazon women was totally different. The time of celebration appeared to turn them into happy women, very pleasant, amusing and quite entertaining. The celebration went on well past midnight, enjoying the music, the dancing and enjoying the delicious drinks, fruits and a great variety food.

The young travelers were quite fascinated with the mysterious culture of the Amazon women. They wanted to take advantage of the time that they had left to learn more about this interesting civilization. After the time of celebration, they were allowed to move with more freedom without the constant monitoring of the leader.

"It seems that this civilization flourished in the jungles to the south of the Amazon River" said Juan, as they walked through the stone alleys of the city.

"It appears that they came from the Mediterranean, but until today their origin continues to be a hard to decipher mystery. They believe in the existence of a mythical figure, a woman who is considered as their goddess who when coming to these lands settled in the basin of the Amazon River. She was the one who founded this city, the center of this secret Amazonian kingdom. In order to please their gods" continued Juan, "the Amazon women established a cult through various rituals. One of them was a human sacrifice; through these sacrifices they communicated with their deity assuring this way the continuation of life for their civilization. Such sacrifices were reserved mostly for the military captives who were offered to their gods as an offering of gratefulness for their help in the battlefields."

"The heads of their greatest enemies remain well preserved by means of a technique not yet known until now," added Chepe.

This city preserves good examples of Mediterranean architecture proper of the ancient civilization of the Amazon women. The fort that protects the city was a sacred space, strategically built in the middle of the jungle. It constituted a true military fortress as witnessed by the abundant treasures and human trophies that were contained therein. The palace of this kingdom hid on the third patio behind the lookout tower. Nearby was also the room that contained the treasures and trophies acquired in the wars.

In the central square, stood the magnificent palace, built of stone, fine wood, gold and other ornaments in addition to precious gems indicating the wealth of this civilization. Its complexity was pronounced in the variety of elements that confirmed it: runners, underground galleries, patios, and walls with unknown inscriptions. The square based tower stood out over the city. The palace on the other hand was the main residence of the queen and her assistants. The majesty of the temple dominated the main square.

This city with its extensive perimeter was the prototype of a lost legendary civilization in the jungle, a splendid scene in the middle of the green forest that covers it and protects it. In order to build it, the amazons took advantage of the natural uniqueness, wealth and character that this magnificent hidden forested land had to offer.

In the main patio, in addition to the field for military practice, there were small sets of buildings; some seem to have been palaces or mansions for distinguished people. In many of these buildings were still present thresholds in the upper part of the walls, a clear evidence of the historical greatness of this people. Chepe and Juan were truly pleased for the opportunity to be there, for the privilege of having found the legendary and fearsome Amazon women.

The next day they got up early after a long and refreshing rest; the women were outside already busy with their routine morning activities. After awhile some delicious fruits were brought to their room and soon afterwards they were taken to the dinning room where a table was served for four people. After finishing breakfast they got up, ready to leave. The queen who had come to send them off said to them:

"Hopefully you will not suffer any hunger during your journey. I know your provisions are small, so I have given orders to prepare your luggage with appropriate provisions for travelers like you; you will lack nothing while you travel through the jungle. I must tell you something else: for the last several days, my warriors and explorers have observed some extraordinary and peculiar objects flying through the skies and have reported the presence of strange beings near the Andes. The sound of the wild is no longer normal. It is as if the wild animals have a presentiment that something unexpected is about to happen. An expectant silence weight over this enigmatic forest and we do not know what it means, but everything seems to indicate that something extraordinary is going to happen. It is as if a great storm is going to take place" concluded the queen.

But then, as if she had forgotten something of high importance she added:

"Come with me. I have prepared something special for you as a token of appreciation which I am sure you are going to need in your long journey."

She took them to a small room, close to the castle where a woman gave them four wool ponchos, some cords and other useful items for the journey ahead.

"I do not want to offer you anything else because your expedition through the mountains is difficult and you must travel light," said the queen.

"I hope that all these things will contribute to the success of your mission. I trust that in the future we will have the opportunity to meet again" exclaimed the queen.

Chepe placed his hand on his jaw thinking in silence for a few moments without saying a word, as if trying to draw up a plan...

"Let's move quickly, there is no time that to lose!" he ordered his companions.

"If you are ready we must start off immediately. In a moment the sun will rise over the forest."

"I would like to have more appropriate presents for the moment of your departure" repeated the queen, at the moment at which they brought their belongings and provisions, "but please accept this small golden blowpipe as a token of our friendship. It could be useful as you step into the enemy's territory. Sometimes the Amazon warriors use them during emergencies. They are made with great mastery and refinement by our best workmanship."

When they were ready to leave, Chepe and his friends bowed to the queen as a sign of respect and in a thankful attitude.

"It was a very positive experience" Chepe said to Juan minutes after they started their new journey.

"I never imagined an encounter as unexpected as this one, to have had the opportunity to establish friendship with a legend… with the legendary Amazon women. It is something absolutely beyond words!" added Chepe.

Back in the impenetrable atmosphere of the dense forest and having left the City of the Amazons, they felt the pure and calm air of the jungle once more. During several hours they walked towards the mountains. They were again in the forest; under the protection of the thick gigantic trees. Through the high branches they could see the sun light on the west, over the imposing mountain range of the Andes. It seemed as if the world ended there. "We must continue on a straight line as much as possible; this way we will be under the protection of the forest for several days and our expedition to the west, our final destination will be shorter," explained Chepe. "But, we must be prepared to ascend through the difficult and steep lands that will take us to the high, impenetrable and yet unexplored mountains.

"In the beginning of our trip, we can walk in the light of the day, but once we are at the foot of the mountain range, everything will be different. We must proceed with much caution; in addition, it is fundamental that we keep to ourselves the objective of our mission."

CHAPTER 28

The path towards the mountains lay right in front of them; long and difficult. The white peaks of high summits of the Andes appeared in the distance from time to time indicating to them that the distance was still quite long. The fog that made its appearance again was scattered once more over the forest, separating them from their previous adventure like a mysterious curtain. The sky in front of them was clear and a full moon appeared in the west in spite of the light of the day; the shade of the high trees extended behind them as black shadows.

They arrived at a thick forest next to the river that came down from the direction of the mountains. The guides walked at the front, very slowly because the path was quite winding. Here the forests grew thicker bordering the river in two long rows from north to south. The trail disappeared among the trees and it was very difficult to follow it, but at the borders of the waters there were short trails much easier to find and easier to walk through depressions and narrow gorges.

The four companions walked well into the night finally arriving at a clear area next to the river. There they decided to spend the night. They woke up in the very early hours of the cold, quiet and humid morning. The moon had disappeared and the last stars sparkled timidly in a blue and reddish sky. The first light of the day had still not shown over the high trees that they had left behind.

Chepe got up trying to reorganize his thoughts about the purpose of his trip.

"Let's march to the west!" Chepe announced to his companions who were still trying to wake up. The river in front of them ran zigzagging through a stony channel among the trees; its cold waters indicated the proximity to the mountains from where it came. The condor of the Andes flew in silence through the clear blue sky as if it was studying the vast forest, which from those heights appeared as an extensive plain.

"The condor is the noblest of all the birds of the Andes," said Juan with his glance fixed on the blue sky, following with his glance the movements of the majestic bird. "It is a bird of indomitable spirit; it has lived in these mountains for thousands of years, where it nests in the inaccessible mountain tops. It is famous for its exploits as an expert hunter from the air. Their speed and ferocity are subtler and more accurate than those of the quickest wind. The old settlers of these lands fear it and they reverence it for the power, the grace and the magic that this majestic bird seems to have."

The four friends followed the trail during several hours in the direction to the west. The guides who went far enough in front of Chepe and Juan, searched for a safe place to cross the river between the gorges and the trees that covered its borders. Suddenly one of them gave out a cry as a sign of danger; the two cousins ran immediately towards them.

"Here is a new surprise! Look!" said, one of the guides showing the corpses of two natives.

They had been struck in a cruel manner but they did not show any signs of blood over their wounds or on the ground.

"What kinds of people have been in these places?" asked Juan. He was very sure that this atrocity could not have been committed by people from that place.

"It is not possible," answered one of guides, "we are still quite far from any towns. It could be possible that some men were here hunting and they found these unfortunate ones."

"I think the enemy is close" affirmed Chepe, "These are clear signs of their methods."

He examined the surroundings without finding tracks or any signs of struggle or anything else that may have offered clues as to who had perpetrated such a despicable and repugnant crime. After a few moments they continued forward. The sun disappeared in the west growing pale in the evening; the stars appeared with a lethargic light which grew slowly accompanying the moon that appeared on the horizon.

Going towards the south they arrived at a gorge where a narrow path allowed them to go by the river. On both sides of the trail there were shrubs and tall grass that served as food to the deer and other wild animals in these places. They spent the night there.

When waking up they discovered over the forest the high mountains emphasized by the morning light that shone like silver on the high summits of the Andes. The red disc of the morning sun rose over the trees in the east. Before them a new world extended, quiet and enchanting. While they experienced the light of the new day and the lively singing of the birds of the forest giving them a cheerful welcome, this enigmatic land woke up, filled with beautiful colors that once again covered the forests of the Amazonian jungle. The white fog rested over the river waters that moved slowly across the wide valley and at the distance the mountains stood high with their summits covered with permanent snow caps. It was a magnificent and delightful spectacle.

"Let's get going!" said Chepe turning his glance from the magnificent forests and looking to the west, searching for the path they were to follow.

The path they followed ascended gradually before them towards Andean mountains that extended before them like a silent and unconquerable giant on the horizon.

"Look," said Juan pointing towards the blue sky "it is the condor again, there! It flies very high. It seems like it is guarding the mountains. I wonder if it is the same condor we saw before, or if they are taking turns to watch over these extensive lands!"

Then Juan continued:

"The condor of the Andes is considered the largest bird in the world weighing up to more than one hundred pounds, their extended wings measure up to three meters from end to end. It is a symbol of power and health for the people of these areas. It lives in the rocky cliffs where it finds protection for its eggs and their young when reproducing every two years. It can live up to fifty years and it prefers to fly in areas of opened fields which allow him to find its prey with greater ease.

"Its habitat extends over the Andes, from Venezuela to Tierra del Fuego in the extreme end of South America. Although it is still possible to find it almost anywhere within these regions, its population has diminished greatly, putting it in the list of the endangered species. Today its home is limited mainly to some regions of Peru, and the north part of Colombia."

"This bird depends on its acute vision to find its food" continued Juan. "People say that it crosses hundreds of kilometers flying at high altitude as it looks for its food. It is almost impossible to follow him with the naked eye to determine its flying routes. His body is covered by delicate feathers with the exception of its head and neck. To conserve energy, this surprising animal allows its temperature to fall during the night, raising it again during the day when it opens its wings for this purpose and to straighten its feathers which tend to bend due to its long flights. It depends on the hot air currents to glide during its long trips. He lacks a larynx and for that reason it does not emit any sounds like other birds. The female has red and shiny eyes, and does not have the fleshy crest as the male does."

When Juan was finished, everyone looked up in the air. The majestic Condor could still be seen at the distance, moving away in the horizon, floating graciously on top of the Andes.

"We must find a route that will take us to mountains as fast as possible. I do not believe that we will find a way faster than the one following the river" said Juan.

So they continued the path that followed the river towards the mountain; they were now walking by the clear light of the day. The path took them to the west through the river bed, and finally they arrived at a steep ascent to the mountain next to a stream that descended noisily through the mountain slopes. By the narrow gorge a rough path ascended to the steep mountain like a soaring set of stairs. At the summit they found themselves suddenly walking on the meadows of a green and smooth turf, like a carpet.

The stream disappeared in the middle of a field of shrubs and green plants covered with flowers. Everyone could enjoy the happy murmur of waters as they slid by rocks, descending quickly towards the planes of the forest below. Here the air was colder and slightly perfumed, as if the spring was in its fullness. Chepe breathed deeply like trying to absorb and to enjoy all the scent that this offered.

"Ah! The smooth scent of the spring in the mountains! The pleasure it offers is greater than many hours of rest" whispered Chepe as he stopped to observe in the horizon the beautiful and mysterious mountains.

Finally the four friends marched forward in a row, following the path towards their destination with great enthusiasm. Suddenly Chepe gave a signal and stopped at the side of the path. "Just a moment!" he exclaimed, and then he ran quickly to the right, moving away from the main path, because he had seen tracks that went in that direction and then disappeared in the waters of the stream. He bended down and examined the tracks carefully; then he returned to meet with his friends.

"Yes," he said, "it is very clear; the tracks of the enemy disappear in the water without any other marker."

There, Chepe found a small object that shone to the light of the sun, apparently left by the men they were seeking. It seemed like a small and beautiful gold and silver jewel of strange appearance; he passed it on to Juan so that he could examine it.

"It is a magnificent jewel. May I keep it?" asked Juan.

"Yes" responded his cousin, "it is a good souvenir, I believe that our search has not been in vain."

"But we need to keep going, we need to push forward!" said Chepe.

Their purpose now was becoming even more important. The noon sun stood in the middle of the sky shining on the distant mountain tops crowned with permanent ice caps and then descended slowly under some clouds that were dragged by the breeze. Finally the sun was hidden leaving behind large shadows drawing up great figures capriciously extending on the horizon.

There were no longer any signs of the men of blue skin in the mountains now that the night shadows were upon them. Chepe stopped on the way trying to make a good decision. The day had been very long and they had only rested a couple of times throughout the day. Ahead of them was a difficult and steep path through the mountains that still separated them from the City of *El Dorado*, according to the information of his guides.

"Well, we must stop here and spend the night" said Chepe.

"We need a good rest before continuing our trip. It is very cold!" complained Juan.

"The cold wind comes from the snow of the high summits of the Andes" indicated Chepe, "but we must recharge our energies. Tomorrow will be another day."

In spite of the intense cold Chepe and his friends tried to sleep under a magnificent, clear sky filled with stars. They covered themselves with the wool ponchos which had been given to them by the Amazon women; they sang songs and told stories until one by one they fell into a deep sleep. Thus they spent the first night in the mountains.

Early the next morning, all of them enjoyed the spectacular rising of the sun as it ascended slowly in a yellow and reddish sky. The wind blew from the east taking with it some light clouds; the dense forest extended like a green ocean at the feet of the mountains. To the west, they observed the high and magnificent mountains which they had seen days before from the base of the Amazonian forest. Their destination was still a long distance beyond the mountainous slopes that disappeared in the distance. Over on the horizon, as floating on a white cloud, was the silver summit of the majestic mountains that hid the city of *El Dorado*.

The guides led them through a narrow path, among deep precipices, following the tracks that the men of blue skin had left in the way. They walked through rocks, going by many streams of water that came down from the mountains. They followed the trail very carefully until they arrived at a wooded area by the slope of mountains.

Far in the distance, Chepe discovered a few figures that could barely be seen on the mountains. Juan standing up next to Chepe took his hand to his forehead to look carefully at the small silhouettes that moved in the direction of the city. Silence reigned in the lands that surrounded them. The two cousins could hear the air that moved in the shrubs next to the path.

The four companions continued towards the top of the mountain, ascending laboriously by the steep slopes. Shortly before arriving at the border of the hill, they sat down on a grassy area and covered themselves with the wool ponchos. The time went by very slowly while they rested. The cold pierced their bones. Juan and Chepe were not accustomed to this cruel and severe climate but they were very thankful to have at least the warm wool ponchos.

"What do we know about these mountain men?" asked Juan "What kind of unforeseen and unexpected dangers wait for us ahead?"

"I do not know with certainty" responded Chepe. "They are very intelligent and they possess a highly developed technology but they live in an enigmatic world. According to our friend Aram, they came to the New World thousands of years ago, shortly after the time of Noah, and the great universal flood; they are audacious, cruel, intelligent and powerful. It seems that initially they were benevolent and compassionate. Initially they helped and protected to the native Indians. They contributed in the construction of the colossal and majestic monuments like those of the *Islas de la Pascua*, and the extraordinary constructions of the Incas. But later they became an evil race, when they decided to take the wealth from the natives and then to enslave them to establish their own empire. But I do not know what has happened with them lately and what plans they have now, but I suspect that they are not good. Soon we will know for sure; we are already close to them.

Now they all could hear the sound of the cold breeze that blew from the mountains; every passing minute grew colder and more implacable against their bodies. Without saying many words, they resumed the long journey, each time more dangerous and more treacherous through the insurmountable mountains. They traveled this path until the afternoon when they arrived at a plain covered with shrubs and small bushes. This was a good place to rest before continuing the strenuous journey. Chepe and Juan lay down on their backs in the meadow looking towards the blue sky. The guides standing up remained at a short distance, having a premonition of an imminent danger.

"Look! There is the city of the Kuélap Indians, which our guides talked about" exclaimed Juan. "Their great constructions are in inaccessible places in that mountain."

From the place where they stood, they could see it at an apparent short distance in the mountain heights, but it would have taken several hours for them to arrive there. Its main center was located in the high forest, at more than three thousand meters of altitude. The four explorers continued climbing, until they finally reached the legendary, extraordinary and prohibited place. In the city were dispersed archaeological remains in an extensive area from the north to the south. Chepe observed how peculiar was this area covered with dense vegetation. Their rooms were characterized by enormous stone constructions of circular form, decorated with tiles and protective walls. The small village was on a small plateau in the confluence of two streams that descended from the mountain. The architectural remains were made up of twenty structures, in their majority in different circular levels, the same as the stone walls.

Chepe and Juan appreciated an impressive wall of approximately thirty meters in height and about six hundred meters in length around the city.

"The spectacular development of these natives culminated at the time of the conquistadores" said Juan. "Their fall was due not only to the superiority of the weapons of the invaders but also to the epidemics and diseases that they brought along. The natives were totally defenseless against the attacks of both. In the first trip of the conquistadores, one of them fell ill and infected the local population. Like uncontrollable gun powder, it exploded extending all over, showing no mercy to the defenseless natives, with new diseases like smallpox, measles, influenza and many others. The colonizers were immune to these evil diseases which were common in Europe. This was the unfortunate contribution of this new civilization. Towns and whole communities in these mountains disappeared due to the epidemics" concluded Juan.

The travelers again looked around the ruins of that old civilization. They tried to locate the city of *El Dorado* which should be not very far from here, to the south of this plain, just as Aram had indicated. The mountains were covered by a dense fog. Chepe stood there for a long while, as if hoping that by magic, this dense curtain would disappear, but nothing happened. From here-on the trail descended for a long distance and then turned into a steep climb up into the mountains.

CHAPTER 29

Suddenly, as if appearing out of nowhere, out of the bushes came out a large number of Indians equipped with bows and arrows, spears and blowpipes. Chepe and his friends were surrounded. Their strong shouts of war resonated in the hills; the leader approached Chepe with a ferocious appearance on his face, while the noises and the military chanting continued. A long line of quick and well trained men of war followed him. The frightful expression of men of war was in all of them; serious and severe features.

They were of medium stature, strong legs and arms; their black hair as the jet stone shone under the sun. Their skin burned by the cold weather indicated that these men lived in high mountains. The troops surrounded the four friends with their glance fixed on them while they moved incessantly in a rare ritual dance. Chepe got up with an amazing speed and agility while the spears and the arrows were pointed at him; a group of soldiers who moved in a circle approached them closer and closer. Chepe stood still, in silence, firm and with great serenity. The others remained seated and immovable, asking themselves if this would be their end.

Suddenly, to a signal from the leader, the noise and the chanting stopped. A circle of spears and arrows were aimed towards the four companions. The leader, a man of medium stature but taller than the rest, came close to Chepe until the end of his spear touched his chest in a threatening way. Chepe remained immovable and calm.

"Who are you and what are you doing in these lands?" the man asked in a threatening voice.

"My name is Chepe and these are my friends, we come from the north with a special mission; to find the men of blue skin up in these mountains and to destroy or to rescue the relic of the power" responded Chepe.

The man remained looking intently at Chepe, motionless and without any signs of bewilderment. Finally he spoke again.

"At first I thought that you were emissaries of the enemy, but now I am convinced otherwise. You do not know anything about the men of blue skin; otherwise you would not be around here. They would eat you alive!" he added with a ridiculing outburst of laughter which propagated to all the group of Indian warriors.

"The truth is that you do not know anything about these enemies. But I see something very odd and interesting in you;" added with his brown and shiny eyes fixed again on Chepe, "You seem to be part Indian and that gives you cleverness, maliciousness and knowledge not available to white men. But your clothes are unusual and not like ours. Are you of Indian blood?"

"No, only two of us are Indian" answered Chepe, with firmness and great calm pointing to his guides. "We have come through the Amazon jungle through great and many difficulties and now we are in these mountains; the favor and the protection of the King is with us."

The leader looked at them with great astonishment, but then his eyes became hard and inexpressive. With coldness then he approached Juan and the guides, as he said:

"Ummm...! You must also be in sorcery and witchcraft!"

Juan rose up from the meadow. His eyes shone with contained fury while the troops of the natives whispered angrily, closing the circle more and more around them.

"Now tell me: Who do you serve, are you friends or enemies of the men of blue skin?" asked Chepe as he approached the leader.

"We do not serve the men of blue skin but we are not at war with them either because that would be a sure suicide. They are very powerful and have many of ours as slaves. We are always under their threat. Now we only wished to be free and to free our people, which is impossible."

"And who do you serve?" asked the leader.

"Really I do not serve any man," responded Chepe with determination, "but I have a mission from the King: to rescue or to destroy the relic of the power. It is now in the hands of the men of blue skin, who use it with macabre purposes. That is our mission, the one that we will carry out at whatever cost and under any circumstances. For this purpose I have not come disarmed."

Chepe raised his poncho. The sheath shone and the leaf of the sword within it shone with the extraordinary brightness of a diamond.

"This is not an ordinary sword" added Chepe. "With it we will accomplish our mission. Now it is your opportunity to choose" said Chepe going to the leader. "Are you with us or are you against us? Choose fast now that you have the opportunity!"

Juan and the Indian guides waited anxiously. Chepe's face reflected the power and the determination to carry out his mission. For a moment his medium stature seemed to grow with great majesty.

Astonished and afraid, the Indian leader took one step back and lowering his glance he answered:

"It seems that you have the determination and the power to do what we have not been able to do for thousands of years. We have always failed."

The Power Of The Relic

"Tell me, what we can do? All attempts in the past have been a disaster!"

Chepe fixed his glance on the eyes of the Indian leader that showed his bravery and courage. He was a true warrior waiting for the opportunity to rescue his people. Chepe took his sword and in a ceremonious manner he briefly touched his right shoulder and then his left one. In spite of not understanding the meaning of that ceremonious act, the man bowed briefly to Chepe and then stepped back.

"Your help will be necessary and decisive" exclaimed Chepe to the native as he moved in the direction of his friends.

"Our destiny now is more clear," said Chepe. "There is no time to lose. We have to hurry; we have to march towards the mountains; towards the city of *El Dorado*! Please give the instructions necessary to our guides of how to find the land of the man of the blue skin. It is very possible that we need your help to carry out our mission." Then addressing the native leader he declared:

"If that is the case, I will send a light signal up to the sky so that you may come to our aid."

The Indian leader took the guides aside with him and gave them instructions, warning them of the precautions they had to take on the way. The Indian warriors moved away into the bushes leaving their leader with Chepe and his three companions. After some final instructions, the native leader put his hand up to wave goodbye and bowed as a signed of respect to his new friends. He stood there until Chepe and his friends disappeared on the way towards the high mountains.

"He warned us that they have seen troops of men of blue skin patrolling these places a few nights ago and that some of them carried strange and powerful weapons" said one of the worried guides in a whisper.

"I am afraid, that if they now dare to leave their hiding place, it is because they are preparing to do something big, perhaps at a global level. On the trail you can observe their tracks quite clearly. These are big, strong and cruel men."

"Nevertheless, we will accomplish our mission one way or another; of that I am very sure" said Chepe. "This is a task for which we are well prepared and perhaps for much more."

"I thank you for your words of encouragement" Juan said "with all my heart I wish I could feel the same way, but I do not think the task will be so easy."

"You are my inseparable companion in this mission, and you have volunteered to do it without hesitation. I feel that your obligation is clear; to continue all the way to the end. Come-on cousin!" exclaimed Chepe, reminding him the blood line that united them. Juan was quiet for a while and finally answered:

"We both have this mission in common and I will go with you to the end. Only this I request from you: that when we have concluded our commitment, I want to return to the normal life and the freedom of my youth in the property of my family in La Mesa…"

They had already advanced a good distance, when Chepe returned his glance towards the plain of the mountain, where they had left the aborigine warriors. They were no longer there.

The tracks that went towards the summit were recent and therefore clearer.

"From now on we must walk slower and cautiously, making sure that we will not be surprised by the enemy." warned Chepe. "The men of blue skin must have noticed that we are following them."

As they climbed up the trail the day became cloudy. White clouds as cotton came down from the high mountain and the fog, wet and cold covered the place. The surroundings of the trail became dark as the sun disappeared. They could no longer distinguish any tracks on the trail but from time to time they found pieces of a gray matter, apparently left-over food.

Finally, at the end of the afternoon, they arrived at an open area forested with bushes and located next to the mountain. At the end of the plateau, looking towards the forest they found the residue of a bonfire, next to a pile of dry trunks and some leftovers of gray mass like the one found previously in the way. They inspected all the area carefully as the light of the day disappeared, then the night came, dark and cold. They did not find any indication as to the proximity of the enemy.

They encamped at a prudent distance from the old bonfire near a leafy tree that protected them partly from the freezing wind of the mountain that whistled with sad and tenebrous murmurs. Juan shook from the cold; he had only brought one wool poncho, and was not accustomed to the harsh climate of these heights.

"Let's make a bonfire" Juan suggested.

"No! It is dangerous and we do not want to attract the attention of anyone" Chepe answered as he extended his own wool poncho to help him sleep in a little more comfort. "We are near the mountains of the enemy and also near their hiding place."

"And how about you, what are you going to wear to protect yourself from the cold?" Juan asked.

"I will guard at night, don't you worry about me."

Saying this Chepe walked away humming a happy song, trying to stay calm and to calm his friends. Then he sat down in the meadow with his back against a rock. Meanwhile his friends fell into a deep sleep. Silence reigned all night, only interrupted once in a while by the murmuring of the ice cold wind.

It was yet quite early, when they resumed the march under the direction of the expert guides who now had new instructions about the journey and its dangers. They climbed in the west direction on the steep mountains. They could see very little; the morning was so cloudy that they could see only a few steps in front of them. The rocky trail made the climb more difficult but thanks to their skill, the guides walked through weeds and rocks like experts, although the steep trail ahead turned into a longer and more laborious route.

All climbed without resting. On the first plain they found they stopped to rest. From there they could see with some difficulty the tops of the tiny trees of the woods that had left back. It was an extensive shade of green.

Then the guide announced:

"Quickly, we must keep going!"

They immediately began to go up through another steep path; the surroundings covered almost completely with low shrubs next to the trail; some yellow flowers were scattered around the meadow spreading a soft and delicate aroma on the hills. The four companions continued climbing untiringly crossing a long path in the middle of rocks. When arriving at the other side of the mountain they stopped for a moment in order to catch their breath; they were much too tired to continue. They sat down to rest and to eat something to fortify their bodies. Then they looked for a cavern between the rocks in which to spend the night.

The next morning a shadowy and reddish sky with a few gray and white clouds greeted the young explorers. From here they could see the high peaks of the mountains in the south covered with snow. Over in the horizon, at a yet very long distance over a mountain extended a large plateau towards the east; it looked gloomy and dark in the middle of the shadows, protected by high mountains in the west and by the steep abyss of the rocks around it.

"There it is! There you have it!" exclaimed Chepe with a feeling of triumph and satisfaction as if he had already obtained his victory. "There you have the city of *El Dorado!*"

As if not yet persuaded, the incredulous four friends stood there for a while observing the mysterious city for a few minutes.

The sun rays over the city made it shine with the color of gold, like an enchanted city with incredible wealth. It had a wonderful and fascinating aspect. It seemed like a dream place, floating in the heights. Chepe and Juan were intoxicated by the emotion; paralyzed by fear. For a very long time they had waited for this moment. There was their destiny, right in front of them, wonderful and challenging.

"So, now which way do we go to get to that city, on top of that inaccessible mountain?" asked Juan.

"This is the moment to think about that" answered Chepe, as he stopped for a few minutes to consider the situation. "We will have to continue towards that fascinating place as soon as possible," he said.

The city seemed to float over a cloud which gave it a celestial aspect. The fog descended from the mountains covering the slopes on its way to the tropical forest that waited for it in the base of the foothills. A reddish glow expanded on the beautiful city of *El Dorado* as the sun disappeared on the horizon. Chepe and Juan ate their supper in silence and then they got ready for a night's rest. The guides remained standing up somewhat anxious with the new discovery, not sure about what was ahead. After a light dinner they sat down on the turf to look faithfully over their masters who soon fell asleep.

Early the next morning they woke up Chepe and Juan.

"Quick! We must take this path towards the city" the guides instructed.

"Quick!" They commanded again as they turned to the west in the way to the mountain, seeking the direction of the plateau where the city was located. "This is the shortest way. We have to travel quickly!" With great agility, like explorers in enemy territory, they slid with quick steps through the mountains of the western edge, under the protection of the steep and rocky ravines.

CHAPTER 30

El Dorado was now not more than a small glitter on the plain on the other side of the mountain. It was still at a considerable distance. The four friends got ready to climb up the rugged mountain.

"Quickly!" commanded the worried guides.

Juan and Chepe did not answer, but followed them through a narrow and steep path, that curved around the mountain becoming a very treacherous and dangerous stretch that soon had sufficient space only for the feet of the four companions who now traveled in a single file. At the end, it finished in a deep precipice which separated them from the mountain where the City of *El Dorado* was. When looking downwards the dark was almost complete, the precipice seemed to have no bottom.

"Be careful!" exclaimed one of guides "missing a step can be fatal!"

"Perhaps, we should go back" thought Chepe for a moment.

"There is no way to get across" said Juan.

"But if we go back, the descent will be very dangerous as well" added Chepe.

A distance of only about ten meters separated them from the other mountain.

"This is as far as we go" warned one of the guides with disappointment and resignation. "There is no other way."

Terribly tired, they did not seem to have the energy to go back the same way. Finally, when they thought that everything seemed to have been in vain, Chepe asked them to be calmed.

"There are only about ten meters that separate us from the other side" he observed with an optimistic spirit.

Passing his fingers through his hair he thought for a moment and then he put his hand on the handle of his sword.

"Everything is possible for those who believe. Yes, we will be able to cross to the other side!" Having said this, he pulled out his word and with agility and incredible speed he touched the end of the trail, next to the precipice. At the point where the sword was, now extended a bridge over the bottomless precipice; it joined the two mountains. The bridge seemed to be of crystal, shiny and transparent, almost invisible.

Chepe took a handful of sand from the trail and threw it over the bridge to assure his friends that it was real. Juan shook in fear as he observed the precipice under the bridge. He felt the sweat on his body; a cold air current coming down from the mountains made him shudder. Chepe approached the bridge as he ordered:

"Ok, let's go!"

The bridge was short but it seemed to extend for several kilometers. The icy wind from the mountain summits and the dark below seemed to discourage them.

A weak light blinked on the other side in the city, and for a moment they could distinguish the shadows of the high buildings in the city of *El Dorado* and the walls that surrounded it.

Chepe marched ahead. Juan and the others followed him very cautiously over the bridge that seemed to have no end. When arriving at the other side they noticed that next to the stone wall, a set of stairs appeared before them. They stopped for a moment before beginning to climb. The ascent was long and exhausting. The set of stairs led them directly to the front of the main wall. Chepe searched around discovering a wide and deep pit between them and the main wall that prevented their access. Juan, raising his glance, saw with astonishment the impressive height of the wall; it seemed almost impenetrable.

"There is no entrance!" exclaimed Juan "This is impossible!"

"Sure there is! Do not shrink or become weak, we just have to find it!" responded Chepe.

"All right, it seems that there is still much to explore in these surroundings" answered Juan in resignation, "but I believe that for now it is good to take a moment to rest. We have had a long and difficult journey."

"Yes, we must rest" agreed Chepe. "Let us look for a safe and secure place where we could rest and recover our energies to be prepared for the next challenge."

Chepe was totally convinced that they could easily find an entrance to the city. He was no longer concerned about the dangers and threats that awaited them. He was focused on only one idea in his mind: to look for a way to enter the city of *El Dorado*. It was about finding the most appropriate way to accomplish his mission. There they rested during the night after a light dinner, part of the last provisions given to them by the Amazon women.

"I would like to know what kind of adventures awaits us at the other side of these walls," said Juan.

"Me too," commented one of the guides.

"Well, I do not know, but of one thing I am sure: it will be one of the most extraordinary adventures that may even change the course of history. Many do not have this privilege in life. The great and important projects are not for those of small heart" concluded Chepe giving emphasis to the importance of this mission.

"We have not yet arrived at our true destiny. It is always good to keep our eyes wide open; when we walk close to the enemy, it becomes necessary to be continuously alert; but I believe that for tonight we will not have to worry about it. We are safe" concluded Chepe as he felt the sword on his waist.

Early next morning they continued their journey. This time Chepe went at the front in search of a place from where they could enter the city. They followed the wall for several hours towards the high part of the mountain. It was silent, the sun warmed up the air in high peaks where the permanent ice caps stood out. A little farther, approximately at a distance of a kilometer they found a stream of water that apparently crossed under the walls. As they approached, Chepe decided that this could be the point they were looking for. They were next to a cold water brook that came down from the mountains, entering under the walls and into the city.

"This is our way in! This is where we enter!" exclaimed Chepe with great enthusiasm.

"Are you sure that this is the only way?" Juan asked, noticing that the water was extremely cold and that it went down with great impetus.

"Yes, yes" answered Chepe, "this is the only way. We will have to go in this way."

Juan submerged his hand in the water and quickly removed it when almost froze due to the low temperature. He shook just at the thought of having to plunge into the water to go across the wall.

"This is the only way" Chepe assured them again. Without thinking about it much more, the four companions jumped into the stream, which took them to the other side of the wall. A few seconds later they were in the wonderful city of *El Dorado*. They left the water quickly to see with incredulity and astonishment the place where they had arrived. They were just barely out of the water when they were greeted by two guards who seemed to be waiting for them.

Still surprised by the wonders of the city that was before them, nobody pronounced a word in the presence of the guards.

"Your perseverance and cleverness are surprising and worthy of admiration" said one of them.

"Let's escape, fast!" Exclaimed Juan using all the energy and resolution he had left in his body.

"No! No! This is our mission and it is our duty to finish it," said Chepe as he put his right hand over the grip of the sword, making sure that it was still there. For a moment his certainty and security shone in his eyes as if a special power had descended on him. The sword shone in the case and the hand that kept a grip on it seemed full of an extraordinary power. Juan contemplated with astonishment the powerful gift that for such a long time his cousin Chepe had within himself; the vitality and the drive that he had not understood and that he had never used in it totality.

Chepe's glance was fixed on his captors and almost instinctive he pulled out the sharp sword with his right hand; immediately the sword lit up like a flame of fire with red, yellow and blue colors. Then, rising up in the air, he moved with firmness towards the captors who vacillated for a moment. The uncertainty and the fear seized them as the light of the sword approached them. Never, until then had they seen a weapon that showed so much power. Slowly they backed up and disappeared in the shadows but with the agility and the speed of a tiger, Chepe captured them to interrogate them and to find more details about their plans.

Juan and the astonished guides remained with their eyes wide open in bewilderment; finally they only dared to exclaim in unison:

"Let's get out of here immediately; out of this place full

of dangers!"

"Our mission is not yet accomplished!" answered Chepe as he looked for a place of refuge that would provide some safety and security.

At a short distance, next to the walls, they found a small space that offered them protection and an excellent view of the city.

"The shrubs are a perfect hiding place" advised Juan as he explored the area.

The two cousins agreed that this would be the most suitable and secure place from which they could watch over the city and its inhabitants.

The city had double fortification with walls that bordered the mountain summit and separated it from bottomless precipices of the eastern mountains. The first stone wall was several meters wide and had an extension of many kilometers. In front of it was a deep ditch, and behind it, at a considerable distance, a second defensive wall of equal dimensions.

The city had several gates. The greatest was a double door, consecrated to the golden idol; the walls were covered with tiles with representations of bulls and dragons, silent witnesses of the gods of their ancestors. The surroundings of the center palace were adorned with beautiful gardens, a wonder of antiquity. In the center of the city stood a large patio with several radars, most probably used for their communications.

There was also a large temple, similar to a pyramid constructed in honor of the "supreme leader" of men. Next to the walls of the south was an extensive area of land cultivated by native slaves, who provided great amounts of foods for the inhabitants of the city. Next to this area was a transport zone, with vehicles for air and space navigation most probably used to spy on their surroundings or perhaps for space reconnaissance. And in the right hand side of the temple, a great golden idol, the figure of a man who represented a leader of the past, the founder of that city. The appearance of his face was hard and cruel, his glance was fixed on the mountains of the west; his right hand was raised in a military greeting.

"It is a monument to Hifar" explained Juan. "It is as it was described by Aram. It is the image of the terrible dictator who had tried to exalt the race of the men of blue skin. That tragic man dominates this race, even many years after his death."

Along the left hand side was an enormous tower that rose majestically towards the skies.

"The tower of Babel!" Exclaimed Juan "It is a copy of the tower of Babel!" he repeated with incredulity.

That building stood up dominant with a sinister aspect; seemingly more like a monument to the past than something useful for the necessities of the empire. The apparently empty building remained beautifully decorated in its external walls. The city rose around the golden idol, which was the central axis of the city; all the streets converged there.

The city seemed to enjoy a perfect atmosphere and absolute peace. Everything seemed to move synchronously, as it was designed by its founder. The afternoon was already declining; the last sun rays projected the long and pointed shadows of the high mountain peaks that protected the city in the West.

Later the darkness came down from the flanks of the mountains, covering the city. The darkness changed its appearance but not its busy pace. The slaves worked incessantly under the constant watch of their bosses. The sun had disappeared completely and the twilight tended on the hills. The city, illuminated by artificial lights, seemed to have a new life. At a distant spot, at the entrance, by the great stone walls several high power lights lit to maintain the security of the city. On the west appeared the imposing Andean mountains whose top shone majestic in the heights, dressed with perpetual ice caps, lonesome and isolated from the rest of the world.

In front of the temple was a large lake. As the legend described it, *El Dorado* was a city of wonders, governed by a powerful monarch, who bathed every evening with gold dust adhered to his body. At dusk the high priest would immerse himself in the water offering the precious metal to his gods. Next to the waters there were four priests with long black tunics and musical instruments used for this ritual. When leaving the water, the supreme leader entered the temple followed by his companions. The spectacle was as strange as it was wonderful. In the horizon, the rays of the sun were reflected on the waters giving it a reddish and yellow tone, a frightful combination of blood and gold.

Juan contemplated the city with great fascination; he had heard so many stories about it throughout this adventure. It was a different world; a sinister world of its own. For a moment, he observed the mechanical and robotic movements of the slaves feeling a deep compassion for them.

Chepe, on the other hand was absorbed in his own thoughts, fascinated by the enigma and the wickedness of this powerful place; but now he felt the responsibility of having to break the mysterious secret of the power of this place. How much he would have liked to close the doors to the city and return freely to his dear lands, to the calm lifestyle next to his family.

He was rather weak due to his long journey; not often he had had a chance to stop for a good rest. Hour after hour during many hard days, he had walked the long journey

The Power Of The Relic

towards his final destination: The City of *El Dorado* on the high Andean Mountains. In spite of everything, he felt very much alone; now more than ever. He was almost at the end of his destination. Now he asked himself in silence the reasons for this long expedition to this strange place where he now found himself. Suddenly he realized the real purpose of this long trip, and the thought shook him. Juan interrupted his reflections saying:

"Perhaps, this is the end of our journey. But we still need to accomplish our purpose; we cannot return until our objective here, either with triumph or defeat, has concluded."

Chepe answered with a smile:

"Our mission cannot fail. If we fail, what would have been the purpose of all our efforts during such a long and difficult journey? But we should not speak about this anymore. We must rest, and at least take advantage of one more night of peace."

The city woke up the next morning with the first daylight. Suddenly, from the great tower a large choir of trumpets sounded in harmony as if uniting into a single sound that vibrated and resounded all throughout. In a few minutes the inhabitants suspended all their labors. Slaves and leaders, all knelt down in the direction of the great image in the central patio. In a single voice they elevated prayers and supplications to the gold statue. After awhile everything returned to normal; the supervisors rose immediately ordering all the natives to return to their daily labor.

CHAPTER 31

Chepe looked at the rough stone wall on the other side of the city; a good part of it was built against the steep rocks of the mountain. A multitude of natives covered every location of the city. At the other side, extending by the walls there were rows of houses and cabins, next to great reserves of weapons always kept by the officers, the men of the blue skin.

The great assembly disappeared in the dark tunnels under the mountains. Although the morning wind coming from summits blew cold and freezing, everyone continued, dedicated to their routine labor. The guards and chief overseers patrolled the city covered with heavy black, long coats that protected them from the cruel climate. Chepe wondered how many guards were actually involved in keeping the city in spite of having the impression that it was a great army, made up of hundreds of men.

The city was almost impenetrable. No enemy could enter it except over the walls but this was practically impossible because they were protected internally by hundreds of armed guards and to the outside was the deep abyss of the mountains that formed an impenetrable natural protection. By air it was totally impossible because the city was protected by an electric shield, impenetrable and impossible to detect.

Guarded closely by commanders, the native slaves were dispersed over the city doing different tasks. They seemed to have lost their will and moved around like robots. Their gloomy eyes looked with sadness towards the mountains as if remembering or trying to remember the good times of the past. The commanders did not lend any attention or pity to them. Chepe on the contrary almost contemplated with surprise and with mercy those figures that moved melancholically in the shadows of the night.

"The inhabitants of this place are similar to those we observed in the city of Mizpah- Harim in its organization and advances" said Juan. "But the similarity ends there. Unlike the city of Mizpah–Harim, these individuals seem to be under a curse, with a certain coldness that makes them evil, unhappy and bloodthirsty."

"The military forces were made up of men corrupted by power and hatred. The only joy for these people was the suffering they caused to their servants and slaves. It did not seem that they have the smallest indication of compassion in their blood. On the contrary they seem to be of cold and malicious blood. Their sinister and imposing bodies were tall, athletic and well trained; their face and nose were rounded and a little extended. Their eyes were a strange combination of green and brown. All are expert and faithful soldiers, with great fear and devotion to their commanders" Juan explained.

"Their only loyalty was to those of their own race. They did not dare to take the potion that was offered daily to their slaves; that was considered as something unworthy of them and dangerous for the supremacy of their race over the natives. The punishment was terrible for those who by simple curiosity dared to try it. Those that dared to do such thing were executed after putting them through long days of tortures; a lesson and an example to their companions."

"Their lineage was maintained at all costs, thanks to their rigid discipline and their way of life. Although they possessed advanced weaponry of high precision, their favorites were the daggers, the arrows and spears poisoned with mortal substances."

After a short while Chepe observed something interesting about the commanders: they communicated through tiny antennas and microphones placed almost in an imperceptible way in their helmets. These allowed them to receive all type of information from the central offices from any location in the city. "This could be the weak point that I am looking for," thought Chepe as he studied the complex and advanced system of communications. At this time he could observe hundreds of transmitters placed strategically throughout the city to control and transfer information. It was an extraordinary and complex system. The guards and commanders who wore the sinister black uniforms were strategically connected with the entire city.

This place had been carefully designed and built like a metropolis, like a secret temple and like a permanent tomb for all its residents, including its leaders. There they had endured the long and brutal years of the past, not only the natives, but also the dominating men of the blue skin. All were eternally separated from the external world.

"But not for much longer" murmured Chepe.

Juan observed the figures of the natives who moved like zombies under the control of the men of blue skin. Suddenly he noticed that the only way to break into the communications system was to find a way to understand its complex operation. At this moment a guard came towards them. Juan noticed that this was a woman with long brown hair, partially covered by the helmet. She was dressed in an armor that came down to her waist; like a warrior. With great skill and agility Juan captured her, immediately taking off her helmet and hiding her between the bushes; along with the other guards they had capture previously.

As he suspected, the helmet contained a sophisticated system of communications that kept everyone well informed about all the activities around the city. Chepe studied it at great length. After a few minutes his face shone with a smile of success.

"I think that now we have a good possibility for penetrating the communication system of the men of blue skin" exclaimed Chepe with a voice of triumph as he pulled his sword.

Close to their hiding place, Chepe sat by himself observing the constant movements of the guards who patrolled the city streets. The dusk already was close, and in the west the hardly visible summits of mountains announced the end of afternoon. In the east the forest already was dark and quiet. The stone walls disappeared slowly under the dark at night. He arose in the shadow of the darkness to go and join his friends but at that precise moment the sound of a trumpet sounded all over the city calling everyone again to render honor and tribute to the golden statute, with prayers and chanting.

Chepe waited standing up next to his friends, trying to understand the meaning of this ritual; the natives knelt before the golden statue over and over again, like robots. Chepe and his friends remained there for a long time observing the strange ritual in silence.

"How can they have so much power over all these people?" asked one of the guides quite intrigued.

"No one knows" answered Chepe, "nevertheless, according to an old legend; there is a secret sanctuary in the enormous central tower. But since these strange beings arrived at this place, nobody has ever ventured into going there to unravel those secrets."

"The legend says that some type of invincible people guards the sanctuary and does not allow anyone to enter these secret places of dark power, with the only exception of the chief and priest. It also says that from time to time, these strange creatures can be observed going to the golden statue. Then the natives of the city bow down and kneel before them with a deep feeling of reverence and terror. These beings come out in rare occasions: only in case of great necessity, imminent danger or to celebrate their enigmatic rituals."

"Also they say that in the nights with no moon, they come out of the tower wearing strange attires and after going around the city disappear in the temple, as if performing some type of special ceremonies."

Chepe saw the desperate situation of the natives under the cruel yoke of the commanders. He thought that the best prospect to gain their freedom would be to find a way to disable the system of communications in the city.

He spent some time considering the different options. Finally he tried to study the different types of wave frequencies used. It was a large number with a rather complex security system, but thanks to guards they had captured and the information gathered from their helmets, Chepe was sure he understood it. Making use of the power of his sword, he raised it in his right hand sending signals that immediately scrambled the sophisticated communication system. After a few minutes the whole city was in total chaos. The commanders seemed lost, with no direction; they did not know what to do. The confusion was short but with disastrous effect.

Suddenly two guards appeared; Chepe couldn't react in time; the attack was too quick. Chepe was taken prisoner immediately to the presence of the supreme Chief. Juan and the two guides had managed to escape. Everything had returned to normal again in the city. With great anguish Chepe noticed that he no longer had his sword. It had been lost during the surprise attack.

The guards took him immediately to the temple, where an old man was sitting, waiting for him. Without doubt he must have been a person of majestic appearance in his younger years, but now he was old, skinny, weak and his hair was completely white. A long beard covered most of his face; he was dressed in black. He remained almost immovable and did not pronounce a word.

As Chepe came into the temple a great voice was heard: a voice that resounded throughout all the corners of the temple. It was a strange language, apparently originally from the old Middle East. Moving towards Chepe the old man said:

"You are an obstinate man. Your perseverance and intelligence are starting to become very annoying to me. I do not see your movements very entertaining as in the past few days."

As he spoke his glance was fixed, always looking straight in front of him.

"It is a great disappointment that a man of your intelligence and power, concerns himself with the value of small people like the natives. Together we can establish a powerful and extensive empire to govern the world. War does not make sense when we all can live peacefully. If you want, you can be part of my empire," offered the old man.

Chepe thought a little while about the meaning of this tempting offer. He took a few steps around the room, and then he answered:

"I am not interested in your empire or in your wealth."

At this declaration the old man gave a resounding and mocking outburst of laughter. He laughed out loud for a long time. Chepe was disturbed; he did not understand what was so funny or the meaning of the joke. Still without recovering, the man said with a hard and serious tone:

"It is not the wealth. It is the power! The treasures and the wealth are of no interest to me. What counts for me is the power! Very soon we will have the power over the world; we can share this power if you decide to join me!"

"We have already made contact with many leaders of the north, of the east and of the west." continued the old priest. "We have spoken about a global agreement of peace, harmony and technological developments. Everything is intelligently coordinated in perfectly synchronous manner. The north has problems of terrorism and is making military skirmishes with the fearsome enemies. In the west there is great displeasure and economic instability. The east has never had political stability or security. In all those lands anxiety, terror and uncertainty reign; unlike our empire which enjoys peace and prosperity, conditions which everyone one else would love to have. The time is appropriate for us... for you and for me," the old man ended with great enthusiasm.

At this instant a commotion was heard outside and the voice of a man calling Chepe's name. Right away the commander of the guards appeared at the door, addressing the old man first with a military greeting and then bowing before him, showing much respect for the leader and chief.

"Your Majesty, there is a guard here who wishes to see you immediately," said the commander.

"Let him in!" ordered the old man.

The guard carried something very familiar to Chepe. It was the sacred and powerful sword! The man who had it in his hands was tall and strong, of green-brown eyes and blue skin, proper of his lineage. He was dressed in a similar manner to the other guards with a black outfit and a helmet covering his head. He also carried in his hand a weapon which he used as a cane, an instrument to rule and subjugate the natives. The handle was black, the rest was of steel. The guard greeted the chief with great reverence.

"Your majesty" he said as he knelt before him to present Chepe's sword to him.

"The sacred sword of the power!" exclaimed the old man as he received it and held it on his hands. He admired it with great joy as if holding an award he had awaited for a long time. His hands shook with emotion.

"The sacred sword of the power had never been seen in this side of mountains! My luck and my future has changed for ever! I believe that now I no longer need you. You should have accepted my offer when the circumstances were different."

"Now I do not need you anymore!" stressed the leader and chief addressing Chepe with an outburst of laughter and satisfaction. "I do not need you!" repeated the old man.

Immediately he ordered the captain to take Chepe out of his presence and to take him to the prison. Obeying the orders, Chepe was taken to a small, dark and cold cell by the city walls. The cell walls were covered with iron bars. The door was made of solid metal. A cold and humid air entered the cell through the cracks of the door and the wall.

Chepe felt abandoned and defeated. The power of his sword in wicked hands was now his greatest preoccupation.

"The situation is really desperate" he said to himself, as he thought about the future of his friends and companions.

"This unlimited power in the hands of these sinister people is a threat for all the nations. There will be no one who could oppose their authoritarian ambitions. The danger is imminent! I have to do something very soon! The future of our people is at risk and cannot be decided within these walls. If the fury of this tide is not contained now, it will be impossible to do it latter; then not even the mountains or the seas will be a safe shelter."

"Yes, the situation is desperate," he repeated, "but perhaps there is still hope and not all is yet lost. It is possible that my friends in the city of Mizpah–Harim can help us. If at least they knew about it… but, how could they know?"

"I have to warn them that the world is in great danger! Perhaps they can come in our assistance now that we still have time. But, how can I let them know!"

He spent many hours desperate and worried, thinking about the fate of his friends and their uncertain future.

"Well, for now I will just have to rest, it is much better to make decisions in the morning, after a good rest; this can help me to think more clearly."

After he had said this, he tried to get some rest in that cold and terrible prison.

"I hope that Juan and his companions are doing well; safe and sound" he said to himself over and over again.

His last thoughts before being able to fall sleep were for the well being of his dear cousin and his faithful friends:

"Good night, my dear friends," he said.

CHAPTER 32

He was in that terrible prison for several days; alone and saddened by the thoughts of a disconcerting and uncertain future; not knowing clearly what he should do under the circumstances or what steps to follow. On the third day the voice of a guard woke him up, taking him by the arm he said:

"Wake up sir, we need you! Wake up!"

Chepe awoke up frightened and not knowing the time or the day, because it was too dark inside.

"What is happening?" he asked.

"The supreme leader needs you."

Chepe tried to think about what could be the reason.

"It is probably not a very good reason, of that I am sure" he said.

"Please hurry!" insisted the guard as the prisoner hurried to get dressed.

He opened the door and looked outside with his still sleepy eyes, trying to get adjusted to the bright light of the outside of the cell. The air was cold and piercing; around the city everything was calm and quiet. Not much could be seen because of the fog that slowly descended from the mountains. A gray and dark sky hid the sun.

Chepe saw a great number of natives who worked around the city like zombies. Their faces were dark and sad and in some of them he could notice a repressed pain. He could almost feel their anguish. With a heavy heart he went to meet the supreme leader. When he entered the room where the supreme leader was, he observed that he was in the company of another man that was familiar to him. It was the mysterious person of the black hat who he had seen for the first time in the bus, long time ago, on the way to Bogota.

"What is the meaning of this clumsy joke with no sense?" Asked the old man quite displease and with an angry tone.

"I do not understand Sir" answered Chepe a little confused, not understanding the meaning of this accusation.

"The sacred sword of the power does not have any power! Everything that was said to me about it is false. This is only a toy for children" exclaimed with an irritated voice. "But if what you are trying to do is to play some trick on me, I assure you, it could be very costly!" he warned in a threatening manner.

"Yesterday, towards the twilight, began the battle nearby the eastern walls and has lasted all night, while you were placidly sleeping in your cell" he said in an accusing way.

"But this is not possible! This city is impenetrable! You know yourself," answered Chepe.

"I do not understand either," answered the old man. "The war has begun. But this is not the end, I assure you." The results of the great battle are in our favor. We have abundant reserves that we have been accumulating, with the specific purpose of being ready for a situation like this one. And most importantly, you will help us to win. The old man opened the curtains of the large window to show him what was happening in the city. The trumpets were sounded to call all the available forces. Chepe passed his hand over his forehead and then he tried to clean his eyes to make sure he was not dreaming:

His friends were ready for combat outside; the swift and skilful Amazon women and the aborigine warriors which they had met in mountains, on their way to the city of *El*

Dorado. It was an incredible spectacle, but definitively it would be an unequal battle.

"Come with me, I will show you what is waiting for them. These are the weapons for the battle" said the high chief as he opened the curtain of the great room to show him a group of soldiers armed with black armors and laser guns, designed to eliminate the enemy in an instant.

"My heart tells me that before the end of day the victory will be ours" said the proud old man, sure of himself, with a sinister outburst of laughter.

"And if it is not, you will help us to make sure it is. As far as the sword is concerned, do not worry; you will have the opportunity to use it at the precise moment."

From that control room the old man ordered the attack. In the darkness of the mid morning the soldiers started to get ready for battle taking strategic positions. In the shadows, the figures of the men of *El Dorado* did not seem as vigorous and energetic as the enemies who surrounded them, but their superior armament was evident in the battle field. It was a highly disciplined army with great loyalty to their lord, the high chief. A mortal destiny awaited them, but they faced it in silence and with certain bravery. Throughout the city they looked for strategic positions. The weapons of the defending army shone in the dark contrasting with their black suits.

The old man observed his troops from the commanding room; very sure of himself. He looked taller and arrogant. His bodyguards contemplated him with astonishment as he stood tall and with great composure. They bowed to him in reverence. In the streets and by the walls that bordered the city, the defending army aligned in numerous groups of soldiers, well equipped from head to toes with equipment highly advanced in technology.

"Their superiority is evident," thought Chepe as he observed through the large window; he bit his lips as a

gesture of helplessness, frustration and anger. "This it is not my place. I should be there outside, with my friends, but now I am forced to be the witness of a clearly unequal, unjust and bloody battle".

Suddenly a trumpet sounded again in the central patio. The old man, the supreme chief and high priest, raised his hand to signal the attack. The soldiers of both sides began to move in silence. As the old man lowered his hand, a siren resonated throughout the city, indicating that the moment had arrived for the battle, in which thousands of warriors were sent to fight a brutal fight. Chepe, the old man and his bodyguards watched with great attention what was happening in front of them. The warriors of blue skin looked severe and ruthless as they marched in long rows. "These soldiers are superior in armament and technology, but ours have great will and determination," thought Chepe as he tried to encourage himself. "Where there is perseverance, tenacity and persistence, there is always a way to victory." Minutes later the old man went to a small room, next to the entrance to the large control room. But Chepe was under the constant observation of two guards. It was impossible to even think about escaping.

The warriors marched outside in perfect military formation, chanting military songs as the Indian drums resonated throughout the city. The armies in black suits, began their first round of attack with laser guns, very sure of their superiority. Much to their astonishment and surprise the Amazon women received them with polished metal shields which sparkled in the light of the day as if they were of silver; these acted like mirrors, reflecting the lasers back in direction of the enemy or in other directions. As the ingenious Roman legions of the past, some of these women formed a protective wall with the shields, while others, with great agility and skill shot arrows towards the enemy. But

the arrows did not penetrate the armors of the men in black suits. The battle of this day was amazing and without greater losses for any of the contenders. Half way through the afternoon and with mutual surprise, all armies returned to their respective fields to plan the next attack.

But the news were not good for everyone; a few hours later came the bad news. The Indian soldiers had retreated to the city walls with great losses. They had not run with the same luck of the Amazon women. For them the enemy was clearly superior, not just about numbers but also about their advanced technology. They had paid a high price the first day of the battle, but less than what they had thought, considering the conditions. The plans had been drawn up. And it was evident that for a very long time they were planning alternative strategies to overcome the enemy.
"At this moment they need me more than ever," murmured Chepe to himself.
It was evident that he was thinking about a way to go to their help. But this was impossible.
The next morning they sounded the trumpets announcing a new day of a brutal war. The commanders shouted with a strong voice, and all the men in black suits marched ready for war. The old man smiled with satisfaction as he watched his soldiers in formation, ready for combat.
"The battle is not yet over. My friends still have control around the walls and are opening breaches within the city. Little by little they will win," continued thinking Chepe, knowing deep in his heart that the advantage was on the

side of the soldiers of the blue skin. A large number of his wounded friends, those that had been able to survive the carnage, the disaster of the previous day, were recovering in the cabins next to the city walls. Chepe watched in all

directions over the city trying to find some clue as to the fortune of his three companions. He was also quite worried about the Indian warriors and the Amazon women. From time to time he came to the windows, as if he wanted to coordinate and command his friend's armies. Sometimes he stopped to listen, hoping to hear some message about what was happening in the city streets; hoping that all his friends would be still alive after a long day of hard struggle.

"The enemy is too powerful. But my friends have come only to achieve victory," reaffirmed Chepe.

"I hope they use all their weapons. This is what all the great soldiers do. I cannot remain here in this room anymore, meditating, observing and waiting for my friends to be sacrificed." His anger and frustration grew as the hours passed by. He got up and walked worried around the room. He longed to have his sacred sword of the power within his reach.

The highly disciplined Amazon warriors had taken the area by the city walls without yielding an inch. They were worthy opponents of the soldiers in black clothes.

"Your friends fight quite well, but the moment has not yet arrived to use all our forces," the high priest said.

"Whatever it may be, we will see the end here. Soon there will be a new battle here; we need to prepare for it."

The Indian soldiers took charge of defending the area around the north walls with great courage and tenacity; they did not yield an inch. At the outset the reinforcements began to arrive in small groups and disperse around but soon with great skill and ability they got organized in perfectly coordinated groups. In the neighborhoods of the north vibrated the fire that seemed to extend within the city, indicating a new strategy. The houses and the buildings burned. Suddenly, from an area near the walls, began to fly arrows of fire, red flames that crossed the skies in the

direction of the soldiers of black clothes.

"It is the enemy," said the old man; angry and very surprised. "There they come, like a violent outburst on the streets; they bring torches."

The soldiers of black suits were confused; they did not understand what was happening in the battle field. The fire grew very quickly. Finally the captains of each group alerted by the emergency system, backed down awaiting new orders. With new instructions they returned to the firing lines that was moving closer and closer to the city center. Suddenly a group of Indian soldiers moved forward shooting arrows with fire into the enemy. The fire quickly propagated into a flood of flames that devoured whatever was found in its way, but neither the fire nor the torches seemed to do any damage to the enemy troops. The arrows did not penetrate their clothes and the fire did not seem to burn them. When they observed that the men of black clothes were not affected by the fire or the different weapons, the native warriors fled in all directions, terrified, shouting and throwing their weapons.

On the other hand, the Amazon women had invoked the aid of the killer bees from the Amazon jungle. These frightful creatures have a terrible poison that in addition to being very painful can also be lethal. From the walls of the east, the women left simulating a simple attack. As soon as the soldiers of the black suites were set in attack formation, the acute sound of a ram's horn was heard throughout the city. Minutes later, thousands of killer bees came over the walls of the city in direction of the sinister soldiers of the black suits. The attack was impressive. The bees penetrated by any orifice in the clothing, what no projectile had been able to do, as well as under the helmets and around the neck. The soldiers of blue skin were completely defenseless. Their high technology weapons were totally

useless before the attack of the deadly insects. Some began to fall in the streets, victims of the lethal insects. Others, filled with terror and great fear, fled with great pain towards the tunnels in the mountains in search of protection and safety. Soon the streets in that section of the city were deserted. Thanks to their cleverness, the battle this time was in favor of the Amazon women. As soon as the soldiers of the black suits disappeared, the acute sound of a ram's horn was heard again over the city and the killer bees returned over the city walls and on their way back to the Amazon forest.

The sound of a trumpet was heard in all the city of *El Dorado*, announcing that that the high priest had issued an order to meet in front of the golden statue. All the soldiers who were still in the city came in silence, organized in small groups. The victorious ones now were defeated. The retreat of the soldiers of the blue skin was now a fact. The battlefield was left covered with dead bodies, wounded warriors and the weapons of the terrified and bewildered soldiers of the blue skin.

CHAPTER 33

The chief and high priest was not ready to give up or to accept his defeat. All his men had come back after their terrible defeat. The olds man's wrath did not have limit. He was looking out from his commanding room with a red face of indignation, his hands trembling, a tense fist and his veins on the verge of exploding. He directed his word to Chepe, who was also reviewing the situation outside.

"This is your last opportunity to be part of our successful plan. Do you not understand that we are peaceful men? We do not want war; we search for a global society where all man can live in harmony, as we must; an ideal society. You can be one of the leaders of that community; it will be just as it was in the beginning. There is no doubt; we can work together in the design of this ideal community. We both have the power, the keys to make it happen. Using the power of your sword we can make this dream a reality" insisted the chief and high priest.

"We can reconcile the enemies. I have the source of power and your friends will be our friends."

Saying this and as a sign of confidence the old man took Chepe to the room of the city's treasures. The entrance was protected by a heavy wood door covered with gold; it was secured with several locks. With much serenity and pride the old man proceeded to open it. Pressing a switch alongside the door, the room was lit up revealing a surprising collection of wealth and precious objects. The room was full of hundreds and hundreds of gold objects and emeralds, masks, pectorals, hangers, command batons, nose jewels, a great number of precious objects, very possibly of native origin. The wall on the foreground was decorated with ornaments and instruments; a remembrance of their ancestors.

A reproduction of Noah's ark and the Tower of Babel stood out in the center as the most important objects of that location; the strategic illumination upon them caused an extraordinary effect. Finally Chepe could admire a sample of the treasures that the Spanish conquistadores had come to look for. The jewels and relics gave the sensation of reliving the ceremonies of the old ancestors. Chepe stopped for a moment with his glance fixed on those pieces and without saying a word, he went to a black door that seemed to lead to a secret place.

"This door takes you to a sacred place where only I as the chief and high priest have access."

Chepe was overwhelmed and astonished. He looked slowly around the room once again. Ha had never imagined a fantastic place like this one, with so much wealth and so much history. The old man felt very proud, keeping his eyes on Chepe, understanding the effect that this wonderful place could have on his spirit and soul; then he said in a tempting way:

"All this is yours if you decide to join me in my plans."

Chepe seemed not to have heard; he remained almost hypnotized by the wonders he could see around the room. After a few minutes the old man spoke again:

"My friend Chepe, it is not the wealth or treasures which I look for, in fact that does not matter to me; it is the power, you and I, we can attain that absolute power." Chepe could not yet understand the complete meaning of the plan from the chief and high priest.

The old man went again to the entrance of the sacred place, and then he invited Chepe to join him.

"Only I, as the chief and high priest have access to this

place of sacred power. But we are going to share my plan; I am going to give you the privilege that no other mortal has ever had previously."

Alongside from the entrance was a closet that contained the priest's clothing. The old man proceeded to put on the sacred ornaments of black and gray color: a mantle, a tunic embroidered with gold, a turban and a strip to the waist. What caught the most attention from Chepe was the great medallion with precious stones with strange designs carved with ruby, inlaid gold sapphire and emeralds; in center of medallion, also in gold was the tower of Babel. The old man directed his glance to the front door as he murmured songs in an unknown language, preparing to go in.

Behind the door was a black curtain covering the entrance. At the other side of the curtain appeared the sacred room; it was simple and austere, with four gray walls; slightly illuminated, resulting in a strange atmosphere. In the center was a small table of wood and on top of it what seemed to be a boat of gold sitting on a blanket also woven with threads of the same metal.

"There it is… the relic of the power!" exclaimed the old man with pride. "There you have it! No mortal has had the privilege to see it and continue to live! This is the original one; it came from the Middle East, from our ancestors. It is the symbol of a pact established with the Creator after the universal flood. It is an inexhaustible source of power, as you can see."

In front of the golden relic the old man seemed to get rejuvenated; his face, his body and even his long and white hair were changed giving him a younger and more robust appearance.

"Can you see it, my friend Chepe? It is an infinite source of magic power!" exclaimed the chief and high priest.

Chepe studied the sacred artifact carefully; it looked like a boat; he was overwhelmed by its enigmatic beauty and its power. It contained eight human figures in it.

"Incredible!" exclaimed Chepe, "the same number of people that was saved in Noah's ark!"

"That is indeed the case my dear friend" responded the old man. "When the human civilization was scattered around the world, leaving the lands of Mesopotamia, our ancestors brought it to this part of the world. It has been an inexhaustible source of power throughout our history; the history of our predecessors."

"Who are you and how old are you?" asked Chepe with great curiosity.

"My age really does not matter" responded the old man who now looked young and full of life. "My name is Nafti, son of Asur, descendant of Nimrod, son of Cus of the territories of the Valley of the Tigris River in Mesopotamia." Chepe was absolutely astonished as he heard this. It is just as Father Nicanor had said.

"Incredible! How can it be possible?" exclaimed again Chepe.

At the front of the table holding the relic of the power was a throne with incrustations of gold, and to its side a small closet. Nafti sat on the throne in front of the relic of the power. He had the appearance of a king; of the kings of the past, perhaps of the medieval times or perhaps even before those times. Without getting up from the throne he extended his hand towards the closet and removed Chepe's sword.

"With this we will be invincible!" Nafti said as he extended the sword to Chepe. "You and I, invincible! Creators of a community of peace and harmony!"

"But I do not understand" answered Chepe with surprise. "If you haven the two sources of the power, why do you need me? I have a feeling that it is not due to your great kindness, or to your mercy and compassion," added Chepe.

Nafti responded, in a direct and honest way:

"We have discovered, much to my surprise and displeasure that the sword is nothing else than a child's useless toy if it is not used by its owner, in this case you Chepe, my friend; you are the owner! The sword only unfolds its power on the hands of its master and owner to whom it was granted. They are one, the sword and its lord."

It had never occurred to Chepe that this could be possible. It never went through his mind that he actually had absolute power over the sword! He approached Nafti to grasp his sword with a deep sense of admiration and respect for this instrument of power. Taking it by the handle, he passed his fingers over the leaf which shone like diamonds on his hand; he wanted to make sure it was in good conditions. Then he roused it up on his on his right hand; it sparkled as an extraordinary alive flame of fire with red, yellow and blue. Nafti saw the sword for the first time in the hand of its lord, in all its splendor and magnificence.

"It is magnificent!" He exclaimed with respect and admiration; he more than anyone else could understand the power of that sacred instrument.

"It is magnificent!" he said again in ecstasy as he arose from the throne.

"One power, one peaceful society; how would you like that, my friend? Something that you can obtain only on your dreams!" Nafti insisted as a tempting proposition.

Chepe looked at the shining relic over the table and then he turned his eyes to his sacred sword. Nafti's proposition was tempting. A single power, a global community of peace and harmony... After all, this would be the best thing for everyone; no more wars, no more violence...

Chepe thought about the offer over and over again for long time. The idea began to germinate, to take roots in his mind. But then he remembered Bachu, Father Carlos, Father Nicanor and his friend Aram; he also remembered the Indian soldiers and their families, the native slaves, the Amazon women. All of them came to his mind. But most of all he remember the purpose of his mission, the purpose of his journey all the way to these high mountains.

"No!" Chepe said finally. "My answer is no! The price is too high. I cannot use this power to dominate my fellow men. The plan you are proposing is macabre and gruesome." Nafti arose from the throne with his face red from anger and exasperation. "What is it that I must do in order to convince you that this is the best way... the only way to establish a community of peace? Just imagine a community of perfect harmony, without wars... without starvation..." the old man continued to insist with great conviction, as if all of this was a reality in his mind.

But Chepe pronounced himself again against the idea.

"In that case, I will have no other recourse but to proceed with my own plans; perhaps then you will change your opinion," said the angered and arrogant old man striking the table with fury and frustration.

"Let's go!" he said as he started towards the control room from where he could direct and control the activities of his subjects. Once there Nafti ordered:

"Send the slaves!"

Hundreds of native slaves came out in military formation, dressed with the same military uniforms as those used by the men of blue skin; black clothes and a helmet on their head with a double purpose: for protection and to receive the orders and instructions from their masters. All marched under their absolute control.

"Their obedience is absolute!" explained Nafti. "They

are ready to obey without a doubt, anything I order them. They ask absolutely nothing; neither the reason, nor the purpose of any order given. These people are perfect! They will defend the city of *El Dorado* even at the cost of their own lives. But the situation is even better. We have similar people in strategic places around the world: in North America, in Europe, in Asia, in Africa and Australia. Everything is ready to create my dream community!"

"But the future is even much more promising," continued the chief and high priest. "As you can see, the natives are under our control. They are like robots, they do not think, they only obey. We controlled their minds and bodies through the magical potion which they receive daily. But this is not good. It has great disadvantages. But now we have a powerful technology that will allow us to control their body and soul."

"Every one under our command, under our power, will be able to use their mind to create, to investigate, to think... but their will is always ours... their total loyalty is for our cause. An absolute power! It will be a perfect society," said the old man with a malicious smile.

Chepe thought about it with incredulity. "People under the total control of someone as despicable as this old man; ready and willing to do anything even at the cost of their own lives!" his body shivered just at the thought of considering the possibilities, the cruelty, the violence and the consequences that this could bring. But now the most important thing were the natives, that dressed in the military uniform of their captors were in the front line, ready to fight without knowing it, against their own relatives and friends; against the Indian warriors and the Amazon women. This would become a massacre of many innocent people.

The old man took Chepe to the large windows of the north. The Indian soldiers prepared themselves for the attack; they seemed to be ready to take the city. Then he took Chepe to the large window towards the east, where the Amazon women were also prepared for the final battle. He said to Chepe:

"What do you think my friend? Do you understand that there is no way to stop this plan? Everything is ready. Even after great heroic battles the victory will be ours, it cannot be prevented. The native slaves have a preparation and weaponry much superior to those of the enemy."

Chepe stood still as he studied Nafti's face without saying a word.

"He is right, the slaves have a discipline and agility that I have never seen before, and their weapons are far superior to the ones from my friends. But, even if my friends fight with greater skill and dexterity there will be a great loss of innocent lives. One way or another it would be a disaster."

Everyone present in the battle field was ready to receive the orders. The native slaves defending the cause of the city of *El Dorado* were well equipped for the battle. The Amazon women after a temporary victory were not prepared for the great surprise ahead of them. The Indian warriors, totally recovered from the horrible surprise the previous day, now were better prepared, with an excellent strategy to take the city and to recover so many relatives who had been enslaved by the enemies. They had waited for this opportunity for several centuries. Their participation for this battle was totally decisive.

Nafti and Chepe kept their eyes on the city streets studying each detail in the formation of the armies. They waited in silence with great expectation. There was still hope before sending the troops to a cruel battle. The morning sun fell a bit warm upon the city. Chepe once again looked all over the city. From there he could also see in the distance the quiet nonviolent green forest as a silent witness of what was about to happen.

"This is a wonderful place," thought Chepe for a moment, forgetting what awaited the people on the streets.

The armies still waited in silence for new orders. Chepe again considered the different options that he had before him. It was a very difficult decision. He preferred to remain calm, as he once again analyzed carefully each one of the alternatives.

"There is no way to win" he said with frustration.

During all the morning the guards crossed the streets, reporting to the central office all the details they would consider unusual. Everyone waited in expectation to see who would be first to break the silence and move to attack.

The natives organized protective trenches using the stone walls and the buildings around the walls. The clouds seemed to dissipate in the sky to better light up the battle fields. The Amazon women suddenly began to move cautiously and slowly towards the city center. At that moment, a roar of drums resonated announcing the attack of the Indians warriors from the north. Chepe watched at all sides with incredulity. He had the impression that many hours had passed since the voice of Nafti had given orders for battle formation. But at that time he finally realized that they ran the risk of mutual destruction between the Indian soldiers and their relatives, now commanded by the men of blue skin.

The native slaves, under the control of the men of blue skin, advanced promptly to the encounter of the enemy. From the walls of the north, the armies of the Indians warriors advanced to the battle fields. In the east, the infantry of the Amazon women continued cautiously in the direction of the city center.

CHAPTER 34

In the north, the forces of the Indian soldiers, once again came together and reorganized, chanting war songs and shouting with the sound of the drums. Minutes latter they advanced through the streets of the city prepared for a surprise attack. The men commanded by Nafti, the high priest, moved forward with great discipline.

The Indian soldiers waited to hear orders from their leader who stood straight and proud in the middle of his army who looked at him with astonishment, inspired by his attitude and composure. They were well equipped and they knew that ahead of them awaited a mortal destiny but they were ready to face it with bravery and resignation. The hours passed quickly; the military drums continued resonating and the spears of the soldiers sparkled under the sun light. For a moment there was silence, then the drums resounded with a great roar and a unanimous shout resounded around the city. The leader raised his hand and his army began to move inconspicuously, very quickly.

The purpose of this encounter was engraved in their mind and shining in their eyes: the liberation of their people and their relatives who have been enslaved for such a long time. At the front marched the most ferocious soldiers, well respected and fearsome men. The leader followed them with an expression of total determination in his face; he looked with much attention at the path that extended in front of him and his troops. Behind came other groups of combatants with a severe look on their faces, they also advanced towards the center of the city.

The Amazon women began the attack; with great

experience and precision they began taking the enemies, piercing their bodies with spears and with arrows impregnated with a poison one hundred times more powerful than the curare; this was known only to them, quite rare and powerful, paralyzing the enemy immediately upon contact. The battle was cruel and ferocious. The number of victims was about the same in both sides. Dozens of women and native slaves fell dead in the streets. Half of the east of the city was occupied by the Amazons but the situation was not secured. Some cabins burned with fire. The native slaves continued advancing with great determination, like human robots in search of their prey.

The situation was desperate. There were two armies of brothers unknowingly who had decided to eliminate each other at any cost and both of them were doing it very effectively. There would not be an evident winner. Chepe looked towards the horizon, at the splendor of the total noon light. He could clearly see the battle field and the soldiers who unfortunately fell on both sides.

The fury of the combat got even worse; the uproar of the weapons grew with the shouts of the soldiers, inciting the battle with the resounding noise of the drums and trumpets. Near the city walls of the south, the infantry of the Amazons attacked the native slaves dressed in black which still remained as a group. The fortune of the men of blue skin seemed to have abandoned them. The violence of the first advance had decimated its army. The astute and ferocious Amazons who were swifter and faster had penetrated with great tenacity the forces of their adversaries. Even though at the beginning the forces of the men of blue skin was superior to those of the Amazons, now the situation had been reversed; the Amazon women seemed totally determined to win the battle at all cost with an agility which totally stunned the commanders of blue skin who ruled over the native slaves soldiers.

Most of the commanders had fallen, but the natives continued receiving orders exhorting them to continue to the end of the battle. The Amazons grasped their spears and arrows, attacking the slave soldiers of black suits in the east, while the Indian soldiers contained them in the north, trying to prevent them from consolidating into a single force. The bodies of a large number of innocent slaves lay on the streets, dressed with the suits of their captors and commanders. In view of this desperate situation, Chepe decided to act. Taking his sword he ran in direction of the sacred room before Nafti could prevent it, with the firm purpose of destroying the golden relic and once and for all eliminate its wicked magic power.

The powerful golden relic was on the table, in front of the throne of the high priest. It sparkled with an extraordinary glow displaying its great power. Chepe grasp his sword in his right hand and aimed at the golden relic emitting a powerful ray of red light. But it remained intact, defiant before the power of the sword. Without wasting time, Chepe gave it a strong blow with his sword. He felt an intense pain that caused him to lose his weapon. When keeling down to pick up his sword from the floor, he noticed that the sacred relic was burning on the table and quickly disappearing in the smoke of a small fire. With great surprise and stupor, he saw it burning, giving up its life as if in the middle of great pain, as it was consumed, disappearing completely before his eyes, leaving only a pile of ashes. That was the end of the powerful golden relic. However, Chepe shuddered at the thought that perhaps this may not have been the end of this mysterious relic. He hoped that he will never see it again in his life.

Nafti, when he realized what had just happened, burned with an uncontrollable rage. He went towards Chepe with the purpose of destroying him with a black weapon he held in his hand, in the shape of a long snake. But it was already too late for him. His power and his energy had already weakened. With the few breaths of energy still left in his body, he managed to sit on the throne, in front of the table where moments before rested the magic and wonderful relic. Without wasting any time, Chepe went to the control room where he hoped to be able to stop the horrible slaughter between the native slaves, their relatives the Indian warriors and the heroic Amazons who continued the ruthless and furious confrontation. Finally he found the location with all the sophisticated system of communications. At the impossibility of deciphering the messages and the complicated instruments, he took his sword and with it he destroyed all the controls. Right away the natives dropped their weapons and suspended the cruel battle. The women did the same, greatly surprised at the sudden change. With some level of distrust, some of them raised white flags and marched towards the city center.

Before leaving the control room Chepe wanted to make sure that Nafti was still in the sacred room. Inconspicuously he entered the sacred room, where he had seen him moments before. To his great surprise the throne was empty; there was no sign of Nafti anywhere. Then he ran quickly to the main patio, looking forward to joining his friends. Moments later he discovered with great joy the two guides and his cousin Juan at the main plaza, in front of the golden idol. With great joy he took them back to the control room. There he offered a toast to celebrate their victory. He told them with luxury of details how he had found his enemy and how he had put an end to a dangerous situation.

"Everything is well now" Juan said.

"Do you really think so?" asked Chepe. "I see that you

have forgotten about the enemies who are still free in the tunnels under mountains."

After he said that, they looked towards the majestic Andean mountain range that had been a silent witness of an era of wickedness, slavery and servitude; the blossoming of a civilization of superior technology and magic powers at the cost of the suffering and the slavery of the innocent natives.

When they realized that this one was the end of a victorious battle, the Indian warriors broke out in shouts of celebration and rejoicing; the Amazon women joined their celebration with exclamations of triumph. The slaves could finally celebrate the moment they had been waiting for such a long time. It had finally arrived... their freedom was now a reality. All were united in a single uproar of triumph and celebration. The Amazon women made sound with the ram horns throughout the city; among all this joyfulness all the people began to shout in a very loud voice that vibrated though the mountains: "freedom!... freedom!... freedom!..."

The voices, the sounds of the instruments and the native's drums resonated with a strong uproar louder than ever before been heard in these mountains. The troops, the men and the women, were chanting victory songs and dancing in rituals of exaltation.

After this they searched for Chepe and Juan to take them to the city center; to pay a tribute to them for having made possible the victory; for obtaining the long awaited freedom. While they continued the celebrations the two cousins remembered with nostalgia and emotion their small town of La Mesa, their family, their friends Bachu, Tachia and Father Carlos. But most of all they remembered the King of kings and Lord of lords, who had taken care of them and helped in the triumphal culmination of this adventure. With this in mind they joined the festivities with the native warriors, their now free relatives and the Amazon women. The sounds from the big uproar and the shouts of joy shook the entire city and beyond, into the distant borders. The festivity and dancing in the streets lasted until half way through the afternoon when the natives and the Amazon women began to organize their return home.

Chepe was very curious to know how it was possible that the brave Amazon and the Indian warriors were able to arrive at the impenetrable city.

"The credit to this success must be given to the cleverness and ingenuity of the Amazon women," said Juan.

"Once you were taken prisoner by the men of blue skin, it was evident that we would need the help of all our friends; the natives and these brave women. Using the golden blowpipe which in fact is an instrument of alarm for help, we called them to come to our aid. With the agility of our guides we were able to use the cords given to us by the Amazon women. They were tied to the walls in the north and the east; they were used to climb up into the city." Chepe was astonished by the ability of his cousin Juan; and approaching him, he embraced him and congratulated him for such a brilliant strategy.

The silhouettes of the beautiful buildings of the city of *El Dorado* stood erected in the horizon. They now seemed sad and downcast, under the weak light of the sun setting behind the mountains. The sorrowful tunnels hid in their belly the slave-driven force of many centuries.

"There is no doubt that these tunnels will be the temporary hiding place for the survivors of the battle" said Chepe. The heavy doors, half way destroyed by the battle kept their guests in silence. At the height of the glory and the splendor of this civilization, now it had lost its luster and its power.

Up in the blue sky, two condors of the Andes observed in silence the results of the battle descending in large circles to take a closer look and better observe the details of the final result. After a while they rose up again in the air disappearing in the distance behind the white clouds. The rescue of the native relatives that had been planned for many years with no positive results was finally a success thanks to Chepe and Juan and the assistance of the Amazon warriors. The atmosphere was a complex emotional mixture of pain and joy, pain for what they had suffered during the years of slavery as well as for those who had been killed in the brutal battle under the influence and control of the men of blue skin. Joy, for the opportunity to finally rescue alive so many of their own blood. The light finally, had returned to that place and now they could feel a new era of joy and happiness for the natives, transforming grief and sorrow into hope and optimism.

But that place was not yet quite vacated. The Amazon women were taking count of the tragedy and the victory. The queen and leader walked through the streets searching for the bodies of the heroines who had sacrificed their own lives for the price of freedom. She comforted the wounded. These honest and loyal heroines we had gone beyond the impossible considered an honor to serve under their brave and courageous queen. All the women fallen in battle as well as the wounded ones were carried to the city wall on their way back to their homeland in the forest.

The queen approached Chepe with a radiating look of gratefulness for the miracle he had performed. She looked more beautiful than when they first met, thought Chepe. Her face had a special brightness with a smile of victory in her lips. Her green eyes shined captivating, her long brown hair slid sensually over her slender body. As she approached Chepe her heart beat faster, perhaps as a sign of gratitude or perhaps as a sign of admiration and respect or possibly as ...

"No, no... it cannot be" she said.

She stopped for a moment and looked away trying to control her emotions. Her obligation was to stay with her own people, her dedicated warriors. But her will weakened and her body shook. She looked down and then closed her eyes in order not to look at Chepe. Suddenly, in the middle of those confused thoughts, she believed to hear the voice of her adored daughter asking her to come home.

She felt comforted and then she moved more sure of herself towards Chepe; step by step with her eyes fixed on Chepe. He pulled out his sword and raising it up, he offered a military greeting of honor. He stood still with his eyes fixed on the beautiful body of the Amazon queen. He remained this way for a few moments. Finally he lowered his sword and placed it back in its sheath. Then he took a few steps towards the beautiful queen and embraced her for the first time with a strong and fraternal embrace, murmuring something in her ear in a low voice. The two bodies separated in silence. Chepe turned around with well calculated military movement and went in the direction of his friends who waited at a short distance. The queen observed him for a while as he moved away, then she looked slowly over the city that now looked dismal and filled with destruction. She stood there for a while like a beautiful statue, and then she went to the walls of the east to join her companions who were organizing the exit from the city. Her beautiful hair shined over her shoulders, smooth, sensual and bronzed. Her green eyes were like the sea; her expression was firm, severe and filled with mystery, but in spite of her hard appearance, some tears rolled down her beautiful cheeks.

The city was deserted. The natives had returned to the plains of the Andean mountains. Only the Indian chief and two of his companions were left looking one last time over the battlefields. The Indian chief came to Chepe to thank him for his help and his heroic acts. Later he observed with great sadness and bitterness the lifeless bodies of his brethren who covered the streets of the city; the high price paid for their final freedom. Chepe looked at him with compassion for a few seconds and taking tow steps backs he pulled out his sword and raising it up on his right hand, he extended a greeting of military honor; the same he had given to the beautiful queen of the Amazons. He remained still in this position for a few moments and finally he placed his sword back.

This great Indian chief and his two friends walked in silence towards the city walls. Before they started their final descent, back to heir homeland, the chief turned back to give one last goodbye raising his hand in the distance. Chepe for his part used the farewell the had learned from Bachu: taking his right hand to his chest, then his lips and finally, extending it in the direction of the native, be bowed in a sign of friendship.

This was finally the culmination of the mission for these two young men from La Mesa. Thus they had prevailed over the men of blue skin. They were now at the city boundaries, next to the walls of the north. Chepe pulled out his sword one last time and pointed in the direction of the control room. The power of his sword unleashed an all-consuming fire that propagated quickly throughout the city. As the sun disappeared, the flames illuminated the skies and the city grounds with red tones. The mountains in the background and the city buildings now looked as if they were painted with blood. The previously great city was now finally reduced to a pile of ashes. Within her there was not a single enemy left alive, except for those who had fled into the deep tunnels in the belly of the mountains; all others were dead.

Chepe, his cousin Juan and the two guides went to the city wall. They were safe and unharmed by the miraculous protection from the King, the power of the sword and the skill, bravery and opportune help from their friends.

Taking one last looked over the city now turned into a pile of rubbish, Chepe put back his sword into its sheath for the last time.

"The King is on His throne and the earth is His footstool; all is well," said Chepe, then he ordered: "Let's go home!" as they took the lengthy and difficult trail on the way back to their hometown of La Mesa.

Jose V. Bonilla

Jose V. Bonilla grew up in a coffee plantation in Colombia, South America. He attended elementary and high school in the small village of La Mesa. Later he studied Chemistry for a period of year and a half at the National University of Colombia in Bogota. His dream since he was a little boy was to become a scientist in a technologically advanced country. He accomplished this dream when he traveled to the United States, where he pursued his studies in Chemistry. He obtained his Master's degree and then his Doctorate degree at The University of Oklahoma.

After his graduation, he participated in a NASA project for the Space Shuttle Program through Argonne National Laboratory. There he also worked as a scientist in Advance Research projects for the Department of Energy and the Department of Defense.

More recently, he has worked in the development of Advanced Engineering Materials and the production of specialty polymers for the pharmaceutical industry.

Doctor Bonilla has published prolifically in the field of technology. "The Power of the Relic" is his first book for the general public and his first book already published in Spanish.